PRAISE FOR THE EMPIRE OF KAZ

"Blaster and laser battles and spaceship rides into hyperspace set a fast pace for adventure."

SCHOOL LIBRARY JOURNAL

"Excellent examples of space opera in the Star Wars *tradition. They seldom have a dull moment, with characters scheming against and trying to kill each other..."*

FRED PATTEN, *DOGPATCH PRESS*

"The plotting is masterful... always exciting... smoothly written..."

DELIA SHERMAN, *FANTASY REVIEW MAGAZINE*

CAT'S GAME

LESLIE GADALLAH

SHADOWPAW
PRESS *Reprise*

CAT'S GAME
By Leslie Gadallah

Second Edition
Published 2023 by
Shadowpaw Press Reprise
Regina, Saskatchewan, Canada
www.shadowpawpress.com

First published by
Five Rivers Chapmanry, 2018

Trade Paperback ISBN: 978-1-989398-70-8
Ebook ISBN: 978-1-989398-71-5

Cover art by James Beveridge

OWR-MARL, ORION

"This is not working," Mawuli said.

Hidden away in the depths of the Biological Sciences Building of the Academy at Owr-Marl, in a small, white-walled laboratory sharp with the smell of chemistry and disinfectants and crowded with too many people and too much equipment to be anything but stressful, once again, a dedicated group of researchers laboured long into a night that was fading into morning. Ehreh, the bioengineer in charge of the project, urged them on even though he knew most of them would rather be enjoying a good night's sleep.

For more than a year, they had donated whatever time they could give, mostly at night, to the detriment of their careers, their families, and their health. Some had not seen their homes in tens of days. The need for rest became nearly tangible, a stronger urge in Oriani than in other races, except for one of their enemies.

"Try bringing the pH down 0.01, then explore slightly higher to slightly lower electric fields. I think we are close," he told his colleague.

Mawuli indicated acceptance, if not agreement, and turned back to his instruments to begin adjusting the apparatus.

Ehreh's right-hand man in the lab was a bright youngster. He had slid from enthusiasm to dogged endurance over the long term of this project. Ehreh was sure others of the team felt the same way, but they had not been so forthright about it. They worked on his project at his behest, and though they all believed the work was desperately important, the long hours were beginning to tell. Ears and whiskers drooped. Tolerance eroded. Tempers grew short.

Ehreh could feel his own mind slowing down.

He eased up from his chair and stretched. Pain shooting up and down his back warned him to be cautious. He was too old to be working such long hours. He needed rest and food and a moment's relief from peering into microscopes as much as any of his colleagues did, and he worried that fatigue might lead him into grievous errors.

But he had so little time. He really wanted to see it through to the end. Age and disease threatened to rob him of the satisfaction. He was unable to achieve the proper emotional detachment.

"I will be at home," he told Mawuli. "Get in touch if you need to."

"Yes."

As he shambled out into the darker hallway, he caught some grumbling in the background about difficult old men.

I am not deaf yet, he thought. He turned back toward the doorway as if to identify the complainer, then changed his mind. *We work so that you have the chance to grow old enough to hear the young ones complaining*, he thought.

He had barely entered the corridor when Mawuli poked his head through the door and called, "Ehreh, you are still here?"

Ehreh limped back into the lab.

Mawuli sat down in front of the screen and adjusted the

resolution. The other researchers had gathered around, their excitement evident in forward-facing whiskers and intent stares, weariness momentarily erased.

And there it was. In the jittery world of the indescribably small, guided by a minuscule electric field and a bit of artificial RNA, a tiny string of dirty silicon and a little string of dirty carbon came together and stuck and became a virus protected by a nanomachine, the novel entity Ehreh had spent a career searching for, a manufactured being he expected to be immune to the usual biological defences complex organisms marshalled against viruses. His whole life's work came to fruition without fanfare at that moment, a sub-microscopic event observed on a screen.

He took a deep breath and held it. This was a monumental event in the future of known space. They knew how to destroy the Kaz.

Elation is not a thing Oriani are normally demonstrative about. But it was obvious in the lab.

Some part of Ehreh wanted to wave his arms and cheer, slap his fellows on their backs, celebrate the success of long years of hard work in spite of its grisly purpose, though his upbringing would have forbidden such a demonstration under any circumstances. His scientific self yearned to rush out and tell everyone. Researchers naturally wanted to make their work public. Most of the time, that was the whole point.

His more rational side reminded him that this time, silence was their only camouflage; if word of all this got out, their people would disown them, their families would shun them, and their government might very well confine them as persons dangerous to society. Not an unreasonable conclusion, after all, though the society they intended to endanger was not Orian.

Ehreh already had acquired a reputation as an anti-traditionalist, a member of an imaginary group that rigid traditionalists thought of as unreasonable troublemakers. All the people who worked with him would be tarred with the same brush, as humans were wont to say. (The significance of tarry brushes was something he had intended to look into but never found time.) He had pointed out the danger to every one of his colleagues as he recruited them, but he suspected they had, as he had, considered official disapproval a problem for some distant future. They all understood they had the more urgent Kazi menace to confront.

If Oriani were more suspicious of one another, the group likely would not have been able to get this far.

Success. He was hard-pressed to contain himself. Perhaps he would finally be able to convince officialdom. The younger ones were less restrained, moving restlessly around the lab, touching one another.

In the meantime, he would take the precaution of copying all the research notes and findings and descriptions of the methods and materials into coded files and sending them to a Turgorn supporter many light years away, where he expected they would be safe. Militaristic Turgorn knew the value of keeping secrets.

He watched a while longer as more and more of the strings came together, savouring the moment. Not all the unions were perfect, but a high proportion appeared functional, and he was confident the system would work well enough for their purposes.

The microscope whined itself down to neutral when Mawuli turned the power off. He took the sample out of it and slipped it into a cryowrap to take to Harl.

The lab was silent for a moment. Everyone was waiting for Ehreh to say something. Nothing momentous came to mind. "I thank you all. We have the weapon," he said, putting their achievement into its sombre perspective. Considering the time and effort these scientists had put into finding it, its purpose was unfortunate. "Now, we must find a way to deliver it. In the morning. We all should get some rest now."

Ehreh himself was the first out of the door.

THE FAMILIAR STONES of the Biological Sciences Building were still warm from the heat of the day when Ehreh started down that same long hallway toward the lab the following evening.

He did not get far.

The person striding toward him was a member of the Academy's administration committee and the fact that she had come to find Ehreh that late in the evening could bode nothing good. He had met her at some time or another but couldn't recall the event. *My memory truly is failing*, he thought. His instinct was to duck away into an intersecting corridor, to flee, to all intents and purposes, to hide in one of the quiet rooms from which sane people had gone home for the day, to avoid the confrontation, but it was not practical on two levels. Firstly, he needed, if not the goodwill, at least the tolerance of the Academy administration for a little while longer. One might pine for the time when an isolated researcher in his garret could make significant contributions to the body of knowledge, but that was no longer realistic. In modern times, to progress, the work needed sophisticated equipment and people sublimely capable in a variety of disciplines.

And secondly, leaving his staff to try to cope with officialdom did not sit well; he had promised he would protect them from just such encounters.

Making a run for it did have its appeal, but the administrator was in the prime of life, so even if he broke into an all-out gallop and dashed for the hills, she could easily catch him. While such a race might be amusing from the outside, as a participant, it would be nothing but humiliating.

Furthermore, Ehreh's bones were heavy this evening, and his muscles weak. He felt the betrayal of his body acutely, long strings of pain climbing up his spine, branching into his limbs. He had drugs for the pain, but they slowed him, mind and body, so he resorted to them no more often than necessary. His healer had said he should not expect too much time; the tumours were entering a fast growth stage. Together, they had fought the disease for many years, but they both knew now that the fight was lost.

He stopped and waited for the official to come to him.

Murr. Her name was Murr. *Congratulations, old fellow*, he thought, *you've dragged one fact out of the murk of muddled memory.*

"The Administration Committee has met at the request of the Planetary Council," the administrator said without preamble. "You are required to cease work, destroy the organism, and close your laboratory. You have one hundred days to accomplish this safely."

Ehreh imagined he detected a sense of self-satisfaction radiating from her.

He paused long enough to stifle the roar of anger that rose from deep within his primitive self. He turned and walked slowly, drawing her away from the lab. He took a deep breath to begin the argument he had made many times before. "The ground-breaking work we are doing here, I believe to be ..."

"The work you are doing here is obscene," she said over him, an egregious breach of Orian manners. She was making it very difficult for Ehreh to remain civil. Perhaps she noticed his flattening ears and rising hackles, for her next words were slightly more conciliatory. "I am merely the messenger. You have argued your case before the committee many times. Nothing has changed. You were authorized to investigate the bonding of nanites to biological entities, nothing more. You were certainly not authorized to test the results in living beings.

You were certainly not authorized to plot the elimination of an entire race of sentient creatures."

"We are working with cell cultures. Surely individual cells do not qualify as sentient beings."

"We both know where this is leading. You cannot expect us to agree to an attempt to destroy an entire species? Who could?"

I could, Ehreh thought, *and you know it. Anyone who considered the cost of inaction for generations ahead could, or anyone willing to learn from history.* Not so long ago, the Kaz had overrun Orion and very nearly extinguished the Orian race. The Empire was expanding again.

Murr was right in one respect. She was just the messenger. Her personal views were obvious, had been for some time, and in the unlikely event he could convince her she was wrong, it would have minimal effect on the committee as a whole, who were largely traditionalists, who all but worshipped the ancestors, and who would not be swayed. He could tell her they had succeeded, that they had built the organism that would hold back the Kazi hordes, but it would be a waste of energy, and he had little enough to waste. He could become defiant, but that would likely bring Security and deprive him of any chance of salvage.

And there, in those first moments, he was already thinking of salvage. He groaned inwardly.

"Please tell the committee I have received their message." It was hard to face the idea that they had achieved their goal just to have it yanked away. What Ehreh really wanted to do at this point was scream his frustration.

"One hundred days, Ehreh." She strode off.

Ehreh turned back toward the lab.

"THEREFORE, we need to complete the next step before the deadline, while we still have lab facilities," Ehreh told Mawuli. That would be to get the virus with its extended genome pushed into a protein coat that could still infect cells. Once that happened, Ehreh had little doubt the virus would do its job. They had derived it from a Kazi disease organism known for its ability to adapt and for its high rate of contagion and had done a little engineering to tweak its morbidity, but not too much. They didn't want infected individuals to be disabled too quickly. The virus needed to spread.

"Harl said that her group has been able to adapt the virus's natural capsule to be big enough, but then it is somewhat fragile and does not hold together long. They have been trying variations. She says they are making progress," Mawuli said.

Once most of the scientists had straggled in, Ehreh called them together and told the group at large what the Council had ordered and asked.

The lab around him was brightly lit and clean and well organized and full of dedicated people who had most likely sacrificed their careers to this work. It should be serving the pursuit of knowledge, not mass murder. It wasn't on any directory or in any budget or other official document. The biologists who worked here would get no recognition. The political machinery maintained a wilful ignorance. Those who laboured to save Orion and many of the worlds of the Interplanetary Community were the heretics of the Oriani principles of benign pacifism. Nobody wanted to know them.

"Anyone who wants to leave before the Council wreaks its havoc should do so," Ehreh said. "Many have families to protect."

"Protecting our families is why we are here," Mawuli said.

"The Council does not see it this way. For those of you who are willing to continue, I ask you to work fast and hard but also carefully. We will not have a second chance to do this. Please pass this information on to Harl's group."

While the others mulled this over, Ehreh took Mawuli aside.

"I must meet with some of the people who have been providing financial and material support. Could you go to Space Central to meet the Brodenli pirate? He promised to find us transport but has failed to deliver. All we have done will be to no avail if we cannot get the organism where it needs to go."

The youngster perked up, pleased to be entrusted with the task.

"Take care, my friend. Dealing with pirates is not without risk," Ehreh said.

"Take care, Ehreh. Defying the Council is also not without risk."

Only death is without risk, Ehreh thought as he left, but did not voice the sentiment. He had not told his colleagues about his disease, thinking they had enough to worry about without his adding to it, but of course, they knew all was not well with him. And he realized illness had changed his perspective on a great many things.

He walked down the corridor toward the outer door and had travelled only a short distance when a form detached itself from a shadowed doorway and moved silently along the wall. It was tall and thin, matte black, with large black eyes that glinted in the last of the twilight coming through the high windows. It called to Ehreh, a sound just loud enough for the Orian to hear but no louder. This was a talent of the Nsfera that many had remarked upon.

Ehreh turned, slightly startled and trying not to show it. "Ryet Arkkad. I was not expecting you here," he said. "I am on my way to Midway. We were to meet there."

Ryet Arkkad had addressed Ehreh in Sindharr, and Ehreh was struggling to understand and answer in the same language.

Ryet Arkkad's diction was nearly perfect, and its grammar fault-less. Ehreh had not used Sindharr, the lingua franca of space-going nations, very often for many years and had forgotten elements he was sure he once knew. *I should brush up*, he thought. *The next phase of his plan would involve people of many races.*

The Nsfera's motion could be a shrug. "Do not change your plans. But there is an unfortunate development you should know about. Previously supportive Gnathans are questioning the time it is taking to produce usable results. They are impatient." Ryet Arkkad displayed a bit of ivory. It often seemed to find life wryly amusing. "They are about to stop payments. They say they will sue for the return of previously rendered funds."

Ehreh failed to see the humour. He saw it as a serious worry. Years of struggle were being threatened by fretful Gnathans?

He stopped walking. A suit would certainly not improve his standing with the Planetary Council, though he suspected there was little to lose in that regard, and the money had long been spent. He felt cold and weak. Too many emotions had buffeted him already today, and he feared losing control. A finger of pain crawled up and poked at the base of his skull.

"Perhaps they would be impressed if you explain to them in person how far along you are in the process," Ryet Arkkad said.

"I do not have the time or the energy to make my way to Gnatha."

"You need not travel so far, my friend. A delegation is attending the Interplanetary Community Strategic Planning Committee on Midway. Speak to them. And fear not; this insult will be remedied in time." Ryet Arkkad often managed to add a hint of menace to a simple statement.

"Time is what I do not have. And insults are not the issue."

"Yes, the Academy has ordered you to stop work, disperse your crew, gather your notes and equipment, and present yourself before the Council to explain why you are doing what you are doing. That also can be remedied."

"You know this how?"

The Nsfera chose not to answer. "Neither the Academy nor the Planetary Council would be able to hinder your work if you were to move it to my homeworld. Fera and Orion are not the closest of allies."

True, they were not. Nsfera favoured expedience and seemed to have few moral strictures.

Ehreh considered it. "It would not be easy. People working on this project have families and other occupations. They will not be anxious to abandon all that. And we have considerable specialized equipment..."

"Simple or not," Ryet Arkkad interrupted, "it had best be done, and soon. Your Academicians are determined. Your work rather goes against the philosophy Oriani profess to live by."

"I think the Ancestors did not know any Kaz," Ehreh said somewhat sourly.

Ryet Arkkad stretched itself as if to become taller yet, brushing the ceiling, and made to extend its wings, but there was not nearly enough space in the hallway. It shook the partially extended membranes, its shadow spread out on the warm marble floor, huge in the failing light. Then it folded its wings away again tightly and neatly between the big shoulder muscles. "Make haste, my friend."

The Nsfera lengthened its stride and turned into an intersecting corridor. By the time Ehreh arrived at the intersection, it was out of sight.

So he went once more down the hallway to explain to his colleagues this new development. As the project progressed, his role had become less and less scientific and more and more political. Having no great tolerance for politicians, he did not enjoy the change of function.

BY THE TIME he finally made his way out of the building, his energy was low, and his pace slowed along the path toward the transit station. He stopped a moment to watch the last light fade as the shadows of the mountains crept up the valley. The biology building was separated by a botanical garden from other buildings of the Academy at Owr-Marl. The numerous small creatures that made the garden their home were stirring. The light-lovers sought safe places to sleep, and the night-lovers peeked out to see what the night would bring.

He sat on a sun-warmed rock and looked out over the valley. Would he be this way again? he wondered. He'd always thought he would die here, near this garden, where he had lived most of his life.

He shook off the feeling and composed a message directly to Harl to tell her what had happened, and that speed was now of the essence. He hoped to head off ruffled feelings that he had not come in person. She was a bit insecure and often thought the others treated her as a lesser member of the team. This had no basis in fact, but only in her atavistic mind. The Ancestors had been wise to counsel avoiding emotional entanglements. Unfortunately, their teachings were being abandoned by the younger generation.

No matter. He had no time to spare for sulks; the team would need to work quickly to complete as much of the experiment as they possibly could in the next hundred days. He knew Harl would suffer renewed moral anguish. He knew of no way to prevent it.

He could not fault the committee; they were acting appropriately to the virtues they held. Once the Oriani were not so divided, and cogent argument could carry enough weight to bring about agreement. No longer.

In the background of his mind, the spirit of the Pacifist of

Owr-Neg groaned unhappily. When the Ancestors forswore violence as a solution to problems, back when Oriani had not yet met another sentient race, they could not have known what eventually would face the Oriani people. They did not anticipate Kaz.

He had thought long and hard before he embarked on this journey and consulted many, but neither he nor anyone else could see a better path. He had tried to curb his conscience, but pangs still surfaced now and then.

A protracted sigh escaped him, an expression of fatigue, he told himself, not of guilt and fear. Perhaps he would not live one hundred days.

He wondered if sending Mawuli to meet the Brodenli was wise. Negotiating with aliens was always exhausting.

Was Ryet Arkkad truthful regarding the Gnathans? Ehreh often did not know how much to believe the Nsfera, who played games with everyone, pursuing its own agenda, whatever that might be.

He would have to forego his quiet time at home. The delay leaving the laboratory and this new addition to his agenda used up that small amount of spare time. He took up his walk again in the new sunshine and then down the stairs to the underground transit system for the day-long journey through the mountains and across the desert to Orion Space Central.

He swallowed his pills and tried to rest on the journey, but his repose was broken with doubt and worry. He had been told more than once that he should delegate some of this work to others. He should. He knew that. He had volunteers willing to take up at least part of the burden. Yet he had not found any way to let go. So many pieces needed to be brought together, and someone had to know where all the pieces were.

The next evening, Ehreh left the transit system at the IP Trade Centre, an ancient building that had been rebuilt after the Kazi occupation, and rebuilt again and again, and remained the pivot around which the life of Orion Space Central swung. Artificial light flooded the area. Smells and noise and confusion and crowding were endemic in the port city, and lifting shuttles pounded one's very being into the pavement. He steeled himself to cope.

Fortunately, he need not remain there long. He had a starship to catch.

DEEP KAZI SPACE

As soon as he saw the swarmbots ripping up from the planet's surface, Whitby Clough knew that he and the crew of the starship *Senator Alice Hester* were in trouble. He just didn't know what the shriek he was going to do about it. He clenched his fists, trying to hold the panic at bay. Sweat poured off him and ran down under the crash harness.

Do something, Whitby, he told himself. Himself came up with no brilliant ideas. "Jesus, we are so screwed," he said aloud.

This was not what he had planned for his life.

"Talk-talk from group leader." Tafillah Rullenahe was Clough's right-hand man and a better soldier by a long shot.

"Later. I'm busy." Whitby concentrated on unclenching his fists so he could work his board.

The fast little missiles flung themselves in their hundreds at *Hester*'s side, each one aiming for the spot the last one had hit, each one clanging and making a little mark. *Hester* staggered. They wouldn't stop until there were no more of them in the swarm or they'd breached the hull. They were too small and numerous to shoot at and hard to outrun.

Hester, a light bomber in Fleet parlance, a flimsy kite in Whitby's estimation, was flashing its distress all over the board. All external sensors were telling him that enemy craft were coming fast from overhead and behind, and he didn't seem to have any place to go but down toward the swarmbots.

"Find us a way between these things," he said to the Lleveci as if Tafillah Rullenahe were not frantically working on that already. The Lleveci gave him the benefit of a two-second beady-eyed stare. Tafillah Rullenahe looked a lot like a scruffy turkey if you could imagine a turkey with a long, black mane. Everybody said Whitby was lucky to have him.

He had to twist himself around in the cramped cabin to talk to Amy Brown, the weapons control person behind him. Amy could hear him perfectly well when he was facing forward, but he couldn't get past the need to look at the person he was talking to. He got a lot of static about that. "Get us out of here. And get rid of the damned bomb."

He turned back to the Lleveci. "Give me the com link." Tafillah Rullenahe detached the comlink from his socket and handed it over. Whitby hesitated a fraction of a second before clicking it into the socket in his own skull. It seemed too intimate an exchange with an alien. But there was no time to be squeamish.

He signalled the rest of the battle group by voice and by code several times each, but no one answered. All that came in was the hiss of the galaxy and an occasional barely audible clicking he feared might be Kazi targeting signals.

Tafillah Rullenahe reached over to Whitby's control board to point out an alarm. Whitby hauled his attention back to the horrors at hand.

"Changing course," Tafillah Rullenahe said, his claw-like fingers dancing over the navigation console.

"I need fifteen seconds," Amy said. She started counting down.

"Go now," Whitby insisted. "Go. Go!" A bit of hysteria lifted the register of his voice an octave or so. He hated that.

The brief delay reminded Whitby that, in many ways, he was captain of this vessel in name only. A small bump bounced *Hester* when the bomb was released, and then Tafillah Rullenahe put them into a sharp turn that the field compensators couldn't fully handle and left Whitby more than a little nauseated.

The vessel touched the upper wisps of the planet's atmosphere and staggered. The hull rang with a number of impacts, and then they dropped into hyperspace, and it was very quiet.

Except for the alarms.

"We're losing air, boss," Amy said.

One by one, Whitby shut off the noises, but the red lights kept flashing. Hull integrity, environmental control, engine temperature, anything that could go wrong, had. "Bring us back into space normal. Engines at idle," he said. "Let's see if we can fix some of this. Tafillah, find us the nearest friendly planet."

"Ferguson Prime," Tafillah Rullenahe answered promptly. "Two hyperspace jumps. Three hours, Terran standard."

Whitby had been somewhat relieved to see the engine warning lights go dark as the engines wound down from max. "Plot the course that puts minimum strain on the engines. Try to raise the rest of the group. Amy!" The weapons-control person raised her head from whatever she had been studying. "See if you can get the fixbots to give priority to plugging holes." His descending into the vernacular for the automated maintenance and repair systems was a measure of his anxiety.

"Boss," Amy said.

"Yes," Whitby answered.

"Shut up."

Whitby didn't like Amy's lack of adherence to protocol nor her lack of respect for authority. He didn't like Amy much either, for all she was a handsome woman, but now didn't seem like a good time to bring any of this up. Besides which, she had a point. He was only telling capable, experienced people to do what they would do anyway. As a leader, he had reached his level of incompetence, and he knew it. He wasn't stupid.

He was, however, extremely worried.

Back when he was planning his career, deep Kazi space had never been in his calculations. When Lieutenant Whitby Clough joined the Fleet at his father's urging, he had not been expecting to shoot at anyone. He certainly had not been expecting anyone to shoot at him. No interplanetary conflicts of note had occurred for a couple of generations when Whitby joined the service; accepting a commission had seemed like a nice way to get out from his parents' muffling control, into a uniform that attracted the opposite sex like a magnet, into a respectable line of work that shouldn't be more demanding than escorting bigwigs around and being decorative at celebrations.

He wasn't in a combat branch of the service. He didn't have much combat training. They had no business sending him here. His father, with all his power and influence, had done nothing to get him out of it.

Whitby had complained mightily, but Stanton had been no damned help at all.

"Just do what your group leader tells you to do," he said. "You'll be fine."

Yeah, right. Thanks, Dad. Does this look like fine?

The board in front of him flashed some new alarm. External sensors were picking up something.

"We got company, right and overhead," he told the others. "Three. Kaz."

He froze for a moment, not knowing what to do. The people who were supposed to be protecting him were nowhere near.

Under the best circumstances, *Hester* couldn't deal with three Kazi fighters on her own.

"Oh, shit." He had a moment of total despair.

Then he remembered something.

He quick-started the engines, which immediately started to complain, warned the others of a rough transition, built up speed for as long as he dared with the Kaz charging after them, dropped *Hester* into hyperspace with a gut-wrenching jerk, and came back out again in a few minutes.

"What was that about?" Tafillah Rullenahe asked.

Space normal was mercifully free of Kaz. That wouldn't last very long. The Kaz would follow their ion trail as soon as they understood what had happened. But maybe *Hester* would have time to slap on a few patches and get headed toward friendly space.

"I heard, read, that Kazi nav systems, or maybe their engines, don't deal well with short hyperspace jumps."

"Well, you might have bought us a little time," Amy said.

"Yeah. Can you get us somewhere else by then?"

The possibility didn't look good. All the engine lights were back on.

Repair and maintenance systems had priority, and they worked full speed. One by one, the engine tell-tales were beginning to go dark. They had obviously paid no attention to Amy's trying to redirect their efforts. Tafillah Rullenahe was busy at the navigation board, trying to find a safe way home. Whitby had nothing much to do at that point.

The planet they had just left, Nidus 23-3-29, had defences much more sophisticated than Whitby had been led to believe it would have. Bombing Kazi nidus worlds into inactivity had become almost a routine exercise, a way of holding back the Kazi hordes by targeting the Broodmothers and their nests of eggs. They were typically hidden deep in Kazi space but not well defended.

So he was told.

Everybody lies.

"Kaz come," Tafillah Rullenahe said.

Whitby wound up the engines and made another short jump. He hoped his stomach would hold out. "Take the helm. Do that whenever you see them show up," he told Tafillah Rullenahe. "Try to vary the course so they don't anticipate and just wait for us to show up."

"Run out of gas real soon," the Lleveci said.

"Yeah, well, let's hope we can hold this bucket together long enough to do that."

He wiggled out of his harness and squirmed his way around Amy's station, following as best he could a high, squealing whistle that he almost couldn't hear into the cramped area in the back of the cabin among engine parts and armaments and life support. He could feel rather than see their life's breath leaking out through a minute crack in the hull where the swarmbots had been pounding them. The process board told him that maintenance was still busy with engine cooling. Whoever programmed the system had a bad idea of what was urgent in times like this. He rummaged through the supply cupboards, trying to find something to stop the leak.

"Hey," Amy said when the squealing stopped. "That's better. What'd you do?"

"Band-aid."

"You're kidding?"

"No. For whatever good it does."

She laughed, a short, sharp bark. She seemed to be facing their imminent demise with better grace than Whitby could manage. He was having a hard time keeping his voice from shaking like that of a whiny child. And he felt like a whiny child, ill-used by fate and the Fleet, put in this impossible position from which there was no acceptable exit.

Hester staggered and shuddered. Whitby nearly fell as he scrambled back to his place. "What?" he demanded.

"Kaz come shooting," Tafillah Rullenahe said. "Energy weapon." The Lleveci was rock steady. His was a warrior race. "Get us out of here."

The transitions were rough.

"Okay. I'll look out for the Kaz. You get us a course to Ferguson Prime since that seems to be our last, best hope of salvation. Amy, put your finger on the trigger and at the first sign of Kaz, give them the heat seekers."

"Not much chance of hitting anything," Amy said.

"Well, maybe we'll scare them a little."

"I don't think Kaz scare very easy. They don't seem to care how many die as long as they get what they want."

"Nothing to lose here, lady."

Amy took a deep breath. Maybe she didn't like being addressed as "lady," or maybe she was not as calm as she pretended to be. "I've heard the Kaz don't bother to clean up once they've eliminated a threat. What if we play dead?"

"You sure they wouldn't blow a hole in *Hester*'s side just to be certain?"

"No."

"I've heard they reprocess everything they can lay hands on. I think we better run."

Whitby was pretty sure his nerves wouldn't hold out for anything else.

But it was too late.

Amy got her blast away, but *Hester* staggered, and the whistle started up again, and Tafillah Rullenahe announced the engines wouldn't start.

WHEN THE SWARMBOTS boiled up from the surface of Nidus 23-3-29, John Kim, group leader and commander of the fighter *General Luis de Silva*, struggled to put down his panic. He divided his battle group into two, sending the halves in opposite directions around the planet.

"Divide and conquer?" came the voice of the group's second in command from the fighter *Tak-tu* on his port side. John rather liked her, a slight Turgorn female, smart, capable, and possessed of a wry humour. They had flown together before and worked well together.

"It's my understanding swarmbots don't have a lot of smarts," he said. "The intel I got says the swarm won't divide. Of course, that same intel said nothing about them being on nidus worlds. I'm hoping they'll take a second or so to agree on which way to go, and maybe that will give us time to get away. Or at least half of us. Stay above the atmosphere so we don't have to slow down," he said, "but keep as close to the surface as feasible. We want to get behind the planet. Go hyper as soon as you're out of sight." He sent her galactic coordinates. "We'll rendezvous there."

Then the bulk of the planet was between them, and he could only hope. The vessels in his half of the group slammed into hyperspace right on cue, barely far enough apart to ensure they wouldn't be dropping out on top of one another. They came out about a lightyear away.

In a moment, the *Tak-tu's* half of the group appeared. Roll call revealed the problem.

"Where's *Hester*?"

"Unknown, Commander." Except for a slight furrow in his brow, Mifornan Rak, the Higant who was John's right-hand man, seemed unruffled, despite his species' reputation for volatility. "I am unable to find it."

"Hail her?"

"Yes. Done. No answer."

Kim stifled the urge to curse. "Sensor sweep, max range." He had good people for the most part. And he also had Whitby Clough. "Give me group-wide," he said to his communications person, a Brodenli with wide, back-sweeping horns that were a bit of a hazard in the tight confines of a fighter's flight deck. This expedition had been put together without too much thought, with no time for people to get to know one another, and Kim would have a word or two for the bureaucrats in HQ when the group got back to Midway. He had been a little uncertain about the Brodenli, but she'd proved to be much less fractious than her species' reputation would suggest.

"Okay, let's take a few minutes to run the sensor logs of the last half hour or so and see if we can figure out what happened to *Hester*."

Mifornan showed him a few seconds of sensor record in which he saw the swarm cluster around *Hester*. John saw that she staggered a bit, then pulled away from the planet's surface and vanished. With his technological wizardry, which John believed to be somewhat akin to magic, Mifornan overlaid the last frame with what he said was *Hester's* most likely course into hyperspace.

John addressed his group once again. "Everybody get your damage reports together. *De Silva* and *Tak-tu* will backtrack to try to find *Hester*. The rest of you get back to Midway and tell them what we found here. Before they send anyone else out into a mess like this."

The main part of the group dropped into hyperspace, leaving *De Silva* and *Tak-tu* behind, and John Kim immediately began to wonder if he was doing the right thing. It seemed very lonely suddenly, and there were a lot more Kaz in this region of space than he had been led to believe.

The two designated ships went back to where Mifornan thought *Hester* might be. She was nowhere in sight. And there was no debris field, which was what John truly expected to find.

After a long time consulting his whizz-bang techno-gadgets, Mifornan said there were ion trails he could follow, so John told him to do that.

"More than one," Mifornan said.

"All going the same way?"

"Yes."

"Okay, then."

There was a hesitation. Beneath the grumbling of the engines, the constant sigh of air handling, and the beep and boop of sensors trying to get his attention, John imagined he could hear Mifornan breathing deeply. "Not the best idea, I think." That would be as far as Mifornan would ever go toward criticizing John's decisions. For him, it was a pretty vigorous protest.

"Yeah, I know. But it seems to be the only course we've got. Let's find *Hester*. Then we'll worry about what kind of shit she's in."

They jumped.

They came out at the designated location some distance apart. John wondered whose navigation was faulty, but he wasn't going to worry about it just then.

"Mass sensors show an object at extreme range," *Tak-tu* said.

As they approached, the mass resolved itself into a number of objects, one of which was the badly damaged *Hester*. Kazi fighters were still hounding her, and she was doing a tolerable job of dodging bullets. The two rescue vessels hastened to join the fray, though John wondered if they weren't just adding injury to insult. They were no serious match for Kazi ships of the line.

"*Hester* is losing air," Mifornan reported. "Energy handling systems are erratic. I expect it will lose life support soon."

"Can you signal her?" John asked the communications

person. To the others, he said, "Go in with guns blazing. It's probably our only chance."

Mifornan questioned him with a slit-eyed look.

"Fire all weapons as often and as quickly as possible," he explained. Then added, almost an afterthought, knowing how literally the Higant could take him, "Try not to hit *Hester*. She doesn't look like she can take much more."

When it came down to cases, John took advantage of the Higant's reflexes and gave him the helm while John and the navigator assisted with the weapons. The Kazi were quite happy to divide their attentions. *De Silva* took a couple of glancing blows, and for a while there, it seemed like they would have to abandon *Hester* or lose all three vessels to the Kaz. Then John got a missile up the tail of one of the Kazi vessels, and the Kaz abruptly quit the battle and went hyper.

So then they had a moment to catch their breath.

"We're low on fuel. We've lost part of our sensor array," *Tak-tu* announced. "Are you getting anything from *Hester*?"

John looked at his sensor board. *Hester* was dark. "You get home. We'll look after this."

"You sure the Kaz aren't coming back with friends?"

"As sure as I can be. They weren't supposed to be here in the first place. Don't blow what fuel you've got worrying about it. There aren't many gas stations out here."

"The reference to 'gas station' is unknown."

"Go."

"Yes. There is no need to be cranky."

John cut the connection before he said something he would regret. Mifornan had *De Silva* approaching *Hester* by then. In a moment, *Tak-tu* was gone.

"Does *Hester* know we're the good guys?" John asked the communications person.

"Unknown. No response from within the vessel. The emergency beacon is operating. Engine is running."

John asked him, "Is there a pressure suit that fits you?"

The creature nodded and did something that might have been a smile.

"Okay, let's go. I hope they don't meet us at the door with weapons levelled."

But before the airlock cycled, *Hester* put on a burst of speed and vanished.

"What the blankety-blank is wrong with them?" John asked in frustration. "How did that idiot over there get a command?"

"'Blankety-blank?'" Mifornan asked.

"I'm trying to avoid bad words," John answered.

Mifornan was silent long past the time John expected some snarky comment. "What?" John asked.

"I am considering the concept of a word being bad."

"Just catch the bloody *Hester,* will you?"

FERGIE PRIME

"Hanna, baby, how are you?"

"Mom, Mom, Mom, are you okay? Can you come home now? I did really good on my math test. I wanted to show you."

"I'll come back as soon as I can, darling. You know I will."

"I want it to be now."

"Me, too. I love you so much."

"Love you too, Mom."

"Could I talk to Aunt Jane for a moment?"

There was a slight delay, a couple of golden seconds ticking by.

"Hey, Lauren, how you holding up?"

"Been better. Listen, this kind of extravagant. Hyperspace communications aren't cheap. Is there any way to explain to Hanna that I'll be home sooner if we don't incur this kind of expense every other week?"

"You want to explain 'incur' to a six-year-old?"

Oh, yes, Lauren thought. *Yes, I do. I want to explain everything that needs explaining. I want to see her beautiful eyes widen when she grasps a concept. I want that like I've never wanted anything.*

"She worries about you," Jane said. "She needs reassurance."

"Yeah. Just do your best, Jane, please."

"Yes, all right, I will. Listen, you should know that lawyer, what's his name, Reiner, sent a letter. It's all legalese, but I think it says the Merriweather family are launching a civil suit, asking for a million credits for pain and suffering and lost income resulting from the death of their son Beau."

"Just when I thought we were done with this. What makes those idiots think I have anything like a million credits? What jurisdiction?"

"Centauri Colonial, I think. I tried to talk to Reiner, but he kept saying he couldn't discuss it with me. I told him you were off-planet, I didn't know where, that they should ask at Double-Chek Security."

"Thanks, Jane. I'm sorry you got involved in this. Can you pass the letter on to Evelyn Cortez and ask her not to rack up too many billable hours? But don't worry; I will look after it. I gotta go."

The connection clicked into static. Lauren wondered how far her bosses at DoubleChek would go to protect her. *Not far*, she thought.

Across the small room that was Howerath Mines' Ferguson Prime office, Marc Duvray raised an eyebrow. "Everything okay?"

Lauren shrugged. "Have you persuaded the AI to accept its new assignment?"

Marc grunted unhappily. "I think I would have liked IT better back in the day when it wasn't so much like teaching kindergarten."

Lauren rubbed the sweat off her forehead that was threatening to run into her eyes. The light of binary suns burned white-hot in a blistering afternoon. Dust devils staggered along the empty street outside. Everyone who could get indoors got in. Ferguson B was just a few centuries or so past the near end of its orbit, and Ferguson A bulged out, reaching for its twin. Its satellite, Fergie Prime, jiggled in its orbit; the tides were insane, and the weather was barely survivable, even hard up against the pole in New Towne while the planet passed between the stars.

Two people and a bunch of machinery ran the Ferguson Prime office of Howerath Mines, and only the machines rated cool air; even so, the machinery idled during the hottest part of the day to keep cooling costs down. Howerath Mines' people spaces were insulated but not cooled. Light poured in from the one thickly laminated window.

One might envy the miners, who had the sense to stay deep underground during the hottest part of the day.

Nathan Howerath Jr. came in and stood behind them. Lauren could feel his impatience, even though he didn't say anything.

The screens in front of Marc flashed for a moment, then went dark. The AI was having a temper tantrum.

She and Marc had been going over the mine's sensor logs, looking for some clue as to where 35.9 grams of heliosite had gone. They had ripped an AI out of a mining machine and roughly re-purposed it as a scanner to help. Sometimes, a totally unprejudiced point of view gave insight, and even if it was pretty damned crude, it was still hundreds of times faster than she and Marc could be. But by the time they had it operational, she had filled up a lot of Nathan's office with equipment, and Nathan found himself squeezed into his inner office among displaced chairs and tables.

He didn't see how any of this was going to find his missing product. He had grumbled throughout the examination of the sensor scans of the number-one shaft, yet to be convinced that they weren't just throwing good money after bad, but his protests were mild because he didn't dare come across to his head office, chaired by Nathan Howerath Sr., as not cooperating. He didn't even complain much when she took his precious production charts down and put up the biggest display screen she could lay her hands on, stolen, over some mild alarm from Marc, from the process monitor. By the time they started on number-three shaft's records, Nathan had run out of complaints he felt confident enough to voice and so had sunk into peevish silence.

The only real reason for anyone to be on Fergie Prime in those days was heliosite, the most valuable mineral there was. A little chip cut as a gemstone glowed like solid rainbows, and such jewellery was sported by a few of the richest (and most ostentatious) individuals in the Community. But most of it was cut a millimetre thick along another plane to become an ambient temperature superconductor; its ability to channel huge energies through a little scrap of crystal made travel through space possible. Without it, hyperspace engines would be too big and cumbersome to be practical.

A hundred grams of raw heliosite would put you on easy street for the rest of time, and Howerath Mines had been the main shipper of heliosite to the Interplanetary Community for the past decade or so, making for some pretty happy, well-heeled shareholders. Then, a couple of months ago, they'd started losing product.

"You're dead sure one of the miners didn't just walk out with it?" Lauren had asked when she first arrived.

"They're subject to a thorough vetting before they're ever hired on. They're very well paid. They go through a thorough check every time they leave the site. They'd have to have a way to get it off-planet and a way to market it. We have the best security system we can get." Nathan had pointed at the "Protected by DoubleChek" sign on the wall.

"But actual people still handle bajillions of credits' worth of the stuff every day."

Howerath shrugged. "I guess that's why you're here."

He had a point. The company automated everything it could in a distant outpost, but some actual people were still necessary. Lauren was currently the agent on-site for Double-Chek System Security IP, a rather grandiose name for a pretty boring company that attempted to protect businesses from the ills of the modern world and the ignorance and stupidity of their owners. Most of the time, it involved persuading people to follow simple security procedures and lock their doors at night. Once in a while, it was more interesting.

"Okay, what's that?" They were playing back the sensor records of the number-three shaft for the period between shifts when it should have been empty.

The AI stopped the playback of the near IR record at Frame 2791. Marc brought up the same time stamp on visible, mass, and motion records and displayed them on lesser screens.

Lauren told the AI to go back a few frames and play them forward a frame at a time, matching all records.

"I don't see anything," Marc said. Nathan leaned in as best he could.

On the big screen, in an image that was already pretty dark —bedrock didn't emit much IR even on Fergie Prime—Lauren pointed out a blurry shadow that appeared in the lower right of the frame, drifted upward off the right edge over the course of seventeen frames, and did not reappear.

"Glitch in the record?" Howerath suggested.

Marc gave him a look.

"Maybe," Lauren said. "If it actually is something, it's absorbing IR. Where would you get a bag of ice around here?"

"Well, now, I don't really—" Nathan looked at Lauren and frowned. Marc was carefully not smiling. "Rhetorical question, right?"

"Yes."

Eye-ball examination of the other records didn't turn up

anything notable. "Can you get the AI to go over all the scans for these eleven seconds or whatever with the finest resolution it's capable of and look for any anomaly it can identify?" Lauren asked Marc. "Talk nice to it; I think it's sulking."

"Yeah, I guess. This is not the optimal equipment for that sort of work, though."

"It is because it's here. If we try to get something better adapted brought in, it could take months, and anything we find will be archival. So, let's do the best we can with what we've got. Nate, I'll want to go to the site later."

"Um," Howerath said. "I'd have to get permission from the company and Fleet HQ to take an unauthorized person into the mine."

"Hustle, then. And hold up the next shift before the site gets any more contaminated than it is. Maybe you should think about getting your security team pre-authorized before the next time there's an issue."

"That would cost thousands of credits in non-productive expense."

"What does 35.9 grams of heliosite cost you?"

Nathan huffed and spluttered.

You probably shouldn't be irritating your employer, Lauren told herself. *That's not going to get you home faster. It's going to get you fired.* "I'm going over to Declan's. I need a break and some food."

"Is that necessary?" Devoutly dedicated to the bottom line, a teetotal, clean-living health nut and general pain in the derriere, Nathan vigorously and vocally disapproved of anything that was not useful, productive, efficient, and profitable. He did not approve of chemical relief of any sort from life's sorrows. "I don't suppose I have any say in the matter?" he continued.

Hot and sweaty and tired and hungry and very uncertain about what was going on here, Lauren felt more than her usual amount of crankiness. "No, I don't suppose you do."

Watch it, she told herself again. *You can't afford to lose this job. Remember why you need the money.*

"Do you have any idea what it's like when these things go wrong?" A small, elderly, dun-coloured man in dun, weathered clothing with an ancient, hollow-cheeked nightmare face of blotchy colours and scarred and unsymmetrical features leaned on the bar, forearms roughly parallel, pint cradled between the three-fingered metal claws that served him for hands. He had a hard time holding the wet glass. It tended to slip until the bulge at the top stopped it. Lauren had always wondered why beer glasses were built that way.

"No, I don't," she said. She was happy to procrastinate going back to the mine office. It wasn't cool anywhere behind the big heat-resisting windows at the front of Declan's, but at least the shelter prevented sunburn. Declan's was better than some—a pretense of air conditioning, at least, a degree or so below boiling, and the shadowed interior and nearly cool beer had psychological value. Fortunately, B's orbit was taking it back into space for a few thousand years to become nothing but a bright star crawling across the sky, making human habitation of Fergie Prime possible. And the worst heat of the year was over. At least, that's what the locals had told Lauren.

"Look at me," the old guy said, bringing a claw up to the side of his head. Lauren did. He wasn't pretty, that was for sure. "Name's Bolek, by the way."

"Lauren."

Bolek gave himself a sharp smack upside the head with one of his claws. It made a sound like a hammer striking a plastic box. "Sarcolite," he said. A partial explanation for why he looked like he was made up of mismatched parts.

"Oh," Lauren said, "What is that, actually?"

Bolek went into an explanation she didn't entirely follow.

Declan himself was behind the long bar, busying himself with the time-honoured polishing and cleaning of things that needed none. The wood and brass were neither wood nor brass and well supplied with nanobots to keep themselves in order. The glass—well, there were machines for that, of course. Could be the long mirror behind Declan's ginger head needed shining now and then. The place was supposed to look like a nineteenth-century Irish pub. Maybe it did, Ireland having gone the way of the nineteenth century, totally subsumed into the grey, grainless homogeneity of the home planet's culture many generations ago.

It seemed a bit pretentious on a frontier world.

In the shadows on the other side of the narrow room, a couple of rough, dusty fellows sat at a table, heads together in deep discussion. Miners, perhaps. Alone in a corner, Rosette nursed a glass of something red, probably not wine, because she was rigorous about not drinking on duty (and being New Towne's lone peace officer, that was pretty well all the time), waiting out the worst heat of the day.

Bolek held his claws in front of his face. "Why did they do this to me? Why couldn't they grow new tissue, you ask?

Lauren hadn't, but Bolek went on anyway.

"It's because anything that promotes tissue regeneration gets the nanites started again. They eat away from the inside out. Do you have any idea what that's like?" He contemplated the claws with a look of old, well-worn sadness. "There must have been something better than this." He negotiated the business of getting another mouthful of beer. "They don't tell you about this when they are telling you how smart you'll be with all the implants, how strong, how young, how every sense will be brighter, sharper, more discriminating than before, and all you have to do to achieve these miracles is your patriotic duty." His thousand-yard stare would have been more effective if his eyes didn't have that vitreous look. "The enemy will tremble at your name, they said. Like hell. Why did I fall for that crap? I was smart enough to know better. I used to be smart. I think I was. I don't how much of what I remember is real and how much is just stuff they stuck in to fill up the holes."

The F-stop of his pupils racked up as he turned to face Lauren. "I lost a lot of neurons. Half my thinking is done with silicon these days. You know what that's like?"

Lauren shook her head.

"Dumb. It's fast, but it's dumb. My wife—I had a wife—she couldn't stand it. She went . . ."

"Lauren."

Lauren turned to greet her saviour, whoever it might be. She was beginning to worry she wouldn't be able to turn Bolek off now he'd got started, and his unmitigated woe was nearly as depressing as the weather.

There were people she never expected to show up in Declan's. One of them stood just inside the door, trembling with urgency and pointedly ignoring everyone else in the room. "I need you right now," Nathan said. "Marc says the AI has found something."

Lauren was on her feet right away. This was her job, after all, and the sooner she got it done, the sooner she could get off Fergie Prime. She and Hanna would vacation somewhere cool and civilized. Ice cubes. Swimming pools. Rain. She thought she would never understand people who chose to come to places like this.

Nathan grumbled away about her not being at her post as they hustled across the street and down the block, trying to take advantage of what shade there was. With two suns in the sky, there wasn't much.

"I don't think me standing around in the office will make much—"

The roar hit them. Lauren turned instinctively, but she was

looking right into the glare of Ferguson A. Then the explosion rolled right overhead and flattened her into the dirt.

The sand burned against her skin, and when her wits recovered enough that she could think about it, she scrabbled for the shadows. In the sudden silence after the explosion, Lauren shook her head, feeling deaf, then staggered up, yanking and shoving Nathan to his feet and, with gestures and pointing, persuading him to continue on into the office, out of the suns' burning rays.

Nathan was shouting at her, but her battered ears couldn't make out what he was saying. He shook his own head and pointed.

A thick plume of black smoke struggled into the sky in the distance. It grew thicker and blacker as she watched. A second detonation, more felt than heard, sent a mass of flame into the smoke. More explosions followed.

Marc Duvray was shaking his head when Lauren and Nathan pushed through the door. He was already talking, it seemed, but Lauren couldn't hear him. Watching him, she thought she made out the word "spaceport."

He motioned her to the screen before him and showed her that Rosette was already on the way out into the desert, sending visuals from her flyer, calling on everyone to give a hand. The crash site was about ten kilometres from New Towne and about a kilometre from the port.

"What was it?" Lauren asked, her own voice sounding small and distant inside her head. Flat planes and right angles amid the dust and smoke declared it wasn't natural.

Marc shrugged, then typed *rosette wants everyone there to help she thinks there are survivors.*

"Humans?"

Marc shrugged again.

"Okay," Lauren said. "Let's see what we can round up in the way of transportation. But I don't know what we're going to do when we get there. We won't be able to get near the thing."

"Hazmat suits," Lauren thought she could see Nathan saying. Then he typed it for the screen. *we have hazmat suits in storage*

"Yeah?" Lauren drew a question mark in the air.

we had to get some when we first started up here industrial health and safety insisted they've been in storage ever since never used

The office door flew open, and Bolek, less flushed than another might have been, came in to relay Rosette's demand that firefighting equipment and men be put in the mine's air sled and flown to the crash site immediately.

Marc translated to the screen. Nathan bristled and shook his head.

Bolek wasn't having any of that. He grabbed Nathan's shirt front in one claw, stuck the other under Nathan's nose, and shook it. Bolek was a little guy, and Nathan was pretty big, but in minutes, miners were in action, and Nathan, released and fuming, retreated to his office to sulk. *People surprise you*, Lauren thought.

"That wasn't very nice," Lauren said, to herself, not expecting to be heard.

A grimace on Bolek's face might have been an attempt at a smile. Words appeared on the screen. *I'm a war vet. I don't have to be nice.*

MOST OF THE miners had been waiting out the day deep underground, intending to emerge only in the relative cool of evening. Everyone Bolek could round up was crowded into Declan's ancient cargo van, whose air conditioning consisted of wide-open windows, and into a strange four-wheeled contraption driven by Bolek, which, from all Lauren could tell rattling along beside him in the passenger seat, was no better.

Fortunately, Ferguson B had almost set. That made the air a little cooler. Ferguson A was about an hour behind. Long red shadows already marked the dunes. But with no suitable generators or lights, the would-be rescuers would be able to do very little once it was dark. So they rattled and clattered out to the scene as fast as they could.

Lauren had never considered Rosette a serious player in the game of life until that moment. Her prejudice, she realized, was born of the woman's silly name, which presumably Rosette hadn't chosen, her frivolous style of dress, which she had, and her insistence on makeup and hair in these most impossible circumstances. But when the hammer came down, Rosette took the rescue operations in hand. As the townsfolk arrived, she organized fire-suppression teams. They exhausted what fire extinguishers they had, then threw sand on whatever they could to try to put out the fire and temper the heat to make the wreck approachable.

Rosette sent others prowling around the wreck to look for a way in, then ordered a second wave of miners to bring their big lifters and earth-movers out to the site. She got everything moving faster than Lauren would have thought possible.

Whatever had crashed had gone in at a small angle, causing a long, shallow gouge with a huge berm of sand at the end. Nearly buried beneath was a pile of tortured and blackened metal. A searcher was calling and waving his arms, then pointing into the smouldering pile. "Movement. Someone's moving in there."

The hull had buckled away from the frame and left a sizable gap. The big digger put its bucket up against the metal and pushed to widen the gap. Lauren joined the excavators frantically working with shovels and pails where machinery would be too crude, each person taking a swipe or two before retreating from the heat. When they had a little trench dug out, Rosette pulled Lauren out of the rotation.

"Here, you might fit into one of these," she shouted as she hauled the hazmat suits out of the van.

Lauren was happy to be able to hear her, suggesting her ears were beginning to recover, but not all that happy with the assignment. Her stomach did a somersault. "Um, yeah, that's maybe not what I should be doing. If anything's alive in there, it would be better off dead."

"I don't want to hear talk like that. We need small, fit people. Take this suit. Find me Bolek for the other one."

When Bolek appeared, a couple of townsfolk were commandeered to help them dress.

"You should be okay for smoke and fumes," Rosette said. "But these things are not rated for heat. You're not going to have much time."

The coverall was antique, dusty and yellowed with age, and, in Lauren's estimation, totally unreliable. It was a-clank with bits of equipment hanging off it and stuffed into pockets. It had a genuine toothed zipper, something Lauren had read about but never seen. As she got into it, she tried to call up whatever she could remember of long-ago first responder training that the military had always said she was exceptionally bad at. And it was still true that while she could deal with dead ones in a numb sort of way, she tended to gag when confronted with broken creatures that were still breathing. Not the best reaction under the circumstances.

The suit's air supply wheezed in her ears. She was hot from the get-go, and it only got worse as she and Bolek crawled along the trench, desperate not to touch any part of the wreck, trying to move quickly and not knock sand down off the walls that would impede their retreat.

The heat was insane. Lauren's diaphragm maxed out at every breath. She could feel her skin crackling before she even reached the gap in the metal. She could hear Bolek behind her and wondered briefly if sarcolite was better or worse than skin in these circumstances. Funny what stress brings to mind.

"Do you see a survivor?" she asked through the headset. With a crack like thunder and a rumbling groan, a metal beam above her bent and the whole wreck shifted. The digger pushed harder, listing the metal a little. *How much adrenaline can one absorb*, she wondered, *before she just falls apart?*

"Go a little left. I think that's the cockpit."

"Hey! There's a boot right in front of me. Can you come alongside?"

With his limbs splayed out lizard-like, Bolek squirmed himself alongside. He tried to move some of the debris out of the way but didn't make a lot of progress.

"Time's up," her headset announced in Rosette's voice. "Get out."

"Wait."

"No waiting. Now."

"You push, I'll pull," Lauren told Bolek.

"We're liable to do more damage," Bolek pointed out.

"He's got nothing to lose at this point except the joy of cooking to death. We have to try." Heart pounding, lungs heaving, dizziness descending, she grabbed hold of a limb and pulled with what strength remained to her while her gut knotted itself. She was trying hard not to look at the ruins she was dragging; her vision was fading.

Bolek had wriggled over onto his back, using both claws to add what he could. The body came free, and they tumbled back as sand cascaded down around them. Bolek pushed her across the loose pile. Rosette's voice was nattering in the headset, but Lauren couldn't make out the words. She latched on to some part of the victim and pulled and scrabbled in the direction of light. She wondered if she would get there. Bolek pushed the body until another landslide occurred.

Then hands were grabbing her, pulling her out, removing the helmet, and for the first time ever, Fergie Prime's air seemed cool and sweet.

"Bolek—"

"We'll get him," she heard Rosette say from a distance. She offered the object she had clutched in her hand, a brass-coloured name tag. "*SS Senator Alice Hester*," it said in a sharp-edged military-style font. "Lieutenant Whitby Clough."

And then there was a big thump, and the ground shook, and then she heard nothing at all.

ORION SPACE CENTRAL

The sun was blazing in through high windows. The office had no air conditioning. As sweat slipped, itching, down his ribs, Ben Lawanda thought he would be more careful in future about what jobs he agreed to. He looked at the Orian next to him as if to ask Mawuli to explain how this had gone so wrong.

"No."

Slouched in the chair, the Brodenli lifted his nose high enough that his swept-back horns made dents in his shoulders. He sniffed as if what he sensed was not to his liking and repeated, "For you, no."

Mawuli thought he was the one who should be sniffing. The pungent creature across the desk apparently did not bathe often. The chair Mawuli was perched on was uncomfortable, and he was tired. Beside him, the human Ben Lawada shifted his weight on a chair no more to his liking, his face a mask of puzzlement.

Mawuli stifled his annoyance and stared past the pirate, looking out of the window of the tenth-floor office at the buildings of the city, looking for some kind of calm in the cityscape and finding only more irritation. He had less tolerance for unreasonable behaviour than Ehreh had, and Ehreh should be the one trying to deal with this irrational creature. Yet Ehreh had asked him to do it, and he had agreed. Having done so, he owed his project leader and friend his best effort. He thought of himself as a gentle and moderate person, a family man well versed in dealing with minor aggravations, but here, his composure was being tested. He continued to stare across the city, trying to keep his temper.

He had not wanted to be in Space Central at all—it was a rough and crowded place—but the pirate had insisted that it was the only place on Orion he could go without being immediately taken into custody. True enough. Orion provided infrastructure and managed the safety of vessels in Orion space but did not police the port. Anyone and anything could be there that was tough and mean enough to survive.

Space Central had been rebuilt after the Kazi occupation with wide, straight streets and tall, clean buildings. Almost immediately, the inhabitants had started reworking the streetscape, filling corners with makeshift structures, letting renovations ooze out onto the roads, and erecting ramshackle instant slums in the few open spaces. No matter how hard some people worked to maintain order, others equally enthusiastically embraced chaos. He knew many of the building contractors active in the port were Oriani, and it rankled. You couldn't trust anyone these days. He felt dangerously close to sliding into "old-person syndrome," thinking of his grandfather's complaints that young people had no sense of propriety; things were so much better when he was young; people had more respect in the good old days.

He wasn't even old, yet he could feel his culture coming unravelled, and it wasn't a pleasant sensation.

"'For me, no?'" Mawuli asked when it seemed likely the Brodenli was not going to continue. "You have some quarrel with me? I do not believe we have met previously. A few weeks ago, you were more than willing to provide a vessel. Something has changed?" At this point, Mawuli was not really expecting much. The meeting had not gone well from the beginning when the Brodenli arrived late, bristling with hostility. Whatever had made the Brodenli pirate decide against providing a vessel for their use, he did not seem about to be swayed by argument. "We have no more money if that is what you are hoping for. Our resources are very limited."

In a somewhat more relaxed posture, the Brodenli shook his head until his ears rattled. "Few weeks ago," he said, "was talking to Nsfera, who is saying nothing about lying, cheating Oriani."

"Eh? Lying Oriani? That's a first," Lawada said. "What's your problem here? Oriani money spends as good as any. If they're successful, the Brodenli will benefit as much as anyone."

"So you say," the Brodenli answered. "Oriani think Brodenli have forgotten the battle of Jengchilea."

"The battle of Jengchilea occurred more than twenty-three generations ago. It has a bearing on the negotiations at hand?" Mawuli asked.

"Brodenli don't forget so soon."

"Put it aside for now," Mawuli suggested. "We have more urgent issues to deal with."

The Brodenli shifted his position, straightening his posture, presenting himself now as a featureless silhouette in front of the window. Mawuli shortened his gaze to take in the office itself, obviously borrowed for the day, and its recalcitrant occupant. The pirate was a rough creature, dressed in an odd assortment of clothing, some bright enough to be Roothian, to which he had attached a gaudy collection of objects made of precious metals and gemstones.

"No," the pirate said.

For a moment, it seemed the Brodenli's attention shifted

from Mawuli to the human. Ben Lawada and the Brodenli understood something that Mawuli did not? It seemed unlikely.

Mawuli leaned back as much as his miserable chair would allow and looked around, and said nothing. Sometimes, a small delay reduced tensions.

The window in the outer wall was the only light. Standard office furnishings included two high-speed data terminals sitting on a desk, no doubt recording the proceedings. Much unidentifiable paraphernalia was heaped in a corner. He heard a squeak and scrabble of small animals there. There was an underlying musk in the place that was not Brodenli.

He wondered if it were possible some opponents of Orion had scripted this event, and the Brodenli was merely their paid actor. But for what reason? Perhaps some opponent of Ehreh's particular project had arranged it. If he were sufficiently paranoid, he could imagine his own government had a hand in it. But it would be an unusual approach for Oriani. If and when the Orian government decided to move, he expected them to be much more direct. Which was why they needed to get their project underway as soon as possible.

Ben Lawada scratched his head around the metal ring that enclosed a thumb-sized hole in his skull, the socket through which he would connect to his ship when flying. No doubt, he was puzzled. When he had offered his services (for a price), he had anticipated a few busy days inspecting a vessel to see if it was space-worthy, talking to mechanics and technicians and potential crew, then bringing it on to Midway, an easy and well-paid few days' work. The Brodenli's refusal likely bothered him, too, though Mawuli very much doubted the pilot understood fully what was at stake.

"What do you need from the Oriani to make it possible for you to work with Mawuli?" Ben Lawada asked.

The Brodenli's snort might not have been laughter, but it

was certainly derisive. "What I get from these hairy pigs but fleas?"

"You have been offered a great deal of money. You have been offered a chance to help defeat the Kaz. You want how much more?" Mawuli said.

Another snort. "Defeat the Kaz? You say this again? Heard this story last time Oriani have big scheme. Bomb nidus worlds, they said. Everything be fine. Look where we are now, back to same place. Not so fine. Here, I think, more lies."

Ben Lawada touched Mawuli's shoulder. Mawuli suppressed the impulse to snarl. Humans were always touching. They did not seem to be able to resist the urge. "Let's go," Ben Lawada said. "We're not getting anywhere. I have an idea."

Mawuli agreed. He was happy enough to leave.

BACK AT STREET LEVEL, elbowing through the noisy crowds, Ben Lawada asked, "So, what happened in the battle of Jengchilea?"

"Long ago, when the Interplanetary Community was just forming, during one of the first efforts to discourage Kazi expansion, when communications were not as efficient as today, a detachment of mainly Brodenli warships were sent to engage the enemy near Jengchilea. They expected to be supported by IP forces assembling near Orion, but those forces did not hear of the plan soon enough. When they finally arrived, the initial assault force had been badly damaged. In the aftermath, a rumour started that Orion had deliberately delayed the support group, that it had sacrificed the Brodenli to protect itself. The Brodenli embraced this idea, and no amount of argument or evidence was able to dissuade them at the time." Mawuli stopped to allow a group of Aragalese to pass by. "Or now, it seems. This one apparently holds it against me that I did not choose my ancestors more wisely. I have encountered closed minds before but have rarely met ones so well buttressed against all input."

Ben Lawada laughed. "It's hard to know how to persuade a guy who denies argument and evidence. What're you going to do next?"

Mawuli did not see the humour in the situation. "This Brodenli agreed to a meeting he was certain, perhaps determined, would be fruitless?"

"Some people like the drama."

"Possibly, some people are being manipulated."

"You think?"

"I cannot be certain, but I believe it to be within the realm of possibility. I will think about it for a time. Perhaps someone would benefit from having me here, at a pointless meeting, instead of back in the laboratory?"

"Who?"

"I do not know," Mawuli said. "Ehreh will be disappointed. I do not think that he has an alternative available."

Ben Lawada scratched around the socket in his head again. "The Brodenli didn't seem that complicated. Anyway, I know a guy who might be able to help."

"You truly have a plan?"

"No, but let's not give up just yet. Listen, we can't discuss this here. I need to talk to some people. If we could lay hands on a drone freighter and fill it with swarm-bots, would that do the job?"

Mawuli thought about it for a moment. "Possibly, with some modification. Our purposes would not be best served with all the bots crowding together as swarm-bots are usually programmed to do."

"I have a hunch that could be fixed. Just tell me exactly what you need and when you need it. We need to go to Midway."

"What I told the Brodenli is real. We do not have much

more in the way of funds. None of us is wealthy in those terms, and we do not have the support of our government."

"You think you'll be able to get your money back from him?" Ben Lawada pointed a thumb over his shoulder toward the building they had just left.

"I will petition the Council but suspect they will consider such an agreement extralegal. Meanwhile, I must return to Owr-Marl and help with shutting down the lab. Ehreh or I will meet you on Midway in a week or so, STD. You should try to connect with a Nsfera called Ryet Arkkad. It may be useful with logistics, and it has many social connections, though I must warn you, it is difficult to control."

"Okay." Ben Lawada strode off toward the shuttle dock, and Mawuli stopped to watch him go. When thinking of Ben Lawada's response to the Brodenli, the thought "mask" had come to mind. Though Ben Lawada's offer of help had come at a crucial moment, it had produced no useful results. Ben Lawada appeared to be accommodating and offered to look for a new solution to their problem. Mawuli normally took people at face value unless he had a reason to do otherwise and had been accused of being naïve because of that.

Today, some instinct had been tweaked. When he got back to the Academy, he would look a little more carefully into Ben Lawada's background.

BACK AT THE ACADEMY, in the bowels of the old stone Biological Sciences building, Mawuli found preparations for moving had not progressed as much as he had hoped. Some crates stood around, but almost no equipment had been packed, and drawers and shelves were still laden. Ehreh was already en route to Midway, Basheh said. Harl herself, though left with the job of organizing the move, had expressed reluctance, and so did several others, and argument was taking the place of packing.

Mawuli asked Basheh to collect as much of the virus as they could spare. "Ehreh has some plan for it. I do not know what it is yet, but he has asked me to bring it to Midway and meet him there."

Seeking a way to motivate his people, Mawuli went down to Harl's lab. She was not overly pleased to see him. She had been expecting Ehreh.

She moved away from the laboratory bench where she was working so Mawuli could get a better look at the screen. The image displayed was the dance of life a few orders of magnitude bigger than the last one Mawuli had studied. Cells seemed so busy at this level of magnification, fluids streaming, membranes stretching and contracting, shapes moving in and out of focus. But even to one whose knowledge of cellular-level biology was not his greatest asset, none of those lumpy, bloated cells looked healthy, and as he watched, one ruptured and dumped its granular contents into the inter-cellular medium.

"We have discovered this much about your organism, if that is what we should call it," Harl said. "The infection rate in Kazi cells is very high *in vitro*. In living Kaz, I cannot say. I expect it to be high as well, but what is not known about Kazi immunology could fill terabytes. The organism survives three degrees absolute for considerable periods and is infectious shortly after warming.

"I have found one peculiarity. The latency is long in juvenile cells, shorter in cells from older individuals. I do not know why this is.

"It seems to be specific; we have not found this strain to infect cells other than Kazi, but we have had no access to evolutionary relatives of Kaz, which would be the appropriate test subjects."

"We can produce it in quantity?"

"I see no reason why not." Harl gestured at the screen. "The culture is not significantly different from other organisms."

"You have done useful work." Mawuli turned away from the carnage on the screen as another cell went down to viral death and leaned against the bench to rest his back. "So, we have our weapon, and we can manufacture it."

"No," Harl said. "We have a good candidate, but given that we have been able to do so little investigating of its properties, that is all it is. We do not know much about its characteristics, even less about its stability. It could change utterly in a few generations."

"I think we must take the risk."

"That is not acceptable." Harl sat on a high stool beside him, with the apparatus of the microscope behind her. Her whiskers drooped, and her ears were slightly back. "I am uncomfortable with our inability to test species related to the Kaz. We can justify putting how many life forms at risk? I am uncomfortable with the whole enterprise. Deliberately attempting to exterminate an entire race of sentient beings must be utterly wrong. Causing thousands of billions to die just because they are who they are and follow their own biological imperative cannot be the right thing to do."

"The only alternative we have is to kill a billion a year for a thousand years, or until they become adept enough at defeating our methods and kill billions of us." This had always been Ehreh's argument. Mawuli could find no fault in it.

"There are not a billion of us."

"We would not be the only victims."

Harl turned away. "Perhaps some of the other billions could do some of these awful things. How can I teach my children that violence is wrong when I am a party to this?"

"Reasonably, we cannot make an evil necessity less evil or less necessary by removing it to a distance." Mawuli straightened, muscles protesting long, long hours without sleep.

"I do not need someone of your tender age to instruct me in philosophy."

"You have children to teach. Let us work to see that your children have the same opportunity."

"I have heard Ehreh say this. I believe that much of what Ehreh says is wrong. He is old and speaks a logic of a different time."

"What is true is true. Time should not change that."

"At times, I do not like you much, Mawuli."

Mawuli was careful to hold his ears up and his tail still, showing no signs of the annoyance he felt. He was standing in Ehreh's stead and needed to respond as Ehreh would. "Affection is not required. Fortunately. At times, I do not like me much, either." He gathered himself to leave. "Basheh will be here looking for as much of the virus as you can spare to send to Ehreh. Ryet Arkkad says it has facilities on Fera that we can use when the Committee shuts down this lab. You should be able to do at least some of the testing when we get to Fera. Perhaps the Nsfera could help find genetic relatives of Kaz. They often have resources no one else has."

Harl sat quietly for a moment. "Fera is far away. I do not want to leave my family."

"I have no alternatives to offer. The Council will take everything and bury it for eternity if we stay here."

"My part of this is done. I do not need to go to Fera."

"You could be held accountable for the entire project if you are the only one the Council can lay hands on. I do not know who is behind this or why they have decided to move just now, but they appear to have argument enough or power enough to move the Academic Committee."

Harl ruffled. "Tell Ehreh I do not want to go to Fera."

"Yes, you have made that clear."

Mawuli left the lab before Harl could express her reluctance further, walking down a long hallway toward the side entrance. Academy officials had made it quite plain they did not want any of this working group coming and going by the front door. A bizarre restriction, to Mawuli's mind. How it could possibly deflect anyone's interest in what was going on in their little corner of the building was beyond his ken, but it was not difficult to accommodate this expression of official paranoia.

He was bothered that Ehreh had no plan in place to cope with the loss of support from the Academy, even though the old man had known from the outset that the Council disapproved, nor had he any plan for the possibility that disgruntled colleagues, disturbed because their fascinating project had become an act of civil disobedience, would not follow him to some barely known distant sanctuary. Mawuli himself had had moments of doubt.

The loss of agility with age was not just physical.

He walked down to the transit station, intending to go home to his family for a while. A day or two of tranquility would be welcome. He was so tense, it felt like all his hair was standing on end.

Just before entering the station, he stopped with a sense of movement at the edge of his vision. He turned, thinking perhaps Harl had followed him, hoping she had not because he was weary of the discussion.

Something charged at him out of the shrubbery. By instinct, he jumped high and to the side, tail arched, hair fuzzed out. The thing passed him on his left side. Collecting himself, Mawuli watched the spot where he had been and saw movement among the leaves. He jumped again, deliberately this time, landing on his assailant with all four limbs. He struggled to hold it, but it had a hard, muscular strength, and Mawuli had as much of the plant as he had of the beast and, like most modern Oriani, his claws were clipped short and blunt; the thing squirmed out from under him and fled with a rattling of branches.

The excitement over, Mawuli spent a few moments thinking. The attack was unlikely that of a predator; predators were encouraged to stay away from centres of population. Therefore, it was personal. The only thing about him that might attract that kind of attention would be the virus.

He headed back to the Academy.

Harl was surprised to see him and more surprised when he told her of his adventure. "Someone thought you were carrying the virus? Attacked you for it?"

"I can think of no other reason."

"Once you are off Orion, you will be more vulnerable."

"So I believe."

"You can take some others with you?"

"In light of this, I do not know whom I can trust."

"You think the attacker was Orian," Harl asked, on the verge of outrage.

"I have no evidence. But the virus needs to get to Ehreh on Midway."

"We need a carrier no one would suspect, and we need to keep the identity between the two of us. Perhaps just the one of us," Harl said. "I have an idea."

"Why are you willing to help when you disapprove of the goal?"

"I disapprove of people being attacked even more."

MIDWAY—INTERPLANETARY COMMUNITY STRATEGIC PLANNING CONFERENCE (IPCSPC)

"Delegate Clough, please. Stanton Clough, wait. I need to speak to you. Can you give me a moment?"

Surrounded by the rough, unfinished walls of disused structures, the walkways leading onto First Avenue and from there to the conference room were narrow and poorly lit, not designed for the size of the crowds attending meetings in modern times. Buffeted from every angle by people pushing their way in, Terran delegate Stanton Clough found himself getting a little testy and was expecting the wider passageway to be a relief. But it was every bit as crowded.

Delegates representing the races and worlds of the Interplanetary Community had agreed to meet there again to discuss strategy in their continuing war with the Kaz. With relatively little squabbling, considering the history of disagreement between them, Turgorn and Beta Ellgarth, the two worlds historically responsible for the place, had scrambled to get it ready in time. Not a simple task, for the conference facilities hadn't seen much use for several centuries. The hosts did their best; still, no one was very comfortable there, but no one felt anyone else was very comfortable either, so it was a kind of democracy.

Barely making out his name over the noise of the crowd, Clough shot a quick glance over his shoulder and saw the pale, shaggy fur of the delegate from Nas Goury. They had encountered one another at a few meetings. Clough dredged up a name: Jorn.

"Mr. Clough, I need a moment."

Clough hesitated. He didn't want to talk to Jorn, but he couldn't really afford to brush off anyone who represented even the slightest possibility of a vote supporting his policy. Jorn embodied many of the characteristics Clough associated with a very large but not-too-bright dog: unrestrained, clumsy enthusiasm; an assumption of friendship on the most meagre acquaintance; and a tendency to get much too close.

The domes enclosing Midway's cold, thin atmosphere had been expanded over the years, first to accommodate administrative branches of the Interplanetary Community and then, inevitably, a military base that eventually dwarfed the rest of the structure. The remnants of many previous occupations of Midway huddled under the original dome, which clung like an ancient wart to the side of the shiny new structures. This older part had been worked and reworked and updated and modernized repeatedly: passages closed off and reopened, walls razed and built until not even the maintenance AIs that were charged with looking after such things really knew what was where. But for all that, Clough didn't see any immediately available escape route.

He sighed and waited to let Jorn catch up. *If he licks my face,* Clough thought, *I will kill him.*

Around them, delegates from a hundred worlds chattered, hissed, and buzzed as they funnelled into the largest space available in the old dome, which had been tricked out as a conference centre for the occasion. Clough fiddled with the flexible gizmo in his hand that Archie called a flimsy, remembering not to fold it into his pocket. That, Archie said, would cause it to fail if he did it very often. Technological whiz-bangs were great and all, but most of them had a downside, like being unable to tuck a document away out of sight.

Jorn had to raise his yappy voice to be heard. "Hi, hi, hi, Mr. Clough. Glad to catch you. I and some others, you know, and the people behind me, would like to talk to you. We are having some doubts about Martin Industries' new fighter design. Particularly, we are concerned about fire suppression."

"Really? At this stage?"

"Yeah, yeah. Some of us are thinking we should look at Lleveci InterNational's proposal. In theory, at least, it is more fuel efficient."

"But not any more fire-resistant, as I understand it."

"My company had a new fire-resistant coating . . ."

"Paint? This about paint?"

"No, no. We just want to delay the vote until we've learned more about the Lleveci design."

"You want me to delay a vote on my own proposal? We've had good service from Martin for decades."

"Yeah, yeah, indeed. Contract renewal for Martin Industries had become automatic, and they are becoming complacent . . ."

"I have to go, Jorn. People are expecting me." A lie, but what the hell. Everybody lies.

"Another thing—can we get together later to talk about this new technique of dealing with the Kaz that the Oriani are proposing? Have you heard about it? If they get the Community to agree, it's going to be a . . . I think it has a real chance."

"Is this the Oriani nonsense about driving some biologic deep into Kazi space?"

"Yeah, yeah, yeah. I'm hoping we can get the Oriani to meet with us to work up a real understanding of the idea. If it could actually work . . ."

"I've heard rumours. It's not that new. But it is total madness on so many levels, not to mention contrary to the Community's charter. As I understand it, the Orian Planetary Council is not on board."

"Can we discuss . . ."

"We don't need to talk about it. I am unequivocally opposed. I cannot support expending resources on some blue-sky scheme at a time when the Kazi Empire is expanding, and all we can do barely slows them down. Enough young people are dying in the fight against the Kaz without sending some out on a suicide mission that has very little chance of success."

Jorn was all but bouncing with distress. "But I understand your United Nations is . . ."

"I'm sorry, Jorn, I really do have to go. I have a meeting, and I'm shortly going to address the Conference, and I need to prepare. There's my aide, come to fetch me. Goodbye." Clough plowed through the crowd and left a deflated Jorn behind.

Clough groaned inwardly. That vote was lost, but even if he had wanted to support the Orian scheme, it would be political suicide. Not only would it be a complete about-face from his previous stance on the issue, but implementing what he understood to be an insanely expensive, untried technology would take huge resources. It would require putting all the Community's anti-Kazi eggs into one very flimsy basket, so to speak, or acquiring new funds. New taxes. No government's constituency would support that, not even the Oriani; those individual Oriani that proposed it and tried to promote it were a splinter group the Orian government was trying to discourage.

Clough gave himself a mental shake and tried to pick up the train of thought he was on before the interruption. He believed that the way to deal with the Kaz was to make it so costly for them to expand into this region of space they would stop trying and go some other direction. More bombs on more nidus worlds; that was the way to go. His firm belief in this approach was why Martin Industries, IP supported his bid to become chair of the Committee. If nidus worlds were being as well defended as the Fleet claimed, then the Community needed to mount stronger attacks. It didn't take high-end math to figure that out. He was puzzled by the number of delegates trying to turn the situation into a complex super-technological issue. *War is never complicated. Kill them before they kill you. Simple.*

Clough pushed on. It was his fate to try to talk sense to idiots.

STRUGGLING THROUGH THE CROWD, Archie Bennett had to shout, and it made his voice unpleasantly squeaky and strained in his own ears. He disliked the sound; it was not in keeping with his personal image. The upcoming surgery to fix that was still some months away. He could hardly wait.

Clough didn't slow his progress through the hordes of delegates as he worked his way steadily toward the conference room and down the aisle to the dais at the end where the Interplanetary Community Strategic Planning Committee was meeting, except for the microseconds required to smile and glad-hand some politico or another. "What, Archie?" he asked over his shoulder.

Archie hustled along in Stanton Clough's wake. "It's personal, Stanton."

"Can't it wait?"

"I don't think so. We've had a communication from the Fifth Battle Group. The starship *Senator Alice Hester* is reported destroyed."

Clough finally stopped and turned to look at Archie. His face had blanched and stiffened in the instant that it took. "Whitby?"

"As far as they know, he was aboard."

Archie could see the information sinking in. Face white, muscles rigid, Clough struggled to breathe. In their brief months of association, Archie had become sure that Clough didn't care much about anything or anyone except his place in the IPC hierarchy and his son, Whitby. Half Clough's world had just gone away, and the fight to hold himself together and maintain his public face in the bumping, nudging stream of folk pushing into the conference room was obvious. Archie found himself feeling a small shred of sympathy for the man.

Clough finally managed a deep shuddering intake of breath. A couple of nearby heads turned, but Clough might very well die before he allowed his pain to be known; he would certainly not display it before those he considered to be his competitors and certainly not before people of other races, whom he uniformly considered to be below the salt.

"I'm sorry," Archie said with a measure of sincerity.

Clough put a hand on Archie's shoulder as if to steady himself. Nodding toward the stage, he said, "Make my excuses, will you?"

"Of course. Did you want me to inform Beatrix?"

Archie watched as Clough struggled to answer. Eventually, he said, "Yes, do that. His mother should know." Clough always spoke of his ex-wife as if she were a piece of necessary but unpleasant equipment, like a dentist's drill. Archie, on the other hand, treated Beatrix with the utmost courtesy and consideration.

He got Clough turned around and ran interference as best he could until the delegate was out of the conference room and headed back to his quarters.

IN CLOUGH'S EAR, the hyperspace transmission hissed with static. Some military bureaucrat blathered on over the noise, giving him the official processed garbage about important missions, keeping the known worlds safe and secure, what hardened targets Kazi nidus worlds had become, increasing casualties, the real need to continue the fight, about how IPC Forces and the Interplanetary Community at large truly appreciated Lieutenant Whitby Clough's sacrifice. Clough kept his temper with some difficulty in the face of all the phony solicitude.

The bare concrete walls of his so-called executive living quarters were rough beneath his hands. One hand on each side of the frame, he stared out of the tiny window, regarding without much interest the way the dome above blurred the stars of Midway's endless night. Alive once, the planet had been dead for millions of years, a bare ball of black rock orbiting a distant stellar remnant, no main player's colony, no one's base, no one's ally's base, no one's special-interest territory, and therefore a neutral meeting place. He had always found Midway bleak beyond measure, and just now, it suited his mood.

"Where is my son now?" he interrupted the babbling bureaucrat when he thought he could sound like he was in control.

"Beg pardon?"

"My son. Where is his body?"

For a moment, he heard only the remnants of Midway's star fizz and whistle in the background. It gave him a second or two to collect himself. Finally, the bureaucrat said, "Uh, *Hester* went down on Ferguson Prime. They were trying to get home." There might have been a minuscule hint of emotion in that last phrase.

"Wherever the hell that is, I need transport there right now."

"Really, sir, we don't have—"

"Please don't tell me what you don't have or can't do. All I want to know is when you can get me to Ferguson Prime, and it had better be damned soon. Am I clear?"

"Yes, but—"

Clough broke the connection.

Silence moved in. For a moment, he could only stand there at the window with the earpiece in his hand and let the awfulness of Whitby's death sink into his soul, and it sank like a rock into snow, slowly, coldly, until it became frozen to the bottom. He slammed his fist into the wall beside him, and the rough surface immediately opened a dozen small abrasions across his knuckles and offered a flash of distracting pain.

He rummaged through the baggage Archie had not yet put away to find something to wrap his damaged hand with and found the bottle of scotch instead. He'd been criticized more than once about using a chunk of his freight allowance for booze, but over the years, he had found a decent whisky very useful for lubricating sticky bureaucrats of many races. He started to look for a glass, then decided it wasn't worth the effort and swigged a mouthful directly out of the bottle. It burned but hardly warmed him. He tried a little more, which had much the same effect.

Some ancient famous person's definition of insanity: doing the same thing over and over again and expecting different results.

After some time, he became aware of a gentle knocking at his door. He thought to get up from the chair he was sitting in but decided it would be too much trouble. "Go away," he shouted at the door, louder and more slurred than he intended.

"I would like to speak to you, Delegate Stanton Clough." Orian accent, a little strained.

"Go away." The second demand was thicker and sadder. One tiny interruption was unravelling Clough's self-control.

"As you wish."

Whitby had once told him that when Oriani used the

phrase "as you wish," they meant, "You're being an idiot." Poor Whitby. He never became the leader of men his father wanted him to be. Tears flowed freely down Clough's cheeks and made his collar wet.

Some uncertain amount of time later, he came back to consciousness in his bed. Archie had been in to tidy up and had left hangover meds and a glass of water on the bedside table. Clough's hand had been painted with liquid synthetic skin, and a padded bandage protected it against further damage. *Good boy, Archie*, Clough thought. He was well aware that his aide didn't like him much, but Archie was meticulous and efficient, and Clough valued those characteristics highly, so they worked together well enough.

Clough had just struggled into a semi-sitting position to swallow the pills when a knock at the door interrupted.

He did seriously consider not answering. He was in no condition to receive visitors. He didn't want to talk to anyone anyway.

It was probably Archie being considerate instead of just charging in as was his wont. Clough had been rescheduled to address the convention, and it might even be now, for all he knew. Once upon a time, people had watches and clocks. Nowadays, they depended on little electronic gizmos attached to their person somewhere to keep them to their appointed schedules. He had no idea where his personal electronic irritant was at that time. Archie always looked after it.

Maybe Archie could look after the speech as well. Clough was in no mood for guiding hidebound bureaucrats along the path to meaningful action. He was tired and hurting. If they wanted to continue banging their thick heads or whatever against walls, he was ready to let them.

For once, politics held little interest.

The knock repeated. Groaning, Clough shuffled over to the door, well aware of his dishevelled appearance. Fortunately, because the room was small, the distance was short, and he arrived on target still upright and with enough energy to key it open.

The Orian standing in the doorway was old. His ear tips were white and his muzzle grey, and he was a bit grizzled at the shoulders. The tawny fur had a shop-worn look, and the frame beneath seemed frail, like some blunt-toothed old lion in its last days. As Clough stepped aside to let him in, he could see the old fellow's movements were slow and awkward, as if he were arthritic.

"My name is Ehreh. I tried to speak to you before. Might I sit down? I am not the man that once I was."

Clough got his only chair onto its legs and indicated it with a gesture, wondering.

The Orian perched on the edge of it with his tail curled to the side. Clough sat on the bed, uncomfortable about its unmade state. And why, he wondered, would that bother him? Why did he care about this alien's opinion?

"I have heard your son has died in a battle with the Kaz. My condolences. It is a hard thing to lose a child."

"You have no freaking idea." Clough believed this to be true. He had no personal experience of Orian family life, but all that he had heard made it seem an unemotional and brief association. In a more diplomatic frame of mind, he would not have made such a reference, but at that moment, he just couldn't give a damn. Usually, discussions with Oriani proceeded without preamble or polite chitchat.

"Perhaps. I, too, have lost family to the endless fight against the Kaz," the Orian said. "When I was younger, I fought myself, back in the days when attacking the Kaz directly seemed like the only way to prevent them from overrunning all of known space."

"It still is," Clough said.

"Perhaps."

Clough realized Ehreh was making concessions to human sensibilities, but then the Orian got straight to the point.

"I do not believe that approach is sustainable. Attacking nidus worlds is becoming less and less effective and more and more costly. This strategy is no longer holding back the Kazi Empire's expansion."

"All we need to do is put a little more effort into it. Increase defence spending—" And then Clough waved away the argument. He just could not be bothered to go on explaining life to this decrepit old alien when his heart was aching for his son. The argument for increased resources for the never-ending battle against the Kaz was a well-worn path for him, and it seemed particularly pointless just then.

"The delegate from Nas Goury suggested I speak to you about a different approach," Ehreh said. "Possibly because they are so numerous, possibly because of their appearance, many peoples tend to think of the Kaz as unintelligent. They are not and are perfectly capable of responding to attacks and devising countermeasures to any threats that we can muster, severally or together. War only means a continuing arms race and endless death and destruction. More parents will lose their children. You must know this."

"Leave me alone," Clough said. "I can't talk about it now."

The Orian went on without pausing, an unusual lack of patience for one of his race. His ears drooped a bit at the tips as if he were running out of energy, so perhaps he hadn't heard. "The treasuries of entire worlds are being ransacked, generations are being spent, and we are not winning. We cannot."

"So we should give up and become Kazi subjects? Or casualties, as the case may be?"

"There is another way," the old fellow said.

"You're not going to tell me about peace negotiations."

"I am not. I do not know that anyone has successfully negotiated with the Kaz. I cannot imagine why they would be interested in a settlement of any kind. They have no reason to compromise."

With a sharp rap on the door, Archie stuck his head into the room. He had been told many times to wait for an answer before he came in, but he never did. "Stanton, excuse me; your transport to the Ferguson system will be ready for you in one hour."

There was some minuscule satisfaction in that. "I have to go," Clough told Ehreh. "Archie, do I have a clean shirt? Is there somewhere on this benighted planet I can wash my face? Would you pack my personal effects into one bag? Everything else can go home with you."

"What would you like me to tell the Conference?"

In his mind's ear, Clough could hear Whitby's voice saying, "Dad, if the universe were coming to an end, you would say, 'Tell it to wait until after this meeting.'" It staggered him, it seemed so near.

He hesitated when another time, he wouldn't. "Tell them I have personal matters to attend to. Tell them I have to bury my son." His voice caught in his throat. He took a few deep breaths, trying to regain his composure, and saw the flimsy laying on the table. He had worked a long time developing arguments he hoped were persuasive. He picked up the device and gave it to Archie. "Tell them this."

"You want me to deliver the address?"

"Yes. And be convincing, okay? We're losing this war," Clough said, echoing the sentiments of his visitor. He paused again; maintaining the illusion of being his usual decisive self took more energy than he had. Realizing the Orian was still there, taking all this in, he added, "And, uh, get this—um—person's contact information, would you?"

IN THE CONFERENCE ROOM, the grim faces of the assembled politicians and soldiers attested to the seriousness of the agenda, which was one item long, as had been the case for as long as anyone there could remember. How can we contain the Kaz?

The lights dimmed slightly, leaving only the dais at the front well-lit. The room quieted a little as the delegates found chairs, stools, slings, or whatever resting places suited their various physiologies. They activated translators and murmured to their aides and assistants.

At the last minute, the hosts' delegates hurried to their places in the last row of seats. A Terran that few recognized took centre stage to deliver an address whose message had not changed much in all the time the Interplanetary Community had held meetings like this. All the worlds represented here had to be more vigorous in their common defence.

In the back of the room, a mossy-green, lizard-like Roothian slipped in behind the seated attendees, careful to close the door softly behind himself. He didn't take a place in the assembly but stood quietly near the door, resting on his tail. Although his race usually favoured brightly coloured garments, today, in deference to the task at hand, he was dressed in dark greys and black. Roothians weren't well thought of by the Interplanetary Community and had not been invited to attend the strategy meetings on Midway.

By invitation or by stealth, it was all the same. He heard nothing new from the speakers, but perhaps it was significant that Stanton Clough was not in attendance. He surveyed the crowd as well as he could from his vantage point, looking for the human, and when the Orian moderator took the floor once more, he left. It was doubtful anyone saw him there.

Beyond the conference room, where the hallways were not well-lit in the interests of saving energy, the Roothian skittered along as close to the wall as possible, trying to avoid the security cameras. His small size relative to the host species and his dark-coloured clothing worked to his advantage. He spent no time at intersections beyond what was needed to be sure the way was clear. Deep within a maze of twisty little passages, all alike, he stopped at a door beneath which a little greenish light leaked out.

He stood up on his hind legs and knocked. "Assiffah iss here," he said, not too loudly.

The door opened. The musty smell of his current patrons wafted out. Giving a little shiver of apprehension, Assiffah went in. He didn't like his Kazi employers, and if he had any other way to make as much money as they promised, he would take it in a heartbeat and be gone. He knew they would not like the message he had to deliver and could only hope they would not seek to take out their ire on the messenger. He stayed close to the closing door.

The two darker shadows stirred in the dim light. They turned toward the entry with a chitinous rustle. One had a sounding device around its neck. "What?" it demanded. The instrument had a tinny voice.

With a silent prayer to the Blessed Saint of Roo, Assiffah said, "Ehreh wass not in meeting. Thiss one cannot ffind him. He sseemss to have vanisshed. Sstanton Clough wass not in meeting. Allso not to be ffound."

Whatever the Kaz said to one another with their posturing and arm-waving, Assiffah could thankfully ignore by shutting his eyes. This allowed him to relieve the tension of trying to guess how they were responding. After a moment, he cautiously opened an eye and saw that both Kaz had reared back on their walking legs, and both of them were waving their forelegs at one another, ignoring him. Which might have been a good time to make his exit, except he hadn't been paid. He waited apprehensively.

Eventually, the one with the sounder around its neck said,

"How is this possible? Has an Orian vessel left Midway? Any vessel?"

"Thiss one doess not know," Assiffah said.

"This answer is not sufficient."

"Iss only answer thiss one hass," Assiffah said. He was pleased to note that his voice was firm, without any sign of the quaver that threatened to betray his unease.

"Go," the Kaz said. "Get a better answer. If Ehreh left this world, determine how and where he went and with whom."

Assiffah didn't move. He was trembling inside but determined to show nothing on the outside. For a moment, when the Kazi fixed him with its glittering, faceted eyes, he feared he had miscalculated.

Then the sounder said, "What?"

"Infformation you sseek iss cosstly. Thiss one iss without ffundss. Thiss one hass not been paid for many scycles."

Again the glittery stare. "The Empire has received no useful data for many cycles." The Kaz waved at one another for a moment, then the sounder said, "It is remedied. Go now and get the information that is required."

Assiffah turned to go. In the split second before the door responded, his heart rate multiplied by ten. When the door closed behind him, he leaned against the corridor wall until it returned to normal and the trembling abated. He checked his implant and saw that his deposit in the Temple of the Immaculate Saint of Roo that acted as his bank had increased substantially. He skittered down the hallway toward the docks and the offices of the Port Authority.

STANTON CLOUGH HAD SUFFERED through all the endless checks and inspections. The security people lording it over everyone in their cold, grey dominion had been at least superficially sympathetic; the bots had been bots. He endured all this with ill grace, truly thinking a person of his position in the current circumstances could be afforded a little courtesy. But all he got were canned apologies, and his mood had not at all improved in the process. He was about to enter the airlock and then head down the long corridor that joined the shuttle bay to the domes. At the last moment, he heard the urgent voice behind him. "Delegate Clough, Delegate Clough, please wait. I have news."

Clough turned to see a Turgorn rushing toward him, arms a-flying, trailing a number of the local constabulary and bots, who seemed to be trying to stop him. The badges and markings on its tunic suggested an individual of some stature. Wrong word, Clough thought wryly, given the being's slight physique.

"Lieutenant Whitby Clough is alive. Gravely injured. He is to be brought here, to the hospital. Delegate Clough, do not go to Ferguson Prime. Whitby Clough is coming here." The creature sounded quite breathless. The constables and the bots crowded around, at a loss now that they had caught up to their quarry.

Clough stopped and looked at the Turgorn. For a moment, he couldn't really process what the creature was saying. The lock indicator chimed and turned green, ready for him.

"They said he was dead," he said quite dully.

"An error." The Turgorn was breathless. "He will be here in a few hours."

Clough felt numb. Too many emotions had him stunned. The Turgorn took his arm and helped him to one of the benches in the secure area. *The little critter is strong enough,* Clough thought. Inconsequential ideas kept him from grasping too tightly onto the one thing that would be devastating if it turned out not to be real: Whitby was alive.

"I need Archie," he said weakly.

IN THE WAITING SHUTTLE, which had been scrambled in great haste, the pilot, hauled back from an impending vacation, listened a moment to his com unit, then turned to his second with a look of incredulity. "Bugger's not coming. Shut 'er down." He called up to the captain of the fast packet *Mercury's Daughter* waiting above. "Stand down. Asshole changed his mind," he said.

Somewhat aware of all the machinery and effort that had been put into motion in order to take one pompous dick from point A to point B, he could only shake his head, which the captain couldn't see. She would chide him about his language later when they were off-air.

Later, nursing that wound to his pride in a small dockside bar called, surprisingly enough, Dockside Bar, the pilot treated the co-pilot to a few helpings of the local brew while they commiserated together about a lost commission and avoided the captain's irritability while the captain and the flight AI put *Mercury's Daughter* to bed.

They became vaguely aware of a disturbance. Neither of them was sober enough at the time to realize they had been causing it and that other people were quite annoyed. Some tall, dark thing touched the pilot's shoulder.

The pilot turned and snarled. "Hey, gechur poochie-pokin' hands off me."

Tall dark said, "You should come with me."

"Oh, yeah? Don't think so."

"Your choice. If you do not come with me, and quite promptly, you will have to go with them." The pilot squinted to follow the pointing digit. From Avenue A, patrol officers were making their way across the open area, headed in their direction.

"'Promptly,'" the co-pilot said and giggled.

After a moment of cogitation, the pilot came to see the creature's meaning and scrambled to untangle himself from chairs and table legs. He lost his balance at one point, and the creature held him up, giving him a look of patient acceptance of incompetence such as your mother might give you after the tenth time she had shown you how to tie your shoes. The co-pilot, possibly less inebriated, managed on his own. They followed the creature down an alley, through a nearly invisible door into another hallway and from thence into a larger, busier passageway. "Stay with the crowd for a while, and you should be okay."

Some carefully hoarded remaining thread of sense caused the pilot to say, "Why you doin' this? Whachu get outta it?"

"Let us say it is in the interests of public service. No good is served by having competent shuttle pilots in jail. Perhaps I will want a favour in return someday. Take care."

By the time the pilot had worked out a reply, the creature was out of sight.

WHEN MORNING CAME AROUND, with heads like over-ripe melons pulsing to the rhythm of the syllables, the pilot and co-pilot endured a few more choice words from the captain about unbecoming behaviour and disappearing without a word and then were sent up to finish the chores on *Mercury's Daughter* while the captain dealt with officialdom.

"How did she know it was us?" the co-pilot wondered on their way through the airlock.

"I have a hunch," the pilot answered.

MIDWAY—YALLAH RULLENAHE GARRISON

John Kim wasn't happy to be summoned into Lieutenant Nes Gow's office. The Turgorn was a bit full of himself, and Kim had been anticipating that a considerable amount of flak would be coming his way after the mess at Nidus 23-3-29. He wouldn't mind if the pencil pushers were somewhere else when it came down. He certainly didn't want to take it from one of them.

Nes Gow offered Kim a chair and told him the base commander would be joining them.

Ominous. "Any idea why?"

"I didn't ask. He's been a bit grouchy this last little while. Things haven't been going so well, as you know."

"Yeah."

"How are you doing yourself? I heard about your last action. That's got to be hard, losing a ship."

"Yeah."

"I can't imagine how a person would cope with losing people you knew, worked with. You must feel terrible. Are you getting counselling? I could recommend—"

"Shut up, Nes Gow."

"Just trying to—"

"You don't get to talk about this until you get out from behind the desk."

"A little touchy?"

"Yeah."

"Okay."

The commander bustled in, a big, rough-hewn man with a gruff manner and a lot of grey hair, a bit on the long side. "Lieutenant Kim, good to meet you. Sorry to be late. Tied up with the delegate from Nas Goury. He's got his tail in a knot over paint. Read your report. Swarm-bots, eh? Nasty. The science people are working on countermeasures. We'll dial back operations until they give us a workable technique. Let's hope it doesn't take long. So, has Nes Gow explained the situation here to you?"

"I just arrived."

"Fair enough. Here it is. We're getting gossip about a group hanging around Midway with a different approach to fighting Kaz. They're being very secretive. Not without reason. There are people heavily invested in the status quo who would not be unhappy if misfortune should befall these folk. Might even help fortune along. I need to know what this bunch is up to. What's their story? Will their scheme work? Should they be encouraged? Discouraged? Moved out of the way? I think you can help with that."

"Me?"

"You're acquainted with a Nsfera, Ryet Arkkad."

"I know it, yes."

"Want to tell me how that came about?"

"It's helped me now and then with a supply problem."

The commander looked like he might ask what supply problem, then apparently thought better of it. "Rumour has it as a member of this group."

"I didn't know."

"I'm thinking you could parlay your acquaintance into the answers to my questions."

Oh, boy, John thought. "I don't think I'm the person for that sort of work," he said, hoping he wasn't shooting himself in the foot. "I just drive a starship."

"You can't do much driving now, can you, until repairs are done, and a new group member is assigned."

Was that a subtle rebuke? The commander wasn't known for his subtlety. "One of the spy guys might be a better choice," John said.

"I like to think I'm a pretty decent judge of people," the commander said. "I think you're the one to do this. Be a change for you. Good as a rest, they say. I'll send you one of the, uh, 'spy guys' to talk to you a bit. Okay?"

John, you just shut up, John thought. *Don't say one damned word you're thinking.*

"Yes, sir," he said.

The commander bustled off.

Nes Gow sat behind his desk, looking smug.

JOHN DIDN'T WAIT AROUND for the spy guy to show up. Instead, he went across the wall, the "wall" being the one that separated the military base from the rest of Midway, to the docks, where Ryet Arkkad hung out quite often. At first, he couldn't find Ryet but then saw it coming out of a small shop off the main thoroughfare, accompanied by a Roothian. The two of them spoke for a moment, then the Roothian scuttled off, and Ryet came to greet John.

"Sit down for a minute," John said, indicating a table with a few chairs beside him. "I want to talk to you."

Ryet leaned on the back of the chair nearest but didn't sit. "I don't know of anyone travelling to the Outer Marches just now, so your mother must do without chocolate for the time being," it said.

"It's not that," John said. He paused and then decided to just plunge in. "I have it on good authority that you're involved with a group of Oriani and friends that are working on a better way to deal with the Kaz."

"What authority would that be, I wonder?"

"I want to do what I can to help."

"Why?"

"I've just come back from an attack on one of the nidus worlds. We lost a ship and three good people. I'm really tired of losing people. There has to be a better way."

"I do not know of any rule in this regard. The Roothian I was just talking to had a similar observation about his dealing with some Gnathans who once supported the Oriani and now are stealing their work and trying to sell it to undisclosed buyers who one can only hope are not Kaz."

"Really, Ryet? Who steals from Oriani?"

"The same who would choose a Roothian to be their go-between? Who can say? I do not have unqualified faith in the veracity of Roothians."

"About the Orian group?"

"I will ask them if they are taking recruits and speak to you later. You do realize such an association will put you at odds with the accepted Fleet doctrine?"

"I'll handle it."

"No doubt you will." Ryet straightened and was gone.

MIDWAY—RESIDENTIAL DIVISION D

Ehreh's hip joints ached, and the joint at the base of his tail felt like fire.

He had persuaded a few of his closest compatriots to come to Midway with the idea that since he had to be there anyway to meet the Gnathans, getting heads together away from the interruptions of daily life and the nattering of the Administrative Council at the Academy would improve their chances of solving the problem he had not had much luck with on his own. But while they were excellent biological researchers, logistics were clearly not their forte any more than his. One by one, they were returning home to places they found more comfortable and to work they better understood.

The group had begun to attract people of other races who seemed eager to help. Ehreh was unsure of their motives.

The human was particularly puzzling.

The more paranoid members of the group insisted on changing venue frequently, and at times, the search among the meagre resources of old Midway for a suitable place to meet took longer than the actual event. The concrete-walled room they occupied in this little, anonymous, out-of-the-way space, poorly furnished, cold, and lit only by a scrap of lighting panel that did not illuminate the perimeter very well, was something Ryet Arkkad had found.

It had also found the human. It introduced him as someone interested in helping, then it went away and left its recruit behind. He and they did not quite know what to make of one another. The human picked up some of the slack, said his name was John Kim, that he was with the military and was passionate about finding a way to deal with the Kaz that didn't involve so many of his comrades being killed.

Passionate, Ehreh thought, was one of those weasel words which meant whatever the speaker needed it to mean at the moment.

He had proved to be more compatible with the group than Ehreh had expected. He had even offered to investigate commercial routes into Kazi space. Though Ehreh thought not much trade passed between the Interplanetary Community and the Empire, an investigation would do no harm and give him time to evaluate the human.

The conspirators gathered around the rough table were also passionate about halting the Kaz, but they often wandered off topic to pursue pointless details, jockeying for position within the group, pursuing imagined slights, looking for whatever advantage they thought they might find, as if, as Kazi vassals, that would make one whit of difference in a miserable, short life. One would think that any free being would be extremely focused on preventing the capture of his homeworld from happening again, but not so. It was exhausting to try to keep them heading in approximately the right direction.

"We must test the organism before deploying it," Walha said. She was Harl's representative here and was as obsessed as Harl was with testing.

"Under normal circumstances, yes," Basheh said, "but circumstances are not normal." Basheh was easily led astray toward subjects he felt more confident discussing. "Testing has no point if we cannot deliver it."

"You are surely not suggesting . . ."

Humans had a saying about herding cats long before they knew any Oriani. Ehreh was not unmindful of the irony. He stretched carefully, muscle by muscle, ear tip to tail tip, trying to get his blood moving again after a long session of sitting with the group and working hard at not getting uncontrollably impatient with the rock-headed, wilfully ignorant, stubborn others.

Many were not Oriani and had no great love of argument. The two Lleveci, daggers ever at the ready, were anxious to charge into the fray as if they could make any difference dispatching Kaz one at a time. The Caparan was searching for a way to turn a profit on the enterprise and was getting cranky because the opportunity had not presented itself and would likely never present itself. Ehereh thought it would leave the group soon. Whatever this undertaking might be, the Interplanetary Community's last, best hope, a suicide mission, or treason of the first water, it was definitely not a money-making venture.

Walha droned on. "I think the nanite hybrid is sufficiently foreign to biology to prevent a rapid build-up of immunity. However, the development of immunity is inevitable in the long run. Ehreh? You are hearing me?" she asked.

Ehreh knew he was gathering a reputation for losing track of conversations. He had been working out how to acquire more information about John Kim as he watched the human across the table. So far, it had been surprisingly difficult to come by. If John Kim was, in fact, a plant into this little band of dissidents by established interests wanting to keep the war going the way it was going, the lack of plausible background seemed like unusually poor tradecraft. He would ask Ryet Arkkad.

"Ehreh?"

Ehreh sighed. In his youth, absent-mindedness would have been considered a symptom of an overactive mind. Nowadays, it was considered a symptom of senility.

"Yes, of course, immunity will build up. I am counting on the organism being distributed in the population before that happens. That's why we need large quantities delivered deep into Kazi space."

"Can we get large quantities?" one of the Lleveci asked.

Wahla placed a small vial with a mound of grey dust at the bottom of it on the table in front of him. "Many billions of particles," she said, "deposited on an inert substrate."

The Lleveci shook it. "Doesn't look like much."

Basheh said, "None of this matters if we can't deliver the product."

"I think we are all agreed on that." Ehreh gathered his waning strength. "Meanwhile, we must move from the Academy very soon. Preparations need to be made. Ryet Arkkad says it has a place on its homeworld we can use to continue the research."

A murmur set up among the group, dissonant in its several languages.

"We cannot debate too long. We have relatively little time."

Wahla said, "Ehreh, I am not going to Fera. Harl is not going to Fera. It is not a good place for us."

The door slammed open. Everybody startled.

"Speak of the devil," John Kim said.

A kerfuffle at the doorway, then Ryet Arkkad pushed through it. It held up a squirming, squealing Roothian by the neck, and brought the struggling creature close for the assembly to see.

"What?" Ehreh said crossly. To his own dismay, he actually welcomed the Nsfera's interruption of what was turning out to be a very tedious and difficult meeting. Embarrassed by that, he kept the feeling inside, where it wouldn't tarnish his image.

For a moment, he feared Ryet Arkkad would throw the unfortunate Roothian onto the table in front of him, but the Nsfera restrained itself. It had everyone's attention without further theatrics.

"This miserable, misbegotten wart has been spying on us."

"Put him down before you choke him to death," Ehreh said.

A swirl of consternation rose over the table. Ryet Arkkad looked at Ehreh, then at the others, its expression unreadable, as it often was. The Nsfera was a bit of a loose cannon, although a sometimes useful one, but Ehreh was certain that sooner or later, it would finally lose patience with careful planning and prudent approaches and go off on its own. It always seethed on the verge of drastic action. More than one of the people around the table would cheer it on.

"Ryet Arkkad, let the Roothian go. You are going to do him serious harm."

"Not an entirely undesirable outcome," Ryet Arkkad answered. It set the Roothian down on his feet. It kept a firm hold on the creature's red-and-turquoise garment, however. The Roothian struggled helplessly.

"Been spying for whom?" one of the Lleveci asked.

"We don't know yet, do we, little beast? But we will find out, won't we, little beast?"

The Roothian's cries grew more desperate.

"Release him," Ehreh insisted.

Ryet glared at the Orian. Its angry face was a little disquieting.

"Harming him will just bring us closer to official attention," Ehreh said.

Ryet Arkkad hesitated, but after a moment, just long enough to demonstrate that it wasn't being bullied, it pushed the Roothian out into the hallway, followed him out, and shut the door rather too firmly behind them.

Silence filled the space it left.

"How much does the Roothian know?" John Kim said. "Maybe whoever hired him could explain why the Brodenli had a change of heart."

"Perhaps," Ehreh answered, "but that information leads to no useful course of action, and it will tell us nothing about how to replace the hoped-for vessel."

"Give Ryet half a chance ..."

"No. That is not the answer."

"We're not getting much in the way of answers here, Ehreh," John Kim said. "Every day we delay, the Kaz come closer."

"Perhaps we should consider alternatives."

"I know of no alternatives. We do not have the resources to acquire a starship on the open market," Basheh said. Basheh was leaning in. He was young and impatient. Others leaned away from this demonstration, bemused by unusual Oriani behaviour and uncertain about what to do.

"I must see to Ryet Arkkad," Ehreh said.

"Maybe you should leave it alone," John Kim said. "It's not your responsibility. Let it rattle the Roothian a bit. Maybe it'll come up with something. Some chance is better than no chance."

"No, it is not," Ehreh said. "A failure might very well alert the Kaz. Once they know what we are planning, they will initiate countermeasures, and we will be far worse off than we are."

"What is more, the Nsfera is a brutal creature," Walha said. Ehreh was surprised that Walha would defend his position. She also showed signs of impatience. Indeed, around the table, several tails swished against the rough floor.

"You seem to think the Kaz are at the doorstep. They are centuries away," Basheh said.

"So we thought the last time."

"What do you know of it, old man? Even you are not that old."

Ehreh looked straight at Basheh for a moment, a breach of Oriani etiquette, then looked away, a little embarrassed. He should do something to reduce Basheh's tension, not add to it. Basheh needed calm, a chance to get himself under control again before the stress did irreparable harm, but Ehreh did not know how he could help him do that. He himself was too close to exhaustion. He could no longer concentrate. He was becoming argumentative, provoking dissent rather than resolving it. He had been sitting too long on this uncomfortable chair with his tail bent to one side. His head ached. Strings of pain burned along his spine and into his limbs. His eyes were heavy. The journey to Midway, the change in gravity, air pressure, climate—all had been hard on him. The pain was wearing him down, and the pills made his mind slow. He needed to sleep.

"Let's break this up for now," John Kim said. "We're all tired. We're arguing in circles. We can get together later when we've all cooled off a bit."

The voice of reason from a human, of all people. This was just the second time John Kim had attended one of these meetings, and he was already assuming a degree of authority.

"I must check on Ryet Arkkad," Ehreh said. "It is inclined to disregard instructions from time to time." He left the room limping and went outside, as much as one could go outside on Midway, hoping to find a moment's peace and quiet.

It was not to be had. On the other side of the door, the chattering crowd attending the Interplanetary Community Strategic Planning Committee conference taxed were flooding the corridors on their way from one meeting to another. The machinery that kept the few hectares under the dome habitable roared along at maximum capacity. The newer constructions that housed the IPC presence in the sector, the military base, and assorted other installations of war were off-limits to ordinary folk. The air handling in the old dome was not unduly efficient, and stank of a hundred species crowded together and bad sewers and the cooking of who knew what fragrant horrors. The temperature was much too cool to be comfortable, the air too thin to be satisfying. Ehreh longed for the desert sun and a wide green sky, and silence.

He did not see Ryet Arkkad anywhere.

SQUEALING, Assiffah squirmed and wiggled, trying to get free, but Ryet held him firmly around the neck, letting its claws dig in just a little, warning Assiffah that it was perfectly capable of shredding the Roothian should it choose to do so. For all he was not a big creature, Assiffah was still too heavy to carry for very long, so Ryet pushed him along a dusty, forgotten passage and into a neglected closet-sized notch at the end that the Nsfera had been using during those times it felt a need to be alone.

"They said I had to let you go, but nobody said you had to be in good condition at the time, so shut up and stop jiggling." Ryet didn't know if the Roothian understood Sindharr, but he apparently understood the tone at least because he settled somewhat, and the squealing got quieter and took on a pleading tone.

Ryet shoved Assiffah into a corner and told him to stay there. It turned its back while Assiffah cowered and whimpered, pushing himself farther into the corner as if hoping to pass through the wall. It waited a few moments for the sake of verisimilitude and to let the Roothian's fear do its work, then said to its captive, "Wait here. Don't move. I'll be back in a minute." It left the tiny room and walked back down the passage the way they had come.

The Roothian was braver than he appeared to be or more desperate, but not smarter, for Ryet was hardly able to slip into an adjoining hallway before Assiffah came running as fast as he was able down the passage past the watching Nsfera, looking neither left nor right. Ryet leaned against the wall and let him go. "Run to your masters, oh brother of a worm," it said to itself in its native tongue. "Tell them all your sorrows. Let them share."

It walked back down to the end of the passage and checked in the notch. Sure enough, the little glass vial it had left behind was gone. Some creatures acted so true to type that the contest almost wasn't fun. Ryet would miss its private space, small as it was, but it wouldn't return to it just in case other Kaz decided to investigate what had happened to their brethren. It wasn't afraid of a single Kazi, exactly, but preferred to slip away from any confrontation at this particular time. A battle avoided was often preferable to a battle won. The less it was associated with coming events, the better.

Coming events came faster than expected. The following morning, a rising of manufactured light, not any effect of the dim and distant star, Ryet joined the group occupying another one of Midway's dismal hallways, a little wider and more often used than the one it had left the previous evening. It stayed well to the back of the crowd, thinking that the Interplanetary Community could save itself a lot of grief if it would raze the old part of the Midway complex and build something modern, more open, well-lit, and better planned. Not that that would serve Ryet's purpose all that well.

The crowd had organized itself the way most crowds did when dealing with some new and intriguing event, but Ryet was tall enough to have a good view of the tight-knit nucleus of cognoscenti, in this case, technicians and medics in biohazard gear, near the eye of the storm, surrounded by their protectors, military types and police being officious and controlling, and the great unwashed milling around and pushing in from the outer reaches to grab a look, the mob gradually thinning out toward the edges until it was indistinguishable from mere passers-by. *An event horizon of a sort*, Ryet thought, and the notion amused it for a moment.

The whole assembly was greatly distorted by the local architecture, and the inner circles had trouble keeping mere onlookers from oozing in along the walls and around the corners. What did the people buzzing around there hoped to learn, Ryet wondered, when everyone had questions, and no one had answers? Its own question, its own reason for being there, was answered when it saw a black-wrapped mass being loaded onto a covered conveyance. It worked its way through the crowd until it was near the centre and could see into the small room behind the technicians that oozed the smell of Kaz.

Beside it, a Sgat pushed its way between the legs of onlookers, but even propped up on its hindmost limbs, it couldn't see much but the butts of taller creatures. Ryet offered to lift it up so it could get a better look, and it accepted. Sgat raised to shoulder height, the Nsfera inched toward a Turgorn soldier who was trying to fend off the crowd while guarding the entrance to the room, presumably the scene of the crime.

"Here," Ryet said. "Could you hold this a minute?" It passed the Sgat, and the startled soldier took it before he realized what had happened. Ryet eased its way behind the Turgorn and slipped shadow-like into the room, picked up a little glass vial that lay on the floor amid the debris in the room and slipped out again, the whole movement taking scant seconds, and it was quite sure no one saw it. The soldier handed back the Sgat. "Carry your own burdens," he said.

The Sgat itself was a bit annoyed. "I didn't expect to be passed around like a game token," it complained.

"I apologize," Ryet said. "You are heavier than I expected you to be. I could not hold you for long."

"Well, put me down now. I have work to do."

"You're welcome," Ryet said.

The creature skittered off just in time for Ryet to turn and meet a human it knew, a youngish, heavy-set woman who had landed on Midway when her parents split up and went their separate ways, seemingly having forgotten they had a child.

"Kiska Babina, what are you doing here?"

"I just came to see what all was going on." She looked up at it and smiled, a ragged attempt at being coy. "I saw what you did there." She nodded toward the cordoned-off room.

Ryet managed to keep its dismay off its face. "Whatever you think you saw, let's keep it between us."

"You know I will." It knew she would. It had looked after her a bit in her early days on Midway, in an arm's-length sort of way. She thought she owed it, and whatever faults her rough beginnings might have engendered, a lack of loyalty wasn't one of them.

LATER, back in their little meeting room, Ryet decided Ehreh smelled of agitation more strongly than Ryet had ever observed in him, for all that he was displaying rigid outward calm. It could not comprehend what was bothering the Orian so much.

"You contemplate extinguishing an entire species and stress over the death of one of its members? This makes no sense to me. You wanted to test your virus." Ryet handed Ehreh the glass vial he had recovered. "You have what you wanted. It has been tested. It works."

"This has been a useless experiment creating considerable risk and offering no information. Yes, one died." Ehreh seemed smaller as if he were shrinking in on himself. "How many Kaz were infected?"

"I have no idea. Does it matter?"

"Yes. If one of one died, it means nothing except that you may have alerted the Kaz to be on the watch for this organism. If one of a thousand died, it means the virus is ineffective.

"And if the killing does not disturb you, two other factors might. Kaz rarely go anywhere alone. At least one other was here, with the one now dead. Do you know where it is? Perhaps only one of two or more died. But perhaps only one was exposed. We have no way to know. Dead or alive, the others will be a warning to their people if we do not find them. They may have already communicated the death of the one to their fellows, in which case we will have very little time to accomplish our goal. Of course, if other Kaz are in the region, they will all know. They sense one another's death."

Ryet worked to control its impatience and the restless anger that was beginning to grow like a living thing beneath its skin. It was doing its best to see that Ehreh got what he wanted. Dealing with Oriani required enormous self-control. "In that case, let us say the talk is over, and we are going to get moving."

"Move how?" Ehreh said. "We still do not have a vessel."

Ryet turned its face away to hide the irritation it was sure was plain there. This entire enterprise was beginning to seem like a colossal mistake. When Mawuli had asked it to help, the project had seemed like an interesting adventure which might incidentally do some good. Now it was beginning to wonder.

John Kim came in, looking as upset as Ehreh seemed to be but would never admit to. "What did you do, Ryet?" John Kim asked.

For a few moments, Ryet watched the play of emotions on the human's face, an almost semaphoric reading of his thoughts. In many ways, humans more genuine than Oriani. For all their willingness to tinker with reality to garner praise and avoid blame, at least they had genuine emotions. Kim was a mature individual with a responsible position in his society, and he still often reacted as honestly as a child. Oriani adhered rigidly to the truth and pretended they didn't react to its meaning.

Ryet debated with itself for a moment about explaining its reasoning, then changed its mind, turned and left the room, and was very careful to shut the door quietly behind itself.

A moment later, Kim followed it out.

Kim found the Nsfera sulking a short distance away. The human looked up at it. "The local constabulary found a wounded Roothian unconscious near the dead Kazi. What did you do?"

"Nothing I feel I need to discuss. The Roothian was frightened but healthy the last I saw him. Ask the Gnathans how they react to an unreliable agent."

"I never know how much to believe you."

"I never know how insulted to be."

"He's in hospital now. What's he going to tell the cops when he wakes up?"

"That he was spying for the enemy? I do not think so."

WHEN JOHN KIM left the Nsfera, he was thinking it was more involved with the dead Kazi and the damaged Roothian than it was ever going to tell him. He made his way across the wall and stopped in at Nes Gow's office to leave a message for the commander, telling him about the disagreements among the Oriani and their followers, their efforts to find a way to get their virus to where it needed to go, and the fact Ryet Arkkad might be involved with the death of the Kaz, but how, he didn't yet know. He added what Ryet had told him about Gnathans stealing the Oriani work and putting it on the market as just a rumour. It would cause grief for some Gnathans if the powers that be believed it, but he decided to err on the side of caution. He put the message in a coded file, mostly just to piss off Nes Gow. There was nothing of real interest in it. He supposed he was proving his lack of value as a spy, but what did anyone expect?

Then he set out for the hospital and a duty call. He needed to deliver a word of thanks to the woman who had arrived there badly injured after trying to save his man Whitby Clough.

MIDWAY—MAIN CONCOURSE

Archie had half a dozen voices in his head at any one time. The implanted communicator had been a good idea, keeping him in hands-free contact and saving him an enormous amount of time not spent looking for a device. The upgrades were a bitch, though.

Surprised to recognize Clough's signature come on, he thought about answering and then reached up behind his ear and shut that contact off. He had no reason not to do so. He was, after all, reasonably expecting Clough to be off-planet for a few days, and he had things to do he didn't want his employer interrupting.

He did wonder what had happened but decided he would find out soon enough.

At the time, he was elbowing his way through the noisy crowd toward the conference centre against the flow of traffic. A session had just ended; the corridors were busy and loud. Several individuals tried to catch Archie's eye. He called greetings and waved but didn't stop.

He was pursuing the featured speaker at the most recent meeting, Michael Martin, the representative of Martin Industries IP, a main supplier of warships and matériel to the Fleet and assorted other militaries in the known worlds.

Martin Industries Interplanetary always sent someone to these strategy meetings; they needed to keep track of which way the wind was blowing, what was in and what was out of fashion in the war business, who supported which motions, and where Martin Industries could apply a little pressure to further their ends. They didn't always send the big chief.

Michael Martin was reputed to be something of a cranky recluse, but given that some members at the meeting were disaffected by the status quo and were becoming vocal about it, this assembly was perhaps more critical than a run-of-the-mill gathering of bureaucrats. The arms trade was largely a recession-proof, non-partisan business, but it was also chaotic. Procedures and recommendations advanced by the Strategic Planning Committee affected the budget for the war effort, and even small shifts in the approach of the Interplanetary Community to the war against the Kaz could dramatically change Martin Industries' bottom line.

Michael wasn't too hard to spot in the milling crowd. Tall, thin, and blond-haired (what pale wisps remained to him), he stood out in the flow of people hustling to and fro, a rock in the stream, eddies forming around him as one or another person tried to catch his attention while he ignored them and talked to his virtual assistant.

Rumour had it that Michael's hair began to recede the same day his mother, Marietta, retired and left him to run the family business. Rumour had it that hair-restoring techniques weren't effective for Michael. Others said he hadn't attempted it, cosmetic procedures being beneath his dignity. Archie ran his hand through his own thick red curls with a measure of satisfaction.

By the time he had pushed his way into Michael's proximity, Michael was in deep conversation with Jorn, the Nas Goury delegate, whom Archie understood to be the brother of a high-level procurement officer for the Fleet. The subject seemed to be paint. Archie moved into Michael's line of sight and waited.

"... not cost-effective," Michael was saying. "Given a fire in a space-borne vessel, paint isn't going to prevent disaster."

"We do want to give our brave fighters every possible chance," Jorn said.

"Of course. Of course. Let me talk to our technical people and see if we can put a price on it."

"One cannot put a price on a life, Mr. Martin."

"But we can put a price on paint." Michael smiled stiffly.

Jorn did not. "You will remember the clause in your contract that does not allow a per unit cost increase of more than ten percent over the life of the contract. I do believe we are very close to that level now."

Jorn moved on, satisfied he had made his point. He knew that Martin knew that if the Fleet couldn't get what it wanted from Martin Industries IP, it could go to Martin's competitors. Lleveci InterNational was hot on his heels.

"Michael," Archie said, "have you had lunch?"

"Archie, hello. No, actually, I was just headed that way." Michael Martin turned and greeted Archie with a welcoming look. Archie had been useful to him on more than one occasion and was likely to continue to be so as long as he was Stanton Clough's right-hand man. Michael knew which bread to butter.

Archie nodded toward the departing person from Nas Goury. "Trouble?"

"His company has developed new fire-retardant coatings. He has some connection in the procurement office. If I can't persuade the Fleet standards division that his paint is no real improvement, it could cost Martin Industries a few million. It won't kill us, but it will bruise."

"As his world's formal delegate, is he allowed to negotiate for his company?"

"Probably not, but what are we going to do about it? Come on with me. I've heard of a new place just off Lane F, and I was going to try it out." He started off in that direction. Archie followed. "Maybe it will be a little better than the average around here."

"A low bar," Archie said, "But yes, I would like that. I have a thing or two I would like to discuss with you. Have you heard about the new plan by some Oriani and friends for a different approach to the Kaz?"

Michael stopped walking and started paying serious attention. He had a nervous tic above one eye that he had nearly managed to conquer, but it showed up now and then. "I have not," he said.

Scanning the crowd around them, Archie noticed that while most of the others who had been trying to catch the industrialist's attention had grumbled to themselves and moved on, one or two hung back, hoping to catch a word.

"Maybe we should go someplace quieter and less public."

"Yeah, okay. I have what has been represented to me as an office, for all it looks like a badger's den. Let's go there. I'll send for food."

Archie followed where Michael led, wondering what a badger was and whether their dens were well-appointed.

The office looked much like all the other rough rooms in the civilian part of Midway, with a bit more furniture. No sooner had they reached it than a minion arrived with a bug-sweep and made sure no uninvited listeners had planted devices, while Michael explained they did this twice a day, regardless. One could only trust mechanicals so far, he said, and the company's rivals kept finding ways around them. Lunch arrived as if by magic, spread out on a low table. Archie understood better than most how much work that sort of magic entailed. All the minions disappeared.

The food was indeed tastier than the average fare, accompanied by wine, a rare luxury, but Archie paid scant attention to it while he laid out Ehreh's scheme to spread a novel biological over the Kazi Empire. Michael didn't interrupt until he was finished.

"I heard rumours about this. Do you think the Oriani might actually make it work?" he asked finally, leaning back in his chair. The thing looked frail, and Archie half expected it to break to pieces.

"I don't think anything like it has been tried before," he said. "As far as I know, the big obstacle in their path just now is getting the organism to the appropriate place and dispersed. Whatever method they originally planned to use has fallen apart."

"Really?"

"You might wonder how that happened." Archie paused a moment.

Michael smiled and said, "I don't suppose you had anything to do with it."

"The Brodenli transporter was easy to convince he should abandon the contract once he could see it would be much less dangerous to do things our way."

"And that stopped the Oriani?" Michael asked.

"Momentarily. They're looking for alternatives." Archie looked into his glass for a moment, admiring the colour. "They'll find some eventually. There's probably serious money involved. Would it be worth your while to . . ."

Michael shook his head. "Annoy clients, irritate govern-ments, break deals for a one-off project? I like the five-year contract with renewal clauses I've got going now. So who are 'they'?"

"A kind of a rebel alliance, if you will; a group of Oriani who are the originators, headed by an elderly bioengineer called Ehreh, some disaffected individuals of other races, some groups of anti-war people who think of bacteria as less violent than bombs, a few wild cards you don't normally hear from, all working outside of government."

"I don't suppose you have a list of names?"

"No."

Michael looked at Archie for a long moment. "Too bad. If we knew who they were, maybe we could just deport the lot to Kazi space."

"They may have the support of one or two planetary governments, which would make the politics of that sort of thing rather touchy." Archie smiled a little, pretending he knew Michael was being morbidly humorous, though he wasn't at all sure that was really the case. Michael could be a bit scary at times. "Making martyrs is always risky."

Michael studied Archie as if he were trying to see how he was thinking.

Archie went on. "A move like that would garner a lot of adverse publicity and turn them from a nuisance into brave souls standing up to the might of the Interplanetary Community, sacrificing everything for our mutual benefit. It would attract a lot of public attention."

Michael waved the thought away.

"All jokes aside," Archie said, "there are already a few members of the Interplanetary Community who are not happy with the 'bomb them flat' approach. If a viable alternative shows up, it will give them traction."

"Yes," Michael said. "I've been talking to a number of them. What wild cards, for instance?"

"Nsfera?"

Michael brooded for a moment, obviously affected by this mote of information. "Those creepy bastards. You never know what they're thinking." Then he asked, "Where does the Orian government stand?"

"Not sure. I suspect they'd be generally opposed. They are very conservative."

"I've heard."

"But I don't think they will take action. They are philosophically inclined to let people go to hell each in their own way."

"If it works, if Ehreh and his followers get exactly the outcome they want, what will happen?"

"They hope the organism will kill off the Kaz completely. Second-best, it will become endemic and keep the numbers down for the foreseeable future."

"That's not good for business. Where has all this supersecret work been going on? Who's funding it? It can't be cheap."

"I have no idea."

Michael reached over and refilled Archie's glass. "See if you can find out, will you?" He contemplated his own glass for a moment.

"Okay, at this point, we need to do two things," he said. "One, see that all our supporters remain firm in their commitments, and two—add a little something to the technical data to suggest the great new solution doesn't work. Do you have any idea where Clough stands on this new approach, supposing it has viability?"

"He's kind of preoccupied right now."

"I understand that. He is also vulnerable. I trust you will keep him pointed in the right direction. I'm always surprised at how much weight he carries in the Council, and I fear business might take a turn for the worse if he wavers even a little."

"I'll need funding. Sometimes support like this will have to be bought."

Michael's slight smile was not amusement. "Of course," he said. "When was it otherwise?" Michael leaned back in his chair again, and Archie understood lunch was over. "Do you think the death of a Kazi on the station is in any way part of this? It seems like a considerable coincidence, though as far as I know, the autopsy has offered no cause of death."

"Dead Kazi?" Archie asked.

BETA ELLGARTH

The camp—one could not call it a base in any real sense —was too cold, too dry, too exposed, too bright, and too far from home. It was perched mostly above ground on a rocky, frozen hillside because icy boulders were difficult to move without heavy machinery. The Kazi team leader could only thank the Broodmother that it was temporary.

The locals, who looked like nothing so much as conical bundles of dried grass, didn't seem to have a language, but if one waved enough credits around, a language wasn't needed. The straw folk only stood blankly before a screen but were able to interpret drawings scratched into the frost well enough, and so the Kaz had a place built of sticks and grass on Beta Ellgarth, close enough to Midway to be convenient, distant enough to be hidden, heated slightly by a smelly pile of fermenting organics, but too chilly even so for its Kazi inhabitants to be at prime efficiency.

The field team leader had come with eleven others to this place. The others had been dispatched to their various duties, and it had been alone here for days, feeling apprehensive and vulnerable.

When the intelligence gatherer's apprentice arrived, the team leader was greatly relieved, though it made no effort to convey this fact to the newcomer. The apprentice was a youngster, with a bright new shell gleaming in the cool, white light while it waited for the team leader's response to its report. It had an attitude of distress and a scent of being unwell out of proportion even to the situation it found itself in, making the team leader wonder if it was getting the apprentice's whole story. An underling attempting to deceive its superior would be unusual but was not entirely unknown. The question would be why, and the team leader could see no benefit the apprentice could gain from misleading it. The apprentice's postures, waving forelimbs, and controlled pheromone release conveyed its story of the intelligence gatherer's sudden illness and death with proper deference to the difference in rank. It noted that the recently recruited Roothian spy had been seriously injured in a separate incident, an attack on his person. This, the apprentice said, was not considered a noteworthy event as the spy had been well known as an abrasive individual inclined to irritate others to the point of retaliation. *I do not believe it would be wise to continue to employ the Roothian, however, as some officials have been trying to connect the two events. The Roothian was doing his best to promote this belief.*

What was the intelligence gatherer working on?

It had heard rumours of a new weapon the Interplanetary Community was developing against us. We were seeking confirmation.

Do you know the nature of this weapon? the team leader asked.

I do not, the apprentice answered. *I do know that it is rumoured to be the source of considerable dissension among the members of the Interplanetary Community.*

Good. Dissension in the Council can only benefit the Empire. I will consult with my superiors. Can we recover the body to determine cause of death?

Doubtful, the apprentice answered. *The authorities there will have performed their own investigation. I do not think they will share.*

Indeed, the team leader said. *You should seek food and rest,* it went on. *I will inform the broodmaster of what has occurred. It may want you to go to Advance Base 5023, where it is currently stationed. Are you able to cope with such a journey?*

The apprentice seemed near exhaustion, but it answered, *Broodmother willing, I am.*

So the team leader guided it to the warmest corner of their shelter and presented food and water. Once the apprentice had settled, the team leader turned back to its other task. The scouts it had sent to Ferguson Prime had all perished. They had been members of its own brood, and it had felt their deaths keenly, though it knew from the beginning they would likely be sacrificed to the Empire's goals.

Conditions on Ferguson Prime, even more bright and dry than Beta Ellgarth and lethally hot where Beta Ellgarth was cold, meant that of the nine individuals dispatched, only four had managed to get into the mine proper and survive long enough to ascertain the presence of heliosite. Some small samples had been returned to the team leader, and though it was not a geologist, they appeared to be of good quality.

Though Howerath Mines' newly installed sensor net had been active while the scouts were there, none of the miners had seemed aware of their presence, which meant either the countermeasures the scouts had been given were effective in defeating the mining company's security or that the miners were not paying much attention to their instruments. For planning the next step, it would be useful to know which it was.

Unfortunately, the scout that brought the samples back died shortly after it arrived, dehydrated and starving.

The team leader was conscious that the loss of so many members of its team was not good for its record. At the same time, it had been given a nearly impossible assignment, and that should be considered. It decided it would recommend to the broodmaster that the Empire gather enough resources to mount a proper invasion of Ferguson Prime. It would recommend that Empire forces arrive in number and as swiftly as possible the instant planetary winter arrived in the northern hemisphere of the planet and that they bring complete life-support systems with them because summer would come all too quickly to that hellish place.

Beta Ellgarth turned, and the planet's slow night began. The team leader decided that no harm would be done by pointing out that it had engineered a considerable coup by presenting the Empire with the opportunity to secure a so valuable a resource and at the same time deny that resource to the opposition. That should also go on its record. With hard work and the blessing of the Broodmother, Empire forces would be established on Ferguson Prime and in a defensible position long before the Interplanetary Community was able to respond. It composed its message to the broodmaster with a sense of satisfaction.

Then the light grew dimmer still, and it stopped functioning until morning.

As the light rose the next day, it arranged for transport to the spaceport and went to rouse the apprentice where it lay beside the compost heater; the apprentice seemed not to have noticed the onset of day.

It was lying flat on the cold stony floor and did not react as the team leader went up to it. It must have been more tired than either of them realized. The team leader prodded it gently, but the youngster did not respond. Then, in a long cold rush, the team leader felt the apprentice die.

After a moment of confusion, during which it found itself alone again, it appended this new information to the message it would now have to deliver itself. It decided that when it met the broodmaster, it would pre-emptively suggest that the Empire's technicians look into the number of deaths that had occurred among a relatively small number of individuals in this sector of space, hoping that would deflect blame, at least a little.

It dragged the apprentice's body outside into the cold. Perhaps, in time, recyclers would come for it.

Little bits of wind-driven ice began to pile up against it almost at once. The group leader left it there and took the transport itself to the spaceport.

MIDWAY—KING GEORGE XIII HOSPITAL

The King George XIII Military Hospital on Midway was the nearest place to Fergie Prime that could offer Whitby Clough any chance of survival, but it was a long hyperspace jump for a patient clinging to life by the tattered end of a heat-fractured nail. The fact that he hadn't died en route was considered by the medical staff a significant miracle.

Lauren made the trip unconscious, attached by tubes and wires to a bunch of machines, wrapped in synthetic skin, while medics set bones and cultured muscle tissue for fast growth to be implanted in the most damaged places in her body. Once she was stable and in the hospital, they woke her up; necessary, they insisted over her loud complaints to ensure neural connections would be made properly.

For many days, it seemed at times infinitely many, she was in a bland white windowless room. Painkillers helped but not that much. She mumbled through the fog that she wanted to talk to her daughter. White-coated people assured her she would be able to do that shortly. She waited in her drug-induced daze. But the promise was only the typical medical head-pat, keeping the patient calm by pretending to acquiesce to her demands with no real intention of following through.

People came and went until she started to recognize certain blurry shapes, mostly in hospital whites but at least one in green- and-gold Fleet colours. After a while, the tubes came out, and the wires were detached.

And then, they brought the nanites.

To say she wasn't very comfortable with the idea of nanites crawling about inside of her would be to severely understate the case. The thought of the things slithering into every nook and cranny and rewriting her entire body from the inside creeped her out, even when the process seemed entirely theoretical. With the practical application staring her in the face, the creep-out factor was up near nine, and she wasn't sure she'd be able to take it. The ghost of Bolek's broken countenance haunted her; in her mind's ear, she could hear his mournful complaints. When the technician came in, she was ready to stand him off with firm refusal or with whatever she remembered of martial arts and whatever weapons she could find— primarily pillows, as it turned out. Pretty ridiculous, she realized later, given the damaged state of her body. It had to be the drugs talking.

The technician was a young Orian; though he was not big for one of his race, on her best day, she wouldn't have had a prayer in any hand-to-hand fight against him. Burdened with numerous packs and bags, he stayed near the door, regarding her resistance with calm golden eyes. His tail twitched ever so slightly. "Do not imagine anything will be forced upon you," he said. His speech was accented but clear. "Do understand that without this treatment, healing will be limited, considerable disability will result, and scars will remain."

"How much disability?"

"To say precisely is difficult; possibly it would be less than you are experiencing at the moment, but how much less is unknowable. Some chronic pain will be present as well. A previous event has prompted your concern?" Then, after a small hesitation, he said, "My name is Aroull," as if just remembering humans wanted labels on things. "You have a child, I understand." He put his things down.

"Yes," Lauren answered cautiously.

Aroull took a small mirror from one of his packs and handed it to her.

Lauren wasn't totally unfamiliar with the red, scarred, and puckered wreck in the glass, the lost eyebrows and the missing ear. After the first shocking, gut-wrenching look that left her physically ill, she had tried to avoid the sight of her reflection as much as she could, or ignore it, a kind of psychological blindness that held the horror at bay a little.

Now she thought about Hanna. The way she looked, she would frighten the kid half to death. Even if she could accept the ugliness, Hanna would always be the kid with the mom who looked like a Halloween joke, though not that funny. *Kids are adaptable, though. Hanna will adapt*, Lauren thought.

Then she tried to imagine doing her job with semi-functional joints and reduced muscles haltered by scar tissue. How would she earn a living when she was barely able to attend to basic biological functions? When the painkillers wore off, would she be able to keep from screaming? Would she become a burden to Hanna, sucking up Hanna's life, making her care for a crippled parent because Lauren was afraid? Did all those things she had been carefully refusing to think about go racing through her mind because the technician handed her a mirror?

She started to tell Aroull about Bolek, a phrase or two at a time, trying to imagine what Bolek's family had felt.

As she talked, the Orian began to prepare his potions and engines. For all he didn't look old enough to have much experience, he dismissed her fears: "That almost never happens," he said. The hiss of the pneumatic shocked her.

"Hey!" she complained.

"The units are inactive. I will flush them if you insist on refusing treatment."

Aroull was putting together a plumber's maze of tubes and plate-shaped objects around her bed. "This will produce the magnetic fields guiding the nanites to where they need to go," he said. Then he asked her to disrobe and get inside of it and assume an all too vulnerable spread-eagle position. As the apparatus hummed and buzzed, Lauren's apprehension morphed into anger. "I wish the Fleet could just bomb the whole damned Kazi Empire flat." She heard herself sounding more like a six-year-old than her daughter did.

Aroull's attention was fixed on the screen before him as he adjusted strengths and polarities. "Lay still, please. Many would die." He sounded more like a six-year-old's mother than he had any right to.

"Ah, that's kind of the point."

"Many of those you consider friends and allies would die. Bombing the Kaz has become very hazardous."

"Yeah, I know. One can't help wishing."

"You are wishing countless brave warriors dead?"

"No, of course not."

"There is another way."

"Really? Why aren't we using it, then?"

"I shall proceed?"

The technician had known all along she would acquiesce. "I think Oriani know way too much about human psychology. I hate to think I'm being manipulated so easily."

Aroull's golden gaze met hers. Lauren fancied she detected a bit of humour in there somewhere. "You believe it is easy?"

AFTER AROULL LEFT, Lauren spent some time with her eyes closed, trying to feel the nanites at work. Her apprehension had not been much allayed by Aroull's assurance. *Almost never is significantly different from not ever.*

Nothing seemed to be happening, and she didn't know whether to worry or cheer.

A tap at the door brought her eyes open. A man came partway in and stopped. "Hi," he said.

Lauren grabbed a sheet and pulled it over her. *Vanity, thy name is idiot.* "Hello?"

"How are you doing?"

"Um, okay, considering."

"You don't remember me, do you?"

"No, should I?"

"Probably not. Last time I was here, you were pretty much out of it."

"Oh."

"I'm John Kim," the man said. "I was leading the battle group when the *Senator Alice Hester* was hit." He stopped for a deep breath, the wound obviously still fresh. He was dark-haired, smooth-skinned, in his mid-thirties perhaps, and a bit more care-worn than a fellow that age should be. Lauren became quite self-conscious of her own appearance. "I wanted to thank you for your efforts to help her people. I can see it cost you a lot." Lauren winced, thinking about the nightmare in the mirror. "I was sorry to hear about Mr. Bolek. Was he a friend?"

"Just a guy I met in a bar who had no reason to love the Fleet. I think he must have been a good man." She realized her voice was hoarse. Funny, she hadn't noticed that before.

"Is there anything we can do for you? The Fleet will pick up the hospital bill, of course, and make a contribution toward lost income."

"Thank you. That's good to know." *More than you probably realize*, she thought. She had been imagining her return home retreating farther beyond her grasp every day she spent lying in bed, with Evelyn Cortez burning up her income much faster than it was coming in. Evelyn was a good lawyer, but not cheap. "If someone could get in touch with my daughter and my sister and tell them I'm okay . . . ?"

"No worries. The Civil Office will be on that. Did they tell you anything about the man you saved?"

Lauren shook her head.

"His name is Whitby Clough. He's from a well-established family; his father is the Terran delegate to the strategic conference going on right now. He is relatively new to the Service and was originally assigned to support and services, but because the attrition rate is pretty high these days," there was a slight pause while John collected himself, "with the increased Kazi defence of nidus worlds, he was moved into a combat branch."

"Does that happen often?"

"More than it used to. I'm not sure it's the best plan."

"This room is full of sensors and recorders, you know."

John looked up and winked at the overhead. "I think my superiors are aware of my thoughts on the practice of putting half-trained precious flowers into combat. At least, I've tried to make it plain." There was some bitter anger in the statement.

He turned back to Lauren and shrugged.

"Isn't that kind of talk cutting off your nose to spite—" and then she stopped. It wasn't a good metaphor in her present condition. "Tell you what—I'm kind of wracked right now, but in a few days, how about taking me out for coffee or whatever passes for it in this place? If this," she waved vaguely at her red, scarred surface, not nearly well enough disguised by a hospital gown and a loose sheet, "doesn't put you off. I'm really hungry for some actual human-to-human conversation. As prejudiced as that might sound. And believe it or not, behind this crispy exterior, there is a real human being."

Kim smiled, and it took five years off him. The stiffness

drained out of his face as if he had just realized the horror he was looking at actually was a person. "I can do that," he said. Lauren thought about that smile until she fell asleep.

SIX DAYS ON, she could walk the hallway, albeit at a slow shuffle, clinging to a pole on wheels. Despite her initial apprehension about nanites, Lauren had to admit the pain of broken bones had eased almost at once, and later she was aware of the difference in the burn scars, more elasticity and more strength, feeling beginning to return in places, with pins and needles that felt more like lances and spears. The burns began to look somewhat less horrible. A hot, tender little bud formed on the side of her head. Aroull assured her it would become an ear.

The hospital was a huge medical complex, and all parts of it looked the same. She was utterly bored with the bland, characterless walls, so similar to one another, and a little uncomfortable with the way the overhead sensors tracked her meanderings.

In the hope of distracting herself from the unease of the sub-microscopic invasion of her body and the macroscopic invasion of privacy, she looked in on Whitby Clough.

There was nothing much to see, a small, sheet-covered mound attached by multiple tubes and wires to an enormous rack of machinery with care-bots hovering around. The room itself was much like hers, brightly lit, featureless white except for the sensors on the ceiling. The difference was the big observation window where she stood looking in.

She had been at the window a few moments when a man came and stood beside her and also looked into the sterile white space. Though he did nothing to provoke it, Lauren felt him as an obtrusive presence. She was about to leave when he said, "That's my son."

Lauren didn't know how to answer that, so she said nothing. He turned to Lauren and held his hand out. *Quaint*, Lauren thought, but took it. "I'm Stanton Clough. I owe you a great debt."

"Lauren Fox. You don't owe me anything. The hero of the event was an army veteran called Bolek. He's dead, scattered across the desert on Fergie Prime."

"Is that so?" After a longish moment of silence, Clough added, "Well, there's not much I can do for him then, is there?"

The remark provoked Lauren to actually look at the man. He was big, past middle age, and pale with rage or pain or some combination thereof. He looked utterly devastated, which provoked a moment of sympathy. He had the round, over-fed, over-dressed, over-groomed look about him that screamed politician. And he seemed to have no clue how unfeeling he sounded. Not a very good politician, Lauren guessed.

"You could let Bolek's family and friends know what happened," she said. "I'm sorry, I don't know much about him, but he was born on Earth in a state called Poland and worked in some government service that uses military-grade nanite enhancements."

"What government?"

"I can't say, but there couldn't be many who do that sort of thing to people."

"I'll get my staff on it." He turned back to the window. "Did you know Whitby?"

"No. We never met."

"He was a good boy."

When she had gone to work for DoubleChek Security and embraced suspicion as a way to earn a living, Lauren had been taught to pay attention to the way people said things as much as what they said. Clough spoke of his son in the past tense and called him a boy. *Can you say "patronizing pessimist"?*

"What's the prognosis?" Lauren asked.

"Not good."

"I'm sorry."

"I'm sure you did your best."

You sound like my mother when she was thinking exactly the opposite, Lauren thought. *Mother was never slow to point out inadequacies.*

She turned once more to continue her shuffle, about ready to go back to her bed for a nice nap. A care-bot arrived, soundless on the smooth floor, looking much like a trash can painted white. A summons for Lauren to return to her room flashed on its screen.

"Could we talk later?" Clough asked.

"Why?"

"I need to do something about this. Maybe you can help."

"I have an assignment at the moment," Lauren said, wondering immediately if that was true. "If you need security service, you should talk to head office. I can give you the contact info."

Clough stopped for a moment, and a certain furtiveness came over him. Lauren could imagine him looking over his shoulder, trying to spot IC agents spying on his conversation. Lauren resisted the urge to direct his attention to the sensors on the ceiling. At a somewhat lower volume and softer timbre, he said, "I have been trying most of my professional life to get the Interplanetary Council to take the Kazi threat more seriously. It is so bound up in red tape and so hamstrung by people who are afraid to take a deep breath lest it cause someone somewhere to take offence that it is unable to act. The current level of commitment is failing to produce results."

"Why are you telling me this?"

"Don't you agree?"

"You've got a better idea?"

"Not yet. Still, if no one works on it, it will never happen, right?"

He's trying to get that hard first word of assent, Lauren thought. Pretty transparent. "Wouldn't it take a lot more knowledge and resources that a bunch of private citizens could gather?" The care-bot made a small dinging sound, reminding Lauren of its presence.

"It's taking time, but we're getting there. We have some serious players. If it takes a change of administration, so be it."

"Who's 'we'?"

Clough shook his head. He wasn't totally stupid.

"I don't know what use I would be to you. I'm nobody, and I don't have a fortune to spare."

"Mm. That's not quite true. There was a time when you were quite well known. I heard about your troubles on Centauri. A champion of women's rights, they were saying."

"If you know that, then you know I have no resources. I don't know what you think about me, Mr. Clough, but I'm pretty sure it's wrong."

"Stanton, please. My friends call me Stan. I met you when you first came here from Fergie Prime, but I don't suppose you remember. They had you pretty heavily drugged."

How many people did I meet that I don't remember? Lauren wondered.

"I'm not your friend, Mr. Clough," she said. "I'm not your ally, either. I'm not out to save the universe for God, motherhood, and apple pie, whatever your concepts of those things might be. I've got all I can handle trying to provide for my family and give my kid a decent life. This," she said, indicating her injuries with a wave across her body, "has been a considerable setback."

"Don't think I'm not appreciative. But remember, the Kaz overran Earth once before. Who's to say they won't do it again? What kind of life would your kid have then?" He paused again. "What kind of life is my kid going to have, or uncountable other kids?"

Now we're playing the sympathy card, Lauren thought. From the end of the hallway opposite the way Lauren had been heading, a young redhead waved and called Clough's name.

"Not now, Archie," Clough grumbled to himself.

Yeah, now, Archie, Lauren thought. *Thank you.* She offered the young man a bit of a smile as he came up and watched his look of curiosity morph into a look of stiff horror as he approached. The robot dinged again, managing to sound impatient. "I have to go," she said.

Back in her hospital room, the communications system dithered, and then Nathan appeared on the screen and said, "You look terrible."

"Thanks, Nathan."

"I sent copies of the sensor records in case you want something to do."

"Marc has the expertise, and he has the machinery where you are."

"Yeah, well, just in case."

"Okay."

"Some lawyer's been on the hyperspace, asking about you."

"Please don't tell him anything you don't have to."

"I told him to get a court order. Get back here as soon as you can. Howerath out."

THE ENTERTAINMENT VALUE of Nathan's records was minimal. Nothing new came out of her review. Lauren grew restless. Aroull brought walking canes for her and told her she couldn't cling to her wheelie pole forever if she expected to regain mobility. This was the next step. He would send a physiotherapist the next day.

So Lauren staggered along on the canes, trying to get the

required (ridiculously large) number of kilometres walked to satisfy Aroull. She felt very insecure.

Two individuals approached at the intersection to the main concourse.

The Turgorn had enough ribbons and badges attached to his person that Lauren assumed he was of some considerable status among his own. Beside him, an unadorned, rather conical, brown bundle of straw rustled softly. The Turgorn introduced himself as Kam Nok of the Civil Constabulary and the bundle beside him as his colleague from Beta Ellgarth, apparently nameless. Lauren thought that being accosted by the local police could bode nothing but ill, though she couldn't think of anything that might have brought her to their attention.

"Can I trust what I am about to tell you can be kept in confidence?"

"Depends."

The straw person rustled his question. Lauren imagined he could be quite expressive once one got used to him.

"If you're about to tell me you have a plan to assassinate the chairman of the Council, then no, I won't keep your secret. If it's the name of a good restaurant, sure, no problem."

The two chattered and rustled together for a few minutes. "Perhaps we should find someplace else to talk," the Turgorn said. "Come with me."

She followed the two to an alcove obviously kitted out for their use. It had chairs, for which she was grateful, and several display screens.

"There has been a most peculiar death," Kam Nok said. "The individual who died was a Kazi. That is, or soon will be, common knowledge. What will not be commonly known is that the manner of death is in question. Also, we have no idea how a Kazi came to be here. The political implications are vast. My superiors have said to me that an unsullied investigator with no previous involvement in local matters would be advantageous. I have been authorized to ask for your assistance if you would be so kind."

"Me? Why me?"

"You have experience in interpreting data from scanners, I understand. I have been told you have been trained in forensic techniques."

"Me?" Lauren realized she was beginning to sound repetitive. "Who told you that? Whoever it was, they were wrong. My training in criminal investigation is extremely minimal. I'm not a policeman, have never been a policeman, have never had any interest. I learned what I had to learn to get the job I've got. That's it. I'm sure your own investigators have been all over the scene with better training and state-of-the-art equipment. What do you think I can find that they haven't already found, collected and filed? Whatever is left there will be stuff they know is not relevant. Do you think they're going to share?"

"I will arrange it."

"But what do you want from me?"

"Only an unprejudiced opinion."

For a moment, Lauren seriously considered it. She was bored witless, and it would give her something to do.

Kam Nok continued, "We need to be utterly fair. Because the victim is an enemy, we need to be seen to be fair."

Maybe the straw person picked up on Lauren's moment of weakness. He rustled a bit, and Kam Nok said, "We will pay for your time."

Lauren sighed. A million credits' worth of debt lay in her future. She hated knowing she could be bought. "So, who is this Kazi, and why do you think its death needs investigation?"

"I will show you what we have found on security sensors."

A skittery, many-legged minion hurried in with the files on a flimsy. Lauren settled down beside Kam Nok and his grassy friend to watch more blurry images from security sensors until she couldn't see straight anymore. Only one thing caught her attention.

"What is that?" she asked about a smear on an image of the outside of the place the dead Kaz was found.

"Unknown. A glitch in the system, perhaps."

"How fast is it moving?" It was a blur in every frame in which it appeared.

"A glitch would not have a speed."

"Is that what you really think it is?"

The Turgorn shrugged.

"Did you have a sensor unit inside the room?"

"It was not operating at the time."

"Why?"

"Unknown. Sometimes they break. Often people turn them off."

"Anybody can do that?"

"It requires some skill."

"Well, let's get the records from sensors from places close by and with as many different perspectives as possible and see if we can figure two things out: what the blur is and how fast it was moving. Send me whatever else your investigation has turned up so far at the hospital. Here's my contact info. I need to get back there. I'm exhausted, and I need to eat."

The Turgorn and his very silent partner went off to collate the existing data about the Kazi's death. They would hand-deliver it to Lauren on this flimsy, Kam Nok said. Transmission over the local communications net, they said, would be too vulnerable to listeners-in.

Lauren began to realize how paranoid these people were. Who would draw vast negative conclusions from the death of a Kazi? Most people, herself included, would see a dead Kazi as a good thing.

Amid the lunch crowds, she made her way to the place near the conference room that delegates and support staff optimistically referred to as the cafeteria and ate some of the anonymous stuff prepared there and sold as food.

"Is THAT FERMENTED?" Ryet asked, sniffing as it joined John Kim in a distant corner of the cafeteria. Around them, the lunch crowds chattered and rattled dishes.

Kim pulled the steaming cup a little closer to himself, an oddly protective gesture, he thought later. As tea went, its contents were less than wonderful, and he could get a much better brew across the wall, but it was, at least, warm.

"Yes," he said, "But it's not alcoholic if that's what you're hoping."

"It is not. I was thinking that humans have an odd penchant for microbially altered food. Speaking of microbes, has Ehreh given up on his plan, do you think?"

"I'm not sure I want to talk to you. You may have wrecked the whole project because you can't control your impulses."

Ryet waited, scarcely moving. Kim didn't know if this was supposed to demonstrate impulse control, but it was disconcerting.

After a moment, Kim relented. "I don't think so, though he's pretty upset about the loss of the transport he thought was certain. And about the death of the Kazi. He tries not to show it, but he's taking it hard. Maybe his age is catching up to him. I can imagine that he's thinking he won't live to see this through. Maybe he's finding it difficult to maintain an interest."

"He is not well."

"Yeah, I can see he needs rest; he's not young anymore, and he probably should slow down a bit."

"It is more than that. He is seriously diseased." Ryet had not taken the chair opposite Kim, instead leaning against the rough concrete wall, preferring that to bending its long legs to sit and finding accommodation for its wings.

"He doesn't look that sick to me. What makes you think so?"

"He smells different."

"Smells different? Mostly I think Oriani don't smell at all."

"Of course you do. Ehreh's biochemistry has changed, is changing."

"Maybe a normal part of aging in Oriani?"

"Maybe."

"Suppose. What does it mean?"

"I do not know the details of Orian physiology."

"He's never talked about it to anyone?"

"He did not."

"If he actually is sick, that would be kind of dishonest, don't you think?"

Ryet's motion might be construed as a shrug.

"That wouldn't say much for the vaunted Oriani commitment to the unvarnished truth."

Ryet paused briefly as if trying to phrase its next words carefully, but they were brutally rough when they came. "His mind is not working well."

"Works better than mine does."

Ryet pointedly made no comment.

"You can smell that, too?"

"No. But he has been unable to proceed now that his original plan has been blocked. Time is short. Every moment of delay means opponents of the plan have a moment more to thwart it. Ehreh must know this."

"He's a biologist, not a tactician. Or maybe he doesn't think it's that urgent."

"Whatever he thinks, we need to deflect him from this course. I think his usefulness is limited. We should get what we need from him as soon as we can and proceed as best we can on a more functional approach."

"You're a callous bastard, Ryet Arkkad. And you cannot out-rational an Orian, even a sick one."

Ryet made a sound not unlike purring but with none of the contentment. "Realistic bastard, John. Mawuli is a good techni-cian but not a leader. The only other biologist among us is Harl, and she is not as committed to the project. She has qualms of conscience, and I am not sure she is able to cultivate the hybrid organism in vitro."

"Anyway, it won't matter if we can't get it off the ground."

"I have met a person who knows her way around security systems. Perhaps she can be persuaded to help."

"Ryet, you can't just go tell everyone you meet what we're trying to do here. Don't you see how dangerous that is?"

"I do not see how we can be less successful than we currently are."

"How about standing trial for God-knows-what awful charges? How about going to jail?"

Ryet was quiet for a moment. Then it shifted its weight off the wall. "Stay here and enjoy your infusion of fermented leaves. I will talk to the person. I do not believe anyone will be taking me to jail."

Before John could react, the Nsfera was almost out of sight down a hallway with its long, loping stride, leaving a swirl of dust, not even jostling the milling lunch-seekers in its wake. John was left behind, open-mouthed, wanting to protest but having no one to protest to.

Stupid critter will get us all killed, John thought and scram-bled away to warn the others that the shit was about to hit the fan and everyone should take cover.

AT ANOTHER TABLE NEARBY, Archie picked up his gear and packed it away. The bug he had planted was scarcely bigger than a grain of rice, with state-of-the-art quantum circuits, cost more than a year's salary, and Kim had put his teacup on top of it as if it were nothing. He hustled over to Kim's table, hoping to recover it before the next dinner sat down or before the cleaner-bots swept everything up and recycled it. It was going to be painful enough explaining to Michael why the recording was so poor without having to explain how he'd lost the bug. He hadn't been able to make much of the conversation himself, except that John Kim seemed quite agitated.

THE CONCOURSE WAS MOSTLY empty by the time Lauren crossed it, and she hurried as best she could while entangled in canes, anxious to get back to her room and call DoubleChek for advice about the strange position she had put herself in. She had no idea how she was going to be helpful to the local police force, though.

"Lauren Fox."

Startled, she stopped, dead still, waiting that fraction of time that allowed a bit of mental processing, but it told her nothing. A little breathless when she caned herself around, she faced the source of the resonant whisper from the shadows.

The creature was leaning against the wall in a shaded corner, hardly distinguishable from the rough concrete until it moved; tall, dark, somewhat satanic in features, not handsome by any means.

"You scared me," she complained. "Do I know you?"

"I cannot pretend to know what you know, but I suspect not."

"So, who are you and what are you and what do you want? I'm hurting and tired, and I have things I need to do."

"I am Nsfera. I am called Ryet Arkkad. Does this tell you something?"

"No. Good-bye."

"Wait." A hesitation. "Please." The word sounded like a considerable concession. The creature pulled itself upright with a soft, dry rustling.

Lauren stumbled half a pace backward. "What?" Communications were spotty in Midway's older facilities, and cameras were not widely distributed in the concourse. Would she be able to get help if she needed it? What made her think she might need it? The thing was tall but frail-looking and had not been in any way aggressive.

"You have been asked to assist with the investigation into the death of the Kazi spy."

"Wow, that was fast. I didn't expect that to be common knowledge just yet."

"It is not. What have you found?"

"Why would I answer that question?"

"I know the cause of death has not been determined. I know the usual autopsy methods will discover anomalies but not the cause. I know it would be best if the cause remained a mystery for the time being."

"Really? Why is that?" Lauren didn't expect it to offer anything, but asking provided a way to keep the conversation going while she figured out what it really wanted.

"I want you to tell the Civil Constabulary that the Kazi's death was accidental," it said, not answering the question. "Or normal. Aging, perhaps."

"The question is still, 'Why?'"

"Let us ask 'What?' instead. What would be required to have you do what needs to be done?"

"Put that way, I'm not sure there is any such thing."

"Bargain with me if you will. Do I need to outbid the Turgorn?"

"You're quite the cynic, Ryet Arkkad."

"About human motivations? Oh, very much so."

"Really? What do you actually know about humans?" Lauren asked. She had been easing herself away from the Nsfera, trying to establish a clear path between the tables to the hospital wing.

Maybe Ryet's toothy grimace would pass for an expression of amusement, that dry snuffling for a chuckle.

"I know Earth very well," it said. "Earth and its people lie at the heart of much of our folklore, as we occupy some of yours. Earth was a vacation spot once upon a time. My people fit nicely into early human myths of night and shadows. And many of the creatures who live there are, to a degree, tasty."

There was a clattering and whispering of wings. Folded, they were nearly invisible, tight between the creature's shoulder blades. Outspread, they formed a canopy that blotted out the blurry stars overhead and were more than a little creepy. Just stretching or an attempt at intimidation?

"But Earth has no shadows anymore," it continued, seeming wistful. "Humans have lighted everything. And they've made themselves civilized and therefore prohibited. And we, we are nearly gone, thanks to the Kaz. Too few of us remain now to tend our own gardens, much less play in others.

"But we have no more time to mourn the good old days. If we do not act soon, we will be gone. And you will be gone. And the Oriani, once again chopping logic while their world burns, will also be gone.

"It is important," it said, "to take action now before the Kaz can prepare." It fanned itself gently. Lauren struggled to keep her balance in the wind.

"I don't see where this dead Kazi comes into this plan," she said, her eyes on the outstretched membranes. Cold fingers moved along her backbone. Could it fly in Midway's thin atmosphere? she wondered. "I don't see many members of the Community accepting a new technique unless there is evidence that it is more effective than what they are doing now. If you have evidence, present it to the IPCSPC. I have no influence there, and I don't see any reason to deal with a person who considers me tasty."

"Evidence is not the currency of politics. Politicians deal with fear and with threats, real and imaginary.

"Somebody else told me that exactly that not long ago."

"The new plan is Orian—Ehreh's, at least, and so more likely to be fact-based than most. Oriani are not so much of one mind as some would suppose, and they have their issues, certainly, but they are realists in the end. They have been at this juncture once before and very nearly lost the fight, entangled in the clinging threads of elegant philosophy. Your people also faced this devastation once before. It was not fine words and lofty thoughts that pulled you back from the brink; it was learning to attack the nidus worlds."

"So, that's been working. Why change now?"

"Perhaps you should ask that of Whitby Clough, or better, his father. We tend to forget that Kaz also learn fast. They will outbreed us and outfight us in the end. They will develop new weapons, given the chance. We must find a less expensive way to hold them back that doesn't cost so much in life and limb and in our combined treasure. I think it will not be oratory."

"And you think this little group of rebel Oriani and their friends have the answer."

"I believe so."

"What do you need from me, in particular? I don't think you picked me out of a crowd by chance. Why do you care what I tell the Turgorn?"

"You know Stanton Clough"—once more, not answering her question.

"We've met. I wouldn't say I knew him. Is this going somewhere?"

Rattling, the wings folded away. "I think you have influence.

He feels he owes you something, and he is one of those obstructing our best chance to stop the Kaz."

"I wouldn't know about that."

"I am telling you that."

Lauren untangled her canes from chair legs and saw her way clear out of the concourse. "But I have no reason to believe you," she said. "and really, it's not any of my business in any case. And even if it were, I wouldn't feel right about taking advantage. I'm going now."

"I will come with you."

"Yeah, no, I don't think so. I think I've had enough of this confusing argument. Tell you what, get back to me when you have some proof that your new scheme is better than current techniques. Or, better yet, get the Oriani to present it to the Committee. Wouldn't that be more efficient?"

"It would, but the Orian government is not in agreement. The Committee is disinclined to hear private citizens."

"Mm. That's unfortunate. So, are you part of Orian folklore as well?"

"Things that haunt the shadows could never be a large part of the mythos for a people with excellent night vision. The Oriani have different demons."

Lauren gathered herself and started away.

"One other thing," Ryet said. "Be wary of John Kim. He is greatly conflicted. I do not think he knows himself which side he is on."

"I hardly know the man," Lauren said over her shoulder.

"That will change," Ryet said, mostly to itself.

THE PHYSICIAN WAS TURGORN, a slight creature in a white robe-like garment that seemed too big for her, and she had asked to meet Stanton in front of the window looking into Whitby's room. Archie stood beside him, offering a bit of emotional support. There, in that cold, echoing hallway scented faintly with disinfectant and the mustiness of strange creatures, with soft, twittery words translated by a tinny machine, the doctor explained to Stanton that no matter how much they tried, Whitby was not going to have any sort of tolerable life. "The most that we could do would be to give him a few months of pain. It is now for you to decide how many."

"What are you saying?"

"I am saying it is time to let your son die."

Once again, the cold thing grew in the centre of Stanton's being and left him speechless and immobile. Archie took his elbow and guided him to a white plastic bench in the white hospital corridor. A care-bot rolled up and stayed nearby, perhaps to administer to Stanton if needed, perhaps to protect the doctor, since Stanton definitely felt an urge to violence, to hit, rip, tear, destroy something, anything. To rage at a universe which would allow this. Fortunately for all, his muscles wouldn't move. He could only push a small, distressed groan from his paralyzed throat.

"The instant we turn the machines off, he will be gone," the physician said, offering the only comfort she could, a quick ending.

Which was no comfort at all. The only thing that gave Stanton's life meaning was about to die. Again.

When he had caught his breath, he turned to ask the doctor for a second opinion from someone human, but the Turgorn had wisely slipped away into the swirling white anonymity of the healthcare apparatus.

"I'll arrange for a second opinion," Archie said in mind-reading mode, "but I don't think you should get your hopes up."

Stanton had already mourned his son once, only to discover his grief was premature. Thrust into that pit a second time, he knew no second reprieve was forthcoming. Guided by Archie, shuffling like an old man, he returned to the bleak, dim austerity of his room and took the pills Archie offered without even asking what they were. A dozen messages were waiting for him, deals not finished or not yet begun, hedged offers of support, veiled opposition, inquiries as to his whereabouts. He ignored them all. He dived into sleep, the only relief he could find.

When he awoke, he found nothing much had changed.

"DON'T ANSWER THE COM," Stanton said to Archie over the course of something approximating breakfast at a well-used table under thin yellow lamplight in the cafeteria.

Archie attacked the food with enthusiasm. Clough had picked at it, drunk a little of the alleged coffee, and mostly stared out into space. The cafeteria seemed cooler than usual, and Stanton shivered. "If media vultures show up, try to deflect them. I don't want to talk to anyone."

"Of course. Um—there's something we have to—" It wasn't like Archie to hesitate to speak out.

"What?" Stanton asked impatiently.

"Should I arrange to have Whitby's—uh—body returned to Earth?"

Stunned by even the thought of that horror, wrenched to his core, Stanton could not reply for a long moment. When his mind thawed enough to consider it, he asked himself, did he really care where the lump of flesh that used to be his son ended up? Did he want to deal with a lot of pomp and ceremony (and a lot of expense) over an event which would serve no purpose except to extend his grief? Did he want to make the long journey to Earth to receive all that phony sympathy from people only trying to advance their own agendas?

Many of the peoples Stanton regularly dealt with had no

funeral customs he understood, but actual humans would expect an observance of some sort, especially from a relatively high-profile family who had lost one who might be considered a war hero.

Then he had an inspiration. "Arrange for burial in space," he said. "Whitby would have liked that."

It was hardly true. Whitby had only joined the Fleet to please his father. Left to his own devices, Stanton's son would have spent his days in dusty libraries reading ancient history and his nights partying with all the other pampered young high-society tadpoles. But a funeral in space would make the right statement and remind folks they were still at war, salvage a minuscule value from the tragedy. And the Fleet would pick up at least part of the tab.

You're a pig, Stanton told himself. Then he did a mental shrug. Nothing he could do would help Whitby.

"I could have that organized by the day after tomorrow," Archie said

"That's too soon. A few days. Beatrix—she might want—"

Nothing he could do would help Whitby. Power, influence, fortune, ending at last his interminable quarrel with Beatrix about their son's future, none of it would help Whitby.

He thought he should inform his friends and associates and wondered if he had any friends here, and then he thought he would go to the room and lie down first, and then, some hours later, he awoke thinking he had a course of action. If he couldn't help his son, maybe retaliation would salve his own anger. Maybe.

He sat on the edge of the bed, assembling enough energy to proceed.

"Stay here," he told Archie when his aide came in. "I have something I need to attend to."

"People will enquire. What should I tell them?"

"Anything you like."

"If something *does* come up, where can I find you?"

"Just do your best to carry on."

"But—"

"I don't care, Archie." Stanton waved his aide aside and left Archie open-mouthed.

"STEAL IT? What, from the Fleet? Jeez, Ryet Arkkad, are you out of your ever-loving mind?" Lauren stared at the Nsfera standing beside her bed while she tried to collect her wits.

She had been dozing while Aroull adjusted the nanites. She awoke to find it there, looking down at her, and her startled heart skipped not one but several beats. Then Ryet started to tell her about its nutbar plan. It still creeped her out, and she was beginning to wonder if it was deranged.

Not only was this a serious and unnerving invasion of privacy from a person she hardly knew, it was talking a crazy kind of something near treason and something she didn't want to listen to. "Go away."

It ignored her demand. "No, certainly not from the Fleet; that would be madness. And not from here, which is closely guarded. Far preferable would be some outlying commercial shipping port, where we can find some old discarded automated freighter nobody cares about anymore. Someplace busy, where keeping close track of everything that comes and goes is difficult. Riga, perhaps?"

"Rigans would eat you alive. Nobody discards heliosite. How could you even contemplate such a thing? Why, indeed, am I not calling the police right now?"

"Maybe you don't want to see me in jail?" Ryet suggested.

"I don't think that's it." Lauren squirmed, acutely uncomfortable, physically and otherwise. She really wanted to be somewhere else, but she was tethered to the machinery. Aroull said they were almost done.

"Why the hell are you telling me this?" She looked over her shoulder at the Orian. "Can you make this person go away?" she asked.

"You experience undue distress hearing what it has to say?"

"Yes, dammit. I think even listening to this stuff would be considered criminal. You do know," she said to the interloper, "that the hospital is lousy with cameras and sensors and whatnot?"

"Aroull turned them off in this room," it said.

Lauren looked up at Aroull, but he kept his attention firmly on his instruments. "You're part of this?" she asked.

"I am sympathetic toward the goal," Aroull replied. "Please be still."

"Well, the whole idea is madder than a hatter's tea party. Even if," Lauren paused, trying to think of a polite way to phrase it but not finding one, "even if you could beg, borrow, or, gods help us, steal a vessel, how far do you think you would get? If you have any experience working in Kazi space, think how deep an unarmed freighter could get into the empire before it was shot to pieces."

"I do not see an alternative. We could arm it, at least a little. But resources are not unlimited."

"Better steal some stealth technology and the best AI pilot you can get along with your vessel."

"I believe an organic pilot would be more effective."

"Yeah, but then you'd be responsible for his death when he got shot to pieces."

While they were talking, a screen had been wheeled into her room. The logo of a messaging company was blinking on it, the machines impatient to get the correspondents in place before wasting precious hyperspace milliseconds.

"Can you give me a moment?" she asked Aroull.

The Orian gave her one of those one-shouldered shrugs and left the room.

"You, too," she told Ryet.

The Nsfera hesitated a moment as if it might argue, then followed Aroull.

She recognized her own paranoia. If anyone really wanted to listen in on her messages, they could. No messaging system in the known worlds was truly private, and Midway's was more compromised than most.

One last screen blink, and Nathan Howerath's worried face appeared. "They've been at it again. We got a new IR recording. Look."

Nice to see you too, boss, Lauren thought. About ten seconds of blurry, dim sensor log played on her screen. "When did this happen?"

Nathan grunted.

It was a dumb question. The time stamp rolled along the bottom of the record. "I'll look at it, Nathan," she said, happy that she had thought to switch on the recorder before they connected. "I'll give it my best shot, but you should really ask DoubleChek for a replacement. I could be here a long time."

"I did. They did. The guy's an idiot."

"Oh." Lauren didn't even try to suppress the satisfaction in that. "What did the AI tell you about the last record?"

"Solid object, 1.3 degrees C below ambient, longest dimension about seventy-one centimetres. Confidence level fifty-three."

"Why didn't it show on the mass sensor?"

"Don't know."

"This one have the same characteristics?"

"Don't know."

"So, what *do* you know about this event?"

"Still processing. Marc will send you the data when he gets them. You're looking way better."

Nathan sounded hopeful. How odd. How uncharacteristic.

"I am better, just not great."

"Hurry up. I need you to get back here."

Do I really want to do that? Lauren wondered as she played the sensor log at the slowest speed this terminal could give her. *Don't I deserve some sort of* hors de combat? *Couldn't I recuperate at home, assuming I could avoid scaring the heck out of Hanna?*

She composed a mental message to DoubleChek and tried to decide if it was worth the cost of transmitting it. "I quit." would be shorter and more in keeping with her mood, but she still had massive bills to pay. Grand gestures in moments of pique were not an option.

After a couple of run-throughs, she stopped the playback on the frame she thought gave the clearest picture of the thing, whatever it was. It didn't look much different from the last one. She zoomed in to the max and studied the fuzzy blob. What could she work out from this that the AI couldn't do better? She walked it back and forth through a few frames. Nothing.

She didn't hear Aroull come back in and started when he spoke. She shut the screen down. Keeping blurry blobs from prying eyes seemed excessively cautious, but she had been taught to err on the side of caution.

"You expect to find something significant in these inferior images?" he asked.

"More hope than expectation."

"A typically human approach to problem-solving."

Did Oriani understand sarcasm? Lauren wondered. "It gives me something to do."

"Indeed. John Kim has asked me to tell you he came to see you while you were not here."

"Okay. Did he say why?"

"He did not."

For a while, Aroull was all med tech, peering at her intently, asking her to turn this way and that, running the portable ultrasound with massive ear protectors on his head, but looking distressed anyway. He prodded her body here and there with soft, quick touches like an arachnophobe might touch a spider. His hands were warm.

"Tomorrow, we will again move some of the nanites to new locations. I believe the treatment is progressing very well. You should have few residual issues by the time it is done."

"That's good to know."

"Yes. I will come tomorrow. Until then, you may return to the study of your poor images of the organism."

Thanks so much, Lauren thought. Then, *"organism"?* "Wait a minute," she said. Aroull stopped at the door and turned toward her. "Why do you call a grey blob on a sensor record an organism?"

"It moves like an organism." His tail twitched like an impatient cat's. "I suppose a mechanical could be built to move in that fashion, but such an inefficient design would be unlikely." He paused for a moment. "In my view."

"You are not an engineer."

"I am not."

"Whatever it is absorbs IR. Infrared radiation."

"Yes. A cold-blooded organism might do so."

For a moment, Lauren was busy rethinking all her previous assumptions. Aroull left the room and closed the door firmly behind him.

After she reviewed the record and thought about it for a while, she sent a message to Marc to ask the AI to look at the sensor records as if the images were of a cold-blooded organism.

Then she lay back on her bed and stared up at the blank white ceiling.

Kaz, she thought.

We are in such deep doo-doo, she thought.

What the hell are we going to do?

She lay there for a moment, trying to quiet her mind, then sighed. This was way too scary to waste time with Nathan's chicken-hearted approach to life.

But from Midway, all she could do was talk.

So, talk, then, girl, for the love of Mike, she told herself. *It's not going to go away if you shut your eyes.*

She asked for a connection to DoubleChek.

Some officious, snippy robotic voice came on and told her she had used up her allotment of hyperspace time and she would have to wait for her turn in the rotation.

"This is important," she said.

"It always is. Your next allotment will be available after 13:53, 11/07 Terran System of Dating. Good day."

She wanted to scream at the discovery that not all hide-bound bureaucrats were bound in hide. But yelling at machinery was completely non-productive. Instead, she beamed a mental stream of servo-mechanical scatology at the communications system, then punched a button to call the care-bot. "I need to speak to the ranking officer in this Fleet Detachment."

Its screen flashed a fraction of a second later: *I will attempt to make an appointment. Subject matter?*

"I don't have time to make appointments. Connect me to John Kim."

John Kim is not in the hospital sector.

"Get me Aroull, then."

Aroull has been paged.

When Aroull arrived, she said, "I need hyperspace communications. Your plan to beat the Kaz? We need to get it in place right now."

MIDWAY—CAFETERIA

"The communications system said you wanted to talk to the base commander," John Kim said.

"I really do need to talk to someone in authority," Lauren said.

"If you want to tell me what the issue is, maybe I can help."

"You'll probably think I'm crazy."

"Then again, maybe I won't."

They sat at a small table in a corner of the cafeteria. John Kim had brought coffee in a thermos from "across the wall." It was a damn sight nicer than the stuff the cafeteria offered. Other cafeteria patrons scattered around the space turned to look as the aroma wafted their way. There she was, having coffee with a good-looking guy: sharp brown eyes, warm smile, thick black hair cut so short it looked like a good-quality brush. He was smiling and attentive. Though the socket in his skull where he connected to his ship was a little creepy. It was almost a pity to spoil the ambience. Be wary, Ryet said. What did Ryet know?

She took a deep breath and got it all out there in as few words as she could manage. "Kaz have been on Ferguson

Prime, and some of them have been into the mines. Howerath is missing some heliosite, and I'm sure the Kaz took it."

"Wow."

Balancing on a slightly wonky wire-frame chair, Lauren cradled the cup in her hands, inhaled the fragrance, and waited to see how John Kim would react.

He looked down, smile gone, and studied the wear pattern on the tabletop for a moment, then looked up at her. "First, I don't think you're crazy."

"But?"

"But that's a lot to swallow."

"So not crazy but seriously deranged?"

A ghost of the smile returned. "Howerath Mines has the most effective intruder alert systems and the most sensitive anti-theft devices in Known Space."

"Yes, I just installed the most recent version a few days before . . . this." Lauren waved a hand across her body.

"So?"

"I don't know. The only sign of them has been on the IR sensor."

"Don't you find that odd?"

"You mean, can I explain it? No. But I've been in this business for a while, and I trust my instincts. The Fleet needs to get out there and protect Ferguson Prime before we lose it to the Empire."

"Based on your instincts? That's a lot to ask."

"My instincts and some missing heliosite and some weird sensor readings. Err on the side of caution."

"Mm. A little above my pay grade, I'm afraid. I can talk to some people, but don't hold your breath." John went back to studying the table. After a moment, he asked, "How did you get into the security business?"

"Pretty much the only thing I know how to do that pays enough to keep my daughter and me fed," she said.

"But you live on Centauri, right, and they have a wealth-sharing plan?"

"Well, yes, but the thing is, wealth-share will give you about nineteen square metres of living space and enough food to survive, but a kid—" Lauren paused, thinking of Hanna's boundless energy that needed a lot of room to keep her from exploding, her delight in everything in the world from some little insectoid motoring down the sidewalk to the curiosities Lauren brought back from far away when she could get home, how constrained Hanna would be in a tiny apartment. "A kid wants more than just the bare necessities."

"And her mother wants that for her, too."

"Yeah, I do. She's such a cool kid. She is curious and . . . joyful, I guess, is the only word, and I want to preserve that as long as possible. She's brilliant, and she needs good schools to take advantage." Lauren stopped and smiled sheepishly. "You probably shouldn't ask a mother about her kid unless you're prepared for the monologue."

Kim smiled. "It's nice to hear. So many parents do nothing but bitch. I suppose your work keeps you away from home a fair bit. It must be hard for you."

"I really do miss seeing her grow up. The plan was to take off-world assignments only until I had enough in the bank to be able to decline them. This," she indicated the fading-but-still-very-apparent scars, "has been a considerable setback."

"I guess. I don't have a child, so I can't really appreciate the issue. I take it your kid's father is not in the picture."

"He is not." That came out a little sharper than Lauren intended.

Kim smiled an apology. "It's none of my business." He paused. "Aroull told me I had to make sure you got something to eat. All this rebuilding you're doing takes a lot of fuel. Is there anything among the offerings here that you would like?"

"You know Aroull?"

"It's a small community." He stood, preparing to fetch.

"Yeah. Anyway, I think that no matter what the server-bot labels it, everything comes out of the same box."

"I'll take a guess, then."

He returned in a moment with a plastic tray containing something speared in its centre with a plastic fork. It looked grey and smelled like the cafeteria. She took a mouthful to be polite. It was sort of warm.

"How old is Hanna now?" Kim asked.

"She's six."

"That's a good age, old enough to be articulate, young enough not to get mouthy."

Lauren smiled and nodded, but a little irritation had started to grow inside. Outside, she kept her pleasant social face on and answered John Kim's chatter, while inside, she watched the uneasiness grow, trying to make out its shape, and finally decided there were enough oddities piling up that she needed to know what the hell John Kim was all about.

"What made you leave the military?" John had asked.

"I got tired of obsessive idiots telling me in exquisite detail the officially approved way of doing things that no one in his right mind would want to do at all."

John laughed politely. "I've felt like that myself on occasion."

"How do you know my daughter's name?"

His smile vanished. He twisted the cup around on the worn metal surface of the table. "Mm, I guess you told me."

"Mm, no, I didn't. I might look like a marginal wreck, but my brain's still working."

Kim was looking a bit flustered. "Does it matter?"

"Yes, it does."

"I don't honestly remember."

"That's not true."

"Lauren, what—"

"All the 'where are you from and what do you do?' stuff. You know the answers, don't you? So what's this all about? Chatting up that crazy, ugly girl for a laugh? Not funny."

"Of course not. What would make you think? Besides, you're not—just—"

"Broken? Let's talk about you for a while. What are you up to these days? I hope you're not planning on espionage as a new career because you're not good at it."

For a moment, John was taken aback. Then he collected himself. "Jeez, Lauren, settle. It's not like that."

Yeah, Lauren, settle, she thought to herself. *No wonder you don't have any social life.* But she couldn't stop herself. "So what *is* it like, John?"

"Okay, so I looked into your background. I was interested. Is that so terrible? You've been saying some pretty strange things."

"Really? Interested how? What did you need to know that you couldn't ask me?"

"Everybody lies."

"What?"

"You left the military under a bit of a cloud, a charge of homicide, as I understand it."

"None of your business, mister."

"A minute ago, you were asking me to tell the commander to scramble the Fleet. I need to know if I can trust you. I need your help to do that."

"Well, congratulations on not getting it. Good-bye."

Lauren was hoping for an exit stage right with a bit of a theatrical flourish, but struggling with chairs and canes made a mess of it. And hobbling off into Midway's barely perceptible sunset had no damned flair at all.

About to re-enter the hospital wing, she chanced a look back. John was still at the table, looking maybe a little downcast but not nearly contrite enough for Lauren's satisfaction.

Congratulations, you idiot, she thought to herself. *Over-*

reacting again. You do have a finely honed technique for pushing people away.

WHEN AROULL CAME in with his equipment, wanting to check on her progress, Lauren put aside the materials from the Civil Constabulary she had been studying. The blurry object continued to bother her. *It's my fate*, she thought, *to try to interpret blobs on screens.* She had found one camera looking from a different angle that was more clear, and she had become quite certain that it was a person going into and then out of the crime scene, moving very fast. She marked it for the Turgorn and suggested he find that individual.

As soon as Aroull was through the door, she asked, "What's going on between you and John Kim?"

Startled, Aroull stopped on the spot, looking for all the world like a man caught with his pants down, if one could imagine an Orian with pants and a hang-up about where they were positioned. But in a flash, he was his calm, collected self again.

"You have a reason for asking this question?"

"Yeah. I had coffee with Kim this afternoon. Your name came up."

"Yes?"

"Yes. Why is he digging into my background? What's going on, Aroull? Have you been helping him out with that? Medical information is supposed to be kept confidential."

"John Kim is a sovereign entity and undoubtedly has his own motives. I am expected to answer for John Kim?"

"Somebody better, or else this story is going straight to Administration, and they can look into who is breaking what rules. I'm sure you've heard about a citizen's right to privacy."

Aroull busied himself with his equipment, but he was obviously uncomfortable. After a moment, he said, "John Kim has examined your history because we have thought to trust you."

"Who 'we'? With what?"

Aroull said nothing.

"So 'we' are thinking about trusting me but not very damned much."

Aroull stopped for a moment, then reached into one of his equipment bags and pulled out a flimsy and a bright-yellow flower. Once again, he hesitated as if he were uncertain, then gave both those items to Lauren. "John Kim asked me to give you these. An attempt to level the playing field, he said. I do not know what that means. But perhaps they will soothe your ruffled feelings."

Lauren could feel her blood pressure rising, which was never a good sign. Her fists clenched. "I don't want to be freaking soothed," she said, a little louder than might be considered polite. "I want to know what the hell is going on."

Aroull said nothing; just went on about his work.

"Where did he get a tulip around here?" Lauren put the flimsy on the chair, away from the equipment, and lay down under the rack of tubes and magnets.

Aroull looked away, a thing he did quite often. Lauren didn't know how to interpret the gesture. He seemed not able to talk to her directly but addressed the room behind her. "A Kazi has died on the station. Officialdom is busy trying to discover the cause. The Civil Constabulary has asked for your assistance."

"Did they put an ad on the entertainment network?"

"I do not understand this question."

"Everyone and his dog seems to have learned about it the instant I did. By the bye, I haven't agreed to do this, you know."

"You have been reading the investigators' reports and studying the sensor logs. The presumption that you are working at the task seems justified."

Lauren regarded the sensor-studded ceiling above, monitoring her heart rate, blood pressure, and every other bloody thing she did. Come to think of it, she had no damned privacy for anyone to violate.

"It is important that, for the time being, the death be attributed to natural causes."

"Which it is not?"

Aroull chose not to answer.

"Why?"

Aroull said nothing.

"Where does the Orian code of ethics position the division between secrets and lies?" Aroull's ears tilted back. Lauren could hear his tail swishing. It did occur to her that antagonizing the person who daily held her life in his hands was possibly not her best move. She seemed to be antagonizing everyone she encountered lately, and she wondered why she had become so cranky.

"I perceive two possible reasons investigators might arrive at this preferred conclusion," Aroull said. "Sufficient evidence is found at the scene to persuade those investigating that the death was natural, or autopsy results are consistent with a natural death.

"There is much not being told: why was a Kazi here; how did it get here, when did it arrive, was it alone? Officialdom appears disinterested in these issues, though one might think them to be of the utmost importance. This suggests information is being hidden. The constabulary thinks it needs to know what happened to this particular Kazi and why. The answer could have considerable bearing on how we proceed—perhaps if we can proceed at all. It would be better for us if they did not find the answer."

"They have plenty of other resources at their disposal if they don't trust their own findings. There's the whole Fleet investigative apparatus they could appeal to."

"Which is why they have appealed to you? Civilians do not trust the Interplanetary military unduly. The military is deeply invested in the status quo, less interested in dead Kaz than in the power struggle with the political system, very unwilling to admit to an error, and not likely to have our best interests centred. The official stance has been to persist with methods that have been proven to be not more than temporarily effective, and which are costing ever more resources and lives, and which the Kaz are learning to counter more efficiently every day."

The apparatus around her buzzed and clicked. "'We,' Oriani generally, or 'we,' your little group of outlaws?"

"A harsh word, 'outlaw.' I think both groups qualify, but our group is probably most at risk. After all, if we are successful, the need for military services is much reduced. The military, with its suppliers and various hangers-on, forms a very large and powerful economic unit, which would not take kindly to being weakened." Aroull turned back toward her and made an effort to meet her gaze—and it was an effort, she could see that. "Also, we can be certain that you were not a participant in this event since your whereabouts have been monitored since you arrived. And you have had training and experience in investigative techniques.

"Our group, incidentally, is not entirely Oriani. A wide range of species are represented."

"Yeah, well, good luck to you and your friends. I really do not want to get into the middle of this, whatever it is. I have a job to get back to and a kid at home I really want to see, and I have agreed to help the local authorities if I can, so no, Aroull, I'm not going to try to bamboozle the local police. And you might be a bit naive, thinking I'm immune to bribery on the one hand and threats on the other. Trusting me with your secrets might not be your best move."

"I can arrange passage to Centauri when this is done. I

might be able to convince your employer that you will recover much more quickly at home."

"Bribery, then?"

"You are setting the parameters, not I."

"I haven't agreed to any of this yet. Tell me what you are trying to do."

Aroull worked at dismantling the apparatus. Lauren could almost see him weighing benefits and risks. Finally, he said, "Come with me. We will speak with Ehreh, who is best able to answer your concerns."

"I don't think I want to talk to anyone else about this."

"You need not talk; merely listen."

For a moment, Lauren almost smiled. "Fine. I'll listen. Then you leave me alone, okay?"

"Everything is a bargain with you."

"Yeah, and I want some real clothes on, too."

"I will see what can be done. I will return shortly."

Once Aroull was gone, Lauren found a cup, got some water, and put the tulip in it. Then she picked up the flimsy. It contained only one file, John Kim's *curriculum vitae*. At first, she was puzzled, then she understood. He was offering her the same information about him that he had about her. A peace offering? Lauren wasn't quite sure it made up for going behind her back, but it was a step forward. She read a little of it, discovered he had been born on one of the worlds at the edges of known space sometimes referred to as the Outer Marches (not that anyone was likely to march there), into a family of nine, the youngest. He had left home early and joined the Fleet as soon as he was old enough, which left a period of four or so years unaccounted for.

What were you doing there, little Johnny? Lauren wondered. She imagined a young, serious boy with big brown eyes. A thread of warmth slipped in alongside her annoyance.

Then she stopped, closed the file, and put the flimsy aside.

Don't do this, woman, she told herself. *Don't go there. You've been down this road before. It didn't end well.*

AROULL CAME BACK in about an hour with a pouch slung on a strap over his shoulder, from which he retrieved a few garments. His idea of clothing suitable for a human female was not so far off as to be totally impossible but hardly the height of fashion and would probably have fit someone a dozen or so kilos heavier.

"At least turn your back while I get dressed," Lauren said.

Aroull looked somewhat bemused but complied.

Lauren rolled up sleeves and pant legs, and Aroull led her out into the warren of old Midway, through a maze of twisty passages, and to a tiny room, scarcely more than a closet, where the old fellow was staying.

Ehreh was far and away the oldest Orian Lauren had seen, grizzled and frail, slouched on the edge of a stool in front of a battered table, hunching over an ancient reader. Without preamble, Aroull went to work, extracting from his pouch various bits of medical apparatus, powders and potions, even though Ehreh tried to dissuade him. "You are wasting time and resources. I will die regardless."

"We will all die, old friend, just not right now."

Ehreh quit protesting and only grunted when Aroull chided him for not eating enough. But he soon lost patience and shrugged the younger Orian away. "Let us get on with it. We have little enough time to waste."

"This human," Aroull said, "needs to know something of our plans. She may be able to influence Stanton Clough and, thereby, the Council. She may be able to redirect the investigation of the Civil Constabulary."

Lauren found another chair and pulled it up nearer to the table.

There was some back and forth between Ehreh and Aroull in their native tongue, and Lauren was about to excuse herself when Ehreh paused, then began in Sindharr to tell her in general terms about the organism he had built and the plan they had to fill a commercial freighter full of micro-drones, drive it as far as they could into Kazi space, and then loose the drones toward whatever Kazi worlds their tiny robot minds could find.

"You're serious," Lauren said when he was done.

"Yes. You have reason to doubt me?"

"I thought Oriani were smart. This is so dumb. You and the Nsfera are a pair."

"I do not believe insults will elucidate whatever problems you perceive. Tell me what you believe to be the error."

"Where to start? The last mission the Fleet sent into Kazi territory: how deeply did it penetrate before the Kaz beat them up, destroyed a starship, and killed its crew, that being a military operation of several heavily armed Fleet vessels and highly trained people? Where do you think you would get on a commercial vessel with no training and no defences? It's absolute suicide. Pointless suicide. Your cargo would be dispersed in open space before it ever entered the Empire."

Both the Oriani offered the one-shoulder-up, head-turned, Orian shrug.

"This is probably the weirdest scheme I've ever heard of. It is so not going to work. No part of it has any chance. Even if you had a manufacturing facility in hand, do you have any idea how long it would take to build your mess of drones, never mind program and test them? I'm guessing decades. You guys are crazy," Lauren said.

"Or desperate," Aroull suggested.

"I confess I am not a tactician. I do not see a better alternative," Ehreh said. "I cannot start sooner than now."

"But the Kaz are in the mines now."

For a moment, Lauren was the object of two intense Orian stares, golden eyes boring in as Aroull and Ehreh processed their surprise.

"This is possible?" Ehreh said at last.

MIDWAY—RESIDENTIAL DIVISION E

When Clough returned to his room, Archie met him with a sizable collection of names on the flimsy. "Everyone is looking for you. The Council chairman has repeatedly inquired regarding your whereabouts. I think you should call him right away."

"Yes, I should do that. I need to inform him I am resigning from the Council. I will need to communicate with IPC Ambassador Li Chang as well. You can tell anyone else who needs to know."

Once again, Archie was speechless. On his list of improbable events, Clough leaving the Council came somewhere after Midway's star re-igniting. As the shock started to wear off, he began to see all his plans coming unravelled. Clough was his leverage. Access to the delegate was what he had to sell. Without Clough, he could not imagine his way forward. "Why?" he asked, his voice squeakier than he wanted it to be.

"It's a long story. The short version is I can no longer support the Council's policy on containing the Kaz."

"But—"

"I really don't want to argue this just now," Clough said. He didn't have a good argument to offer, truth be told. Eventually, he would have to think up something to tell his backers and his associates. Vengeance seemed petty in the bigger picture, but it truly was what was most on his mind. "Can we get some food in here? Before I talk to the Ambassador, I want to meet someone as high up as you can manage in the civilian government here. As soon as you can manage."

"Should I give him a topic?"

"No."

Okay, Archie thought, *things really have changed.* Clough was usually forthcoming to his aide about his plans.

He put on his most sincere voice and said, "Are you sure about giving up on the Conference, Stanton? You've put a lot of effort into building up support. If you do this, that support is going to disappear fast. Chances are, you will never get it back."

"It doesn't matter."

"But—"

"Nothing I can do now will help Whitby."

Well, that's true enough, Archie thought. *But where does that leave us?* "Okay," he said. "I'll get started."

"Set up a meeting with the Orian called Ehreh."

"Okay."

As soon as he had left their room, Archie activated his implant. As he manoeuvred his way along the corridor, he ignored all the frantic incoming calls inquiring after Clough and initiated a search for Michael Martin. Michael's virtual assistant came on the unit and informed him Martin was in a meeting and was not to be disturbed. "Tell him I have important information that I don't think he will want to miss. Tell him I'm on my way to his office right now. Tell him he should meet me there."

Could a chunk of software give you a dismissive sniff? "I will put it on his calendar."

"Put it at the top of the list. This won't keep." *And if you don't,*

I'm going to come over there and rip your code out, you virtual jerk, Archie added to himself.

The electronic presence simply went offline.

Archie parked himself in the hallway close enough to Clough's room that he could watch the door while he picked at the flimsy to get food delivered and then started working his way through the various barriers to reach a government official high enough in the system to satisfy Clough's ego. It was worth the trouble to stay on Clough's good side, at least until he knew where this was going.

The cafeteria's delivery-bot came trundling down the hall with the food. Archie's stomach reminded him he hadn't eaten himself for quite some time, but he decided to stay where he was for a while.

His patience was rewarded. A short time later, Clough left the room, walking quickly, looking determined.

Archie put lunch on hold and followed.

⸻

Since Midway had become a major military base, its diplomatic role had been much curtailed. Most major IPC functions had moved to bigger, more modern facilities, and so the civilian accommodations had not been upgraded as much as one might hope.

Stanton longed for a map. No doubt Archie had maps on one or more of his ever-present machines, and Stanton, not for the first time, regretted his own lack of skill with information-processing devices. Usually, it was a minor inconvenience, at most. Someone was always at hand who could do that sort of thing. He almost never went anywhere alone. But at the moment, pursuing a course that was definitely illicit and probably illegal, Stanton did not trust anyone quite enough to accept him as a guide. He had the information

Archie had acquired from the Orian earlier, but it was proving to be less helpful than one might hope. Stanton found himself blundering around in a maze of half-lit passages, stumbling over broken walkways, trying to find the place that was described to him amid places that all looked much the same.

That period of immobility he had experienced when he got the news of Whitby's fate—the thought made him pause and take a deep breath—had given him this chance. If he had been able to act on his feelings then, he would probably be in somebody's jail by now, and no doubt his hands would be damaged again. But he was through waiting for the IPC and its bureaucracy-bound committees to move. And a physical attack would have been pointless anyway; those who were directly responsible were forever out of reach. Those who were indirectly responsible, however—

They had become a closed little clique, power brokers and bureaucrats and policymakers, talking to one another about one another, reacting to each other and not thinking about much else, and he had long been a part of it. They had lost sight of what they were there for, busily arguing about who should fund the firefighters while their houses burned. The rest of the circle would undoubtedly see Clough's present course of action as a betrayal of their unwritten covenant. Stanton found it hard to care a lot.

The baby-blue door was before him, the paint flaking away. If it had ever had any identifying marks, they were gone now. He raised his hand to knock.

A furry hand grabbed him by the shoulder and turned him away quite forcefully.

"Hey," he protested.

"You are at the wrong door," the Orian said. "Follow me."

She led him down the passage and around a corner to another blue door and in. The room was small and dim and displayed the unfinished concrete interior that was the theme in civilian Midway.

Ehreh and a third Orian were seated at a small, battered table in the middle of the room, where the light was best. The others, hugging the shadows, represented several races, some Stanton couldn't identify.

"Thank you for coming, Stanton Clough," Ehreh said, leaning forward, ears up. "The person beside me is Aroull, our systems expert. I will not identify the other people here."

"That's not fair," Stanton said. "Everyone here now knows who I am."

"I believe a human cliché suggests that little in life is fair," Ehreh said.

Stanton grunted a sound that was not agreement but decided against belabouring the matter. "You said you have a way to defeat the Kaz that doesn't involve people getting shot down in flames."

"What you remember is not accurate. I said there was a way that is different from the one currently being pursued by our several governments. I must add that the process is by no means without risk."

"Okay, fine. So tell me about it."

"First, you should tell me how we can be assured that you are not here to identify our people and disrupt our efforts."

"I beg your pardon. You came to me not so very long ago. Why would you do that if you thought that all I would do would be to spy for the establishment? I'm planning the funeral of my only child. If all we're going to do is hurl accusations back and forth, I'll be on my way." Righteous indignation had served Clough well on many occasions.

"As you wish. However, this group and this plan may be your best chance to serve your vengeance."

"Vengeance?" Clough was startled. Was he that transparent? Did it matter? He took a moment to regain his centre.

While he struggled, a creature he could not identify even as to race came in and spoke briefly to the Orian, but Stanton couldn't follow the conversation. Ehreh seemed to wilt as the discussion progressed, as if his energy were being exhausted.

"Find Ryet Arkkad and send it here," Ehreh said. He turned back to Clough. "Please forgive the interruption. A Kazi has died on the station, and one I know might have information about the death."

"There are Kaz here?"

"There were," Ehreh. "One has died, and another, we believe, has left Midway, undoubtedly to carry the news to its kin. Depending on what information it has, it may mean the time available to take effective action has been considerably shortened. If we do not act quickly, we may lose our only opportunity."

"Ehreh, you can explain it to me, and maybe I can help, or you can stand on your demands, and I will go away."

After a moment of thought, Ehreh explained. Clough listened. He understood better than Ehreh clearly expected he would. "Presently," Ehreh said, "we are unable to proceed due to lack of the means to deliver the virus. We are trying to find a vehicle. If you have a starship handy, that would be good. Otherwise, the project needs funding."

"Everything always does," Stanton Clough said. He managed to sound a bit put off; of course, he did, though he didn't know if tactics like that worked with Oriani. In truth, he had relaxed considerably. This was old, familiar territory, the kind of battle he knew how to fight. "A spaceworthy vessel can probably be had, though the price would be well beyond my means, even for a second-class freighter. You wouldn't necessarily have to go through official channels, but unofficial channels will raise the price. So, where does the Orian government stand on this project?"

"They are opposed."

"That's too bad. Let me ask around, see what I can do."

"Many oppose us: individuals, companies, and governments. If they were to join forces, they could easily destroy the venture."

"The trick, then, is to keep them arguing with one another."

"A trick you know well."

"I do." *Everything is politics in the end.*

MIDWAY—KING GEORGE XIII HOSPITAL

Lauren had put in a few hours with the sensor logs from Howerath but couldn't come up with any better interpretation than the one Aroull had suggested. Earlier, when she had communications time built up again, she had asked Marc to send someone into the number-three shaft and watch what the sensors reported. Marc sent her the resulting record. Nothing showed except IR, which was as bright as ever. "I don't get it," Marc said. "They can use each other's circuits and power sources, and they use the same reporting software. It's networked. But only the IR sensors are working."

"Thanks, Marc."

She called DoubleChek. "The sensors we set up for Howerath—is there a way to defeat them? Would someone be able to switch them off for a while without us knowing?"

Sillah Waell was on communications. "I don't think so," she said. "I'll find out."

"Thanks. Tell the boss I need to talk to him soonest."

A few hours later, the tech division sent her some pages of math and a brief note at the bottom: *Not easy take some seriously sophisticated technology not impossible either wish you hadn't asked this question.*

Kaz had plenty of sophisticated technology. Cold-blooded creatures might not think about IR because they were close to ambient temperature most of the time.

The sense of terror that had assailed her earlier returned and was not so easily put down. She got back on the hyperspace link, hoping her allotted time would hold out.

"Nathan, the shadows we saw in the shafts are Kaz. There are Kaz in the mine, and you need to evacuate as soon as possible. Maybe sooner."

"Oh, my God," Nathan Howerath gasped, he who never swore. She could almost feel his shock coming over the link. "They can't be here. How would they get here? Why didn't we see them on sensors? No, no, no, you're mistaken."

"Nathan, I'm sorry. The Empire knows heliosite is there. A few Kaz have been in the mine already. I don't know how they beat the sensors."

"How can you be sure?"

Precious seconds ticked by as she repeated herself. "That's what we've been seeing on the sensor logs. I don't know if any of those ones survived the heat on Fergie Prime, but they will have surely phoned home. The Empire will be preparing to come and get the heliosite. No way they won't. They are coming, and you need to evacuate Fergie Prime. Right now. Before the hordes show up. I don't know how much time you have, but I'm thinking not much. I haven't got much time on the link here, and I have to talk to other people. You get on to Nathan Senior if you need to. I'm pretty sure he'll agree with me. Don't fool around with this, okay?"

"No, not okay. You can't just call me and tell me it's the end of the world, so pack up and go. What am I going to do? I can't just leave the mine to the Kaz. Did the Fleet agree to this?"

"I've told them, but I'm not asking permission. That would

take way more time than we've got. For the love of Mike, Nathan, don't argue. Just get your people safe. Then you can deal with the Fleet and all the rest of the IPC bureaucrats and your father and the shareholders. I suspect there will be serious panic in those quarters. You need to be gone before protocol and process and procedure start delaying every move. You need to get everyone to safety as soon as you can. Then destroy the mine. I don't know when the Kaz will arrive in force, but I'm damned sure they will."

"Yes, but the sensors—"

"I don't know why they didn't pick up intruders. Our tech people are looking into it. Let's err on the side of caution."

"I don't know about that. A lot of money, lost production. If you're wrong . . ."

But Lauren decided she could not waste any more precious hyperspace minutes. "I'll check back later and see how you are getting on."

She had to spend a few more of those precious minutes explaining to her boss at DoubleChek what was happening and received the same incredulity but with somewhat more threatening overtones. "This is not okay. You were supposed to be looking after that place. Didn't you get proper sensors into the shafts? That was your first order of business. What the hell happened there?"

"I don't know. The sensors were installed and were functioning. I know that for certain. Then they weren't. I've asked the tech people to see if there might be a way they could have been turned off when we weren't looking. Can we hash through it later? Can you do anything to help evacuate the mining community? Not having people die at the facility should help the bottom line at least a little."

"Yeah, okay, I hear you. But next time you have a notion to play superhero, remember you have a job to do, and it doesn't include getting busted up and spending months in hospital. You see what happens when you leave clients alone?"

"I have to go," she said. "Yell at me later." At least they were talking about a next time.

And then she did the hard one.

"Mom, Mom, Mom, you'll never guess. We went to this farm place at the University, and there was a cow. I touched it. It's an animal, Mom, did you know?"

"Weren't you scared, such a big thing?" Lauren imagined that perfect little hand reaching out to a creature twenty times her size.

"Nah, it was cool. Not fierce or anything. It smelled kinda strong, though. Oh, you're supposed to talk to Aunt Jane."

"Okay, put her on. Love you, babe."

"Love you, Mom."

"Lauren," Jane said, sounding brittle over the hyperspace link. "Where are you? What are you doing? I thought you would be coming home after your accident. Are you okay?"

"I have eyebrows."

"Okay. That seems like a good thing."

Lauren smiled, thinking of the puzzled look on Jane's face. "I'm getting recovered. But there's some stuff here I have to deal with. Listen, Jane, don't be upset, but you're going to get some legal documents in the next little while giving you title to the apartment in Centauri City and formal guardianship over Hanna in case anything happens to me. I'm going to put the money I have there into a trust for Hanna, with the intention of keeping it away from the dear Merriweathers. Okay?"

"What? No, no, not okay." *That does seem to be the consensus,* Lauren thought. Jane continued, "You've never talked like this before. What's going on? Why now? Is something likely to happen to you? What are you up to, Lauren?"

"I don't think you'd believe me if I told you. I don't half

believe it myself. Can you just trust me to do my best to come out of it in good shape?"

"Trust you? Little sister, you're the craziest person I know."

"You just don't know enough people." Lauren disconnected the link and hoped that Jane wouldn't hold her craziness against Hanna.

Then she climbed back onto the bed and let Aroull to do his thing.

LYING inside her cage of pipes and plates, Lauren half-imagined she could detect the nanites protesting their deactivation. She was restless herself and had a hard time keeping still.

"I am not entirely in favour of this approach," Aroull said. "Interrupting the programmed sequence could have unintended consequences."

"How likely is that? Is it better or worse than if they continue to work without your supervision?"

"I do not know that any studies have been done."

"Now you tell me."

"I had not anticipated the need."

"Me neither. Anyway, at this point, I'm more concerned about the Kaz than the nanites. The probability of surviving an encounter with the Kaz is far smaller."

"You originally expressed deep concern about nanites."

"Funny how one's priorities change. With luck, we won't encounter any Kaz, I'll be back in a couple of days, and the nanites can carry on."

"A poor thing to depend on, luck."

"It's what I've got."

Aroull looked like he might have something to say about that, but Ehreh and his crew were crowding in and finding places. Ehreh took the only chair; he seemed to be moving even more slowly and more carefully than he had been a few days ago. The others sat on the floor or leaned against the walls. John Kim was with them, which surprised Lauren on more than one level. She watched him watching her, trying to assess her mood.

"Quite the fashion statement you've got there," he said with a smile.

"Aroull's choices," she said.

Ryet Arkkad, a black creature in a white room, settled into a corner and managed to become nearly unnoticeable. Something about the way it moved scratched an itch, but Lauren couldn't quite identify the source.

The little room became crowded. Aroull busied himself with putting away the machinery.

Ehreh had insisted that the group was not "his crew" but merely a gathering of like-minded individuals, but it was obvious from the first meeting that they looked to him for guidance, regardless. He was the person she had to convince; the others would follow his lead. Lauren had suggested they meet in her hospital room, which was way more comfortable than the cubicle Ehreh was in and probably just as secure once Aroull had turned off the spyware. The time when secrecy mattered was probably over anyway.

It was Ehreh to whom she explained her plan.

"It looks to me like we can build the perfect trap. If we do it this way, you will only need to borrow a hyperspace vessel, and you won't have to worry about building drones. You won't have to send a pilot to certain death," she said, an argument she hoped would appeal to the Oriani. "But if you can think of a better way, I'm all ears." Pairs of Oriani ears waggled and made Lauren feel inadequately endowed even though her new one was almost full size.

"We have this short window of opportunity, and we either take it or it's gone forever. Howerath will evacuate Ferguson

Prime." *I hope*, she thought to herself. "And once that's done, they will collapse the mine shafts and possibly raze the buildings. There will be traffic back and forth from the planet for a while, but once everyone is off-world, there won't be any more. We need to be in there before the mine is destroyed, and since you guys have been hurting for transport, I think we need to be gone before the last ship leaves, or we'll have to stay and greet the Kaz. Not something I would look forward to."

"Why would Howerath destroy the mine?" Kim asked. "Surely, they would be expecting to return someday. That's how big business thinks. And personally, I hope that's the case. There aren't many sources of heliosite in the known worlds. I'd hate to think we were giving one up permanently."

"Howerath IP hopes destroying the mine will keep the Kaz busy excavating until the Fleet arrives." At least, that was what Lauren hoped they hoped, or would do, or whatever. "They are pretty sure the Fleet will arrive as soon as they can get themselves organized. Nobody wants the Kaz to have a reliable source of heliosite. I'm thinking there is going to be a huge battle for Fergie Prime. And until the Fleet gets its act together, it's the bait we've got."

Ehreh shifted uncomfortably. "I believe this to be an ineffective strategy. Kaz are expert tunnellers. They will reopen the mine in a very short time," he said.

"Yes, of course. That's the whole point. That's why we'll spread the virus in the shafts. They will tunnel in as fast as they can to get at the ore and will infect themselves. They will take the heliosite back to secure Kazi worlds and infect others. This could work." She said all this with a much more positive tone than she felt.

There was a moment of quiet while everyone chewed this over. One might imagine she could see a slow smile begin to grow on Ryet's face. The Oriani were as still as stone, cogitating.

"Provided you're sure the organism doesn't infect humans, it seems like a solution to the question of delivery," John said.

"Even if it infects all of us, humans being no special case, I believe Lauren is correct in saying this will be perhaps our only chance," Ryet said.

"Do we have a suitable antibiotic?" Lauren asked.

"We do not," Ehreh said. "The laboratory is working on that issue."

"Then it *does* matter if it infects all of us."

Ryet shifted in its corner. "If the Kaz succeed in securing this source of heliosite, they will have all they need for quite some time, and they will have crippled the IPC's ability to function. We will be defenceless until another supply is found, a strategic masterstroke for them. But I do not see them bothering to invade Ferguson Prime or to bomb. From what I understand of the planet, it would not support a population on its own. They would expect the current occupants to perish once their supply lines are cut. They could simply picket the area, possibly destroy the spaceport, then stand off any attempts by the Fleet or anyone at rescue, or at resupply with drones, drops, and so forth."

"That could take quite a long time, depending on how well the site is supplied now," Kim said. "On the other hand, the Fleet won't just stand by and let it happen. Fergie Prime is likely to become a bad place to be."

"Kaz have time. They think in generations," Basheh said.

"Will the organism survive generations?" Lauren asked Ehreh.

"Unknown." The old fellow was hunched over, and his attention seemed far, far away. "They would not need to wait if everyone abandons Ferguson Prime." He grunted a little Oriani at Aroull, who fetched a glass of water and a pill. "But I think this scheme is too local. It won't give the organism enough dispersion. The Kaz will have time to discover counter-measures."

"There's no reason you can't go on with the original plan later."

"Yes, there is. The supply of virus is small."

"Grow more virus; build your drones; make them the second wave."

"Our laboratories are being closed, so the possibility of producing more is in doubt."

"I'm not happy about this idea either." John Kim stood up and walked a couple of tight circles. "Here we are, running away from the Kaz again and leaving behind the stuff we need most."

"You sound like a Nsfera I know." Ryet raised its head and looked her way. "The Kaz need heliosite too, which is why it makes such good bait."

"You're planning to blow up the mine, bury everything, and delete the maps and the records. Funny way to plant bait."

"Howerath will send the records to the head office. If we make it too easy for the Kaz, they'll be suspicious."

"If I was a Kazi, I'd be suspicious anyway. People don't normally run away from massive treasure just because they don't like the weather."

"Fortunately, you're not a Kazi."

John smiled at Lauren, misinterpreting.

"By now, I'm sure they know we know they've found the heliosite. Evacuation ahead of an invasion makes sense. Let's hope their need outweighs their caution," Lauren said.

"What do you need for this trap?"

"All we have to do is to get the virus there. The mines are full of ventilation blowers we can use to spread it around. We need a supply of the agent, and then we need to hitch a ride to Fergie Prime."

"I believe I can do something about that kind of transportation," Ryet said. "Do we have any liquid assets we can use to grease the ways?"

"Our resources are limited," Ehreh answered. He still sounded a bit breathless but looked more focused than a few minutes ago. "Speak to Stanton Clough. He has offered to help."

"Someone should tell the Community what we know."

"Do we have to? Next thing, they'll quarantine the Ferguson system and start blasting away," someone said.

"Yes, we must. It would be unconscionable to have this information and not share it," Ehreh said.

"I can do that," John Kim said.

"That would not jeopardize your position?"

Kim made a face. "Might. Message. Messenger. Sometimes they get confused."

"Let me inform the authorities," Ehreh said. "There is not much they can do to me."

"If Ryet can get transport, then the next order of business will be to get a supply of the virus," Lauren said. "Ehreh?"

"Some time ago, I asked Mawuli, my colleague, to bring all he can find here to Midway. I do not believe it will be excessively large quantities." He was agreeing to the plan in his own way.

"The sooner we can put this together, the less likely somebody will organize a way to stop us. How long, do you suppose?"

"I myself do not suppose anything since I have no way of knowing how much time he would need to collect the supply, nor do I know the transportation schedules between Orion and Midway."

"There's nothing quite like a smart-ass Orian."

"I do not understand that remark," Ehreh said.

In its corner, Ryet rustled its dry chuckle. Lauren glowered at it. It did not look the least penitent.

John stepped in. "Terran System of Dating, Ehreh, are we talking about days, weeks, months?"

"If not days, then not ever."

"Okay," Lauren said, "We all know what to do? Ehreh will talk to officialdom. Ryet will find transport. I'm going to locate maps of Howerath Mines before they disappear from the records and figure out what we need to take with us. Who's going to talk to Clough?"

"Me," John said.

As the others left, the room grew quiet. Ryet shifted out of its corner. It seemed to glide more than walk.

It was a motion Lauren recognized this time.

JOHN KIM REMAINED BEHIND after the others had left.

"I'm beginning to understand why it takes Oriani such an age to accomplish anything. They have to argue out every detail," Loren said

"Can we talk?" John asked.

Lauren took a deep breath. "Look, John, I get the point of the flower and the file, really, I do, but I'm not sure I'm ready to forgive an invasion of privacy just yet; I need to think about it."

"Okay," he said, striking just the right note between sadness and acceptance. He had the puppy-dog eyes figured out, too.

"We have a lot to do right now. Could we have this discussion later?"

"I guess. "

In a moment, he said, "So, getting on with it. First, you tell me, on what authority did you order the evacuation of Fergie Prime?"

"Order? Really? I don't do orders, John. All I can do is tell Howerath Mines IP what I think they should do to stay safe. That's pretty much my job."

"Get out of Dodge; abandon strategic materials to the enemy."

"Stay alive. Open up an opportunity to do some serious damage to that very enemy."

"There's a good chance your scheme won't work."

"I think there's a chance it will. I think it's the best chance we'll get in a while. If you don't want to help, get out of the way."

For a moment, John looked like he might argue, but then he turned, stiff-backed, and left.

I'm sorry, Lauren wanted to say. I didn't mean it like that. She wanted to call him back and explain.

But she didn't.

OWR-MARL

Dawn had barely begun when Harl made her second request to meet Murr and/or the Academy's Administration Committee and stressed the importance.

"Very well," Murr said this time, perhaps intending to forestall endless repetitions of this request. "I have a few minutes this morning."

Murr was reluctant, expecting, Harl supposed, that Ehreh's fellow researcher would be petitioning for the continuation of Ehreh's work and not seeing a reason why this had to be done face to face. Harl could not offer a reason either, except that sometimes discussions were more effective in person.

She stopped to admire the sun streaming through the leaves of the garden before she began the walk down the hill to the administration building. Most of the valley and the lower mountains were still in shadow, but the tallest, Ent-Kowal Itahi, was brilliant in sunlight, bearing a cap of cloud. The air still had its morning scent.

If Harl was successful this morning, she might very well damage beyond recovery her own career and status, as well as that of two colleagues. Ehreh had been her mentor and had her respect; he was a better person than she was, she understood that, and his arguments were rational. But overshadowing all else was his intention to destroy an entire race of beings, and that had to be wrong. Waiting around for them to destroy you was also wrong. The duty of defence, it was called in the teachings of the Pacifists.

Then there was Mawuli. Mawuli was her friend. They had worked together for many years. He was a shy, gentle person, too young, she thought, to have a family to care for. When he first came to the group, he had been a conventional proponent of the teachings of the Pacifist of Owr-Neg. Yet, in time, he had come to believe Ehreh's plan was the right one. She wondered if Mawuli had information that Harl did not, that Mawuli did not share because she was still ambivalent. He had secrets he needed to keep? She could not imagine that to be the case. But he would be caught up in this, too.

Harl could see no right path. The fate of the whole project depended on what she did next. She had not asked for this burden. She did not like what she was about to do but could not find any rational way to avoid it. For all this action violated what she believed to be the proper way to live, it was at the same time necessary. But that did not make it easy.

She ruffled her fur in the sunshine and started down.

WHEN SHE ARRIVED at the administration building, Murr escorted her into a small office. It was sparse, containing only a desk, two stools, a few screens, and a shelf of antique books. A communications headset and a carry-all lay on the desk. A long window occupied most of one wall. Murr was a mathematician working on set theory and needed little in the way of apparatus, just a connection to the computational centre in the bowels of the building. Harl understood Murr's grasp of biology was not the strongest and wondered how she was going to make the administrator understand that she had serious concerns about her work.

Murr sat on one stool and offered the other to Harl.

Harl would try to present everything she needed to say quickly before her superior lost patience. Of course, Murr knew the basic issue. It was recent developments she needed to hear.

"I cannot in good conscience work with this group any longer. They are proceeding as blind people. The outcome is very much in doubt. So many things are still unknown about the virus. It might be infectious toward any number of other species. Little work has been done, can be done, toward understanding the biology of Kazi worlds. I realize testing these potential problems is nearly impossible, but to proceed without any idea of which non-target species might be affected is surely irresponsible at best, immoral at worst. Truthfully, we do not know how it will affect the target species. It might not even infect living Kaz. We have not been able to test even this most basic characteristic, which in itself defies morality. To try to eliminate the entire species is not only unethical—"

"Eliminating, as you put it, even one individual is generally considered unethical," Murr said.

Harl sputtered a moment. Oriani do not expect to get interrupted. Harl paused to collect herself and continued, "I perceive it to be also dangerous. Everything in biology affects everything else. When a biological niche is opened, an organism will evolve to fill it. We could be creating a new problem worse than the one we face now."

"Or a replacement organism that is no problem at all. Or a shuffling of the roles of existing organisms. These are also possibilities?"

"Yes, of course."

"Surely a new, possibly hazardous species would be many

hundreds of generations from now," the administrator said. "By which time we might have a better understanding of Kazi-related biology. And it might not be aggressive in any case."

"We do not know. The data are not available. The work has not been done. No one can say what is poised to step in. Maybe, as you suggest, nothing to concern us at all, or maybe a species far more dangerous than the Kaz."

"Which is to say, your objections are based on hypotheticals."

Harl turned away. She was well aware of the weakness of her argument. Her primary objection had always been one of ethics. She had intended that the suggestion of concrete danger might add enough weight to move Murr, who until now had been disinclined toward action. "I believe when one does not know, one should err on the side of caution."

"The Administration Committee has told Ehreh to stop work and shut down his laboratory. Even if your worst fears are realized, surely that should preclude dangers to and from distant places. I do not understand why you are still apprehensive."

"Ehreh has asked for quantities of the virus to be sent to Midway. He wanted it shipped at once, and Mawuli is on his way to Midway right now with whatever he could collect."

Murr sat up and took notice. "This would serve Ehreh's goal?"

"I do not know. I can see no other reason for his request. I am very uncomfortable about this development. I am certain it was not part of the original plan. Something has changed, and Ehreh is not communicating."

"Midway has a special significance?"

"I am not informed. I understand Ehreh himself is there. I believe he intended to petition members of the Interplanetary Community Strategic Planning Committee who are meeting there. But that would not require quantities of the virus."

"He is working against the wishes of his own government?"

Harl shrugged and looked away. She had said all she knew how to say to accomplish her goal. She had made her case. She had done what she had to do. What happened next was out of her hands. She would go home now and spend some time with the children.

She thought she should be more comfortable with what she had done.

We tell others we do not know how to lie, she thought.

Everybody lies.

MIDWAY—FIRST AVENUE

Ben Lawada caught sight of Archie Bennett just outside of the conference room, talking to a group of delegates who seemed intensely absorbed in what he was saying while others leaving the room milled around them. Lawada had previously visited the location Martin gave him as a place Ehreh's group often met and found nothing there but a Sgat and a bot, apparently cleaning up. The Sgat responded to his inquiries with much friendly-sounding twittering, but neither of them understood the other. In any case, he was not on the hunt for Sgat.

He decided he would try a few other things before he went back to Martin and told him that his information was bad.

What little he'd been able to discover about the Orian was that he spent a fair bit of time with various delegates to the IPCSPC, and particularly with Stanton Clough of late. Clough had just lost a kid in the war.

He'd been keeping out of sight of the Turgorn police people mostly out of habit; he didn't have a weapon with him just then because the sensor net was pretty sensitive in some areas.

Armed, he would have to spend too much time looking out for sensors, and it would be easy to miss one.

For a moment, he thought to break cover to see if Clough's aide might tell him where his target was, but Martin had told him to keep this project to himself. No one else needed to know.

Then the group broke up and dispersed. Lawada followed Archie. Clough had not been in the conference room nor among this little group, and there were no Oriani there other than the official delegate, but Archie worked for Clough, and they roomed together. Clough had been meeting the Orian. Hang around Archie and find Clough and then find his target. It seemed like it should work.

But Archie Bennett merely went back to the room he shared with Clough, and nothing more happened for quite some time.

Lawada had thought the job Martin had given him was simple enough, but step one was turning out to be ridiculously difficult. Who knew it would be hard to locate a person in modern times? He should have asked for more money.

Growing restless with waiting, he decided to be a bit more proactive. He knocked at the door and, when Archie answered looking annoyed, asked for Clough. He didn't say why he wanted to find the delegate. He might be pushing Michael's boundaries a little, but what were his options? Archie snorted. "If you do find him," he said, "tell him I need to talk to him. Tell him the Committee chairman wants to talk to him. Tell him there are a hundred sub-committee heads and delegates who want to talk to him."

"I'm guessing you don't know where he is," Lawada said.

"No, I don't," Archie said crossly.

Lawada left.

So, that strategy didn't work. Ehreh himself wasn't registered at the conference. Lawada found himself not really knowing how to proceed. Oriani didn't necessarily hang together. They didn't have a favourite bar or anything like that. In fact, he hadn't seen a single Orian other than the official delegate all day. He checked out a few of the places that he had been told Clough liked to go but didn't see the Terran delegate or the Orian.

Finding his man in a chaotic situation like this was going to be a problem.

He wandered along the hallways toward the central area, scanning the crowds but not expecting to see anything useful. He found a data terminal and looked up the index. People who wanted to be found were listed there, but those who didn't want to be found or who didn't care one way or the other were not. He found Clough's name, but he already knew where the delegate was staying, just not where he was now. People with implants could be located exactly if their implants were turned on. He could see exactly where Archie was. That also did him no good.

He had a wry notion to put a CQ call out on Midway's intranet. Not exactly a clandestine approach. Martin would not approve. Would the Orian answer? Probably not.

This is stupid, Ben, he told himself. He found a bench near the wall and sat down to think it over.

NOT FAR AWAY, the airlock cycled, and Murr took her first steps onto an alien world, her carry-all clutched tightly to her side, her ears up, her eyes wide. The flight had been weird and, in a way, terrifying; though intellectually, she understood that it was not exceptionally hazardous, some atavistic instinct insisted that she had truly been in the middle of nowhere and that she had to depend utterly on someone she had never met and some piece of machinery she didn't understand to get back to somewhere. She felt enormous relief when she arrived back in normal space intact. Hyperspace was fine as a mathematical construct but not a place (non-place) she wanted to inhabit. She had never had much interest in travel; as a place to live, Orion suited her perfectly, and her curiosities led her to matters of vast abstraction rather than to odd environments and strange customs.

The first thing she noticed about Midway was the noise, and then the crowds, and then that the air was heavy with moisture and had a peculiar, not very pleasant, smell. None of the data she had consulted before this journey had made any mention of noise and stink. Her companion also lifted his nose, so she concluded it was not just her lack of experience that made her uncomfortable with it. The companion, Raish, was well-travelled, experienced in the business of getting from one place to another, and had saved her considerable discomfort.

Midway was crowded and in restless motion. Many kinds of beings she had previously known only as images were there before her, pushing and shoving their way around. Many of them were not the least bit polite. They spoke myriad languages. Murr knew Oriani and math. It was a lot to take in. Among all these busy creatures, just finding Ehreh might be the hardest part of her chore.

She tried to ask a passer-by how to find the Orion delegation to the conference now in session. The individual crooked his long neck and said something, then moved on.

Her companion said, "He said he didn't understand you."

"Well," Murr said, turning away in embarrassment. "Since you understand at least some of these people, perhaps you should ask the questions. Find our delegation."

Raish knew that most people who travelled used Sindharr as a common language, so the problem was easily solved. They were directed to the upper floor and found the appropriate suite without further difficulty. It was a primitive-looking living space and poorly appointed: a couple of small rooms crowded with a half-dozen people. They looked the way Murr expected people to look and spoke the language she understood, so that was a relief, but they all seemed very young, which was less reassuring. The official delegate was at a meeting, they said; they were the communicators and researchers assisting him. Unfortunately, not one of them knew where Ehreh was, but they were curious about why Murr had come all that way to find this particular individual.

Murr decided the only reasonable thing to do was tell them about Ehreh's plan for genocide and thus enlist their aid in the search. But when she finished her explanation, she found the youngsters were about equally divided between revulsion and what Murr considered to be morbid interest. *That could be the whole problem with our people these days*, Murr thought. *We cannot decide on a direction.*

One of them said, "Another, Mawuli was his name, came looking for Ehreh not long ago. I wonder if they found each other."

"Mawuli is Ehreh's colleague. They are quite likely to be together."

A fair bit of discussion ensued, and though disagreement was rampant, they did agree on one thing: Murr would have trouble finding Ehreh on her own, so they would help. "Does Ehreh have a communications implant?"

"I do not know," Murr confessed. "I do not actually know much about him at all."

"Yet, you are anxious to find him?"

"What concerns me is not who he is but what he is about to do."

She sat down on a small bench near the door. The stress was tiring. Raish brought her water and a seed cake, which she accepted gratefully. One of the youngsters looked up from her screen. "I have a bot scanning the security records for the last two local days."

"That is legal?" Murr asked.

The other shrugged. *That's another thing*, Murr thought. *No one has any sense of morality anymore.*

"Well, presumably you found something of interest?" she said.

The other leaned back and turned her screen toward Murr. "A view of the port just after the arrival of a scheduled carrier, with passengers coming through the lock. That is Mawuli?"

"I believe so. The strange creature meeting him is?"

"Unknown. Searching now," someone else said, then after a long moment, "Nsfera. That should not be hard to find."

"It should not?"

"Not many Nsfera inhabit the known worlds. That one is here is remarkable."

The person breaking into the security system set her scanning bot to look for sightings of Nsfera in the security records later than the first one. She did not expect to find more than one Nsfera on Midway.

"There it is, a few minutes ago, leaving the hospital wing, headed toward the port."

"Let us see if we can intercept it. Someone who speaks the language, come with me."

"No one knows the language of the Nsfera other than Nsfera," Raish said, "but one might reasonably suppose it knows Sindharr."

Most of the people there followed them out. Their duty was dull, they were stressed by the close quarters, and they were naturally curious creatures.

"AM CALLED ASSIFFAH," the Roothian said as he hiked himself up onto the stool at Lawada's invitation. He was a twitchy little critter and seemed to be recovering from a number of injuries. "I know where iss a bunch of Oriani sstaying in a ssuite on upper level. What you want with thosse I do not know. They don't treat people nicsely, you know. At leasst their hhenchman dossen't. Damned near killed me, didn't hhe?"

"Really?" Lawada said. He'd moved on from looking for a particular Orian to Oriani in general, and in this quiet bar near the port, this battered Roothian and a little beer had given him his first lead. "Would the one called Ehreh be there?"

"Not likely. Hhe doesn't sstick to the government line sso much. That'ss the one who hhurt me. Much damage. Near death."

"Hmm. I understood Oriani were pacifists. If I can find him, I might be able to return the favour."

Assiffah brightened. "I assk around." He held up a hand, and his spatulate little fingers rubbed together in the universal sign for money.

Lawada smiled. "I haven't got much on me right now, but bring me good news, and I will make you happy." He transferred a small amount to the Roothian's account. "What about the henchman you mentioned; do you know where he is?"

Assiffah spat, a short stream of stinking liquid. "That Nssfera I kill mysself."

Yeah, Lawada thought. *Good luck with that.*

Assiffah left, getting along at quite a speed for a small beast.

Nsfera, Lawada thought. *There can't be many of those around.*

When the Caparan tending bar came by to ask about refills, Lawada asked, "Have you heard anything about a Nsfera being on Midway?"

The bartender's brow furrowed, and she wrapped her several arms into a knot as she leaned on the bar. "Actually, I might have. Someone mentioned the other night that he had seen one. Over by the docks, I think."

"Perfect," Lawada said. "Thank you." He left a generous tip and headed for the port. He went around by way of his room and picked up his blaster. He was beginning to feel naked without it, and the port was a sometimes dicey place. He would put up with watching out for sensors for the time being.

WHILE SOME RACES eschewed all badges and symbols of rank and merit, Oriani among them, others bedecked themselves like flamboyant holiday icons. The Higant who met Ehreh at the wall was an extreme example of the latter, but all that flash and brass didn't help Ehreh interpret where this person was in the hierarchy that managed Midway. Nevertheless, he followed the bright display through a sensor-encrusted and guarded gate into the newer part of the building, to be faced with a large sign made of shiny metal letters affixed to a second wall that bid him welcome to the Yallah Rullenahe Interplanetary Security Service Military Garrison. The walls were white, the lighting harsh, and the letters large and sharp-edged. Ehreh did not feel all that welcome.

He was ushered along the corridor into a room through a door with many polysyllabic words in brass letters on it that did not seem to mean much as far as he could tell. From there, another, less colourfully decorated, individual asked his name, escorted him into an office, and said someone would be in to talk to him shortly. Ehreh had the impression that he was not being taken very seriously.

The newer part of the Midway complex was better finished than the old part, and the furnishings much more modern. Framed prints of old pictures of spaceports hung on the walls;

one, Ehreh recognized as Orion Space Central before the Kaz. There was a rug in front of the desk and a padded chair.

In due course, a third person bustled in, sat down behind the desk, switched on various devices, and said while he watched them boot up, "Sit down, please. My name is Lieutenant Nes Gow. What can the Fleet do for you, Ehreh?"

"Not very much, I suspect," Ehreh said as he perched himself on the edge of the chair. "However, I have some information I believe you should know."

"Really. What would that be?"

"You are doubtless aware that a dead Kaz was found on Midway a short time ago."

"Yes, I am. It was something of a surprise."

"It was not alone."

Lieutenant Nes Gow finally looked up. "You know this?"

"Yes."

"We swept the station pretty thoroughly. We haven't found any others."

"You did not find the one until it was dead."

"Well, true, we didn't, but then we weren't really looking for Kaz then. What makes you sure there are others?"

"Kaz rarely travel alone. But that is not the most important issue right now. What is important is the threat to the IPC's heliosite supply. Other Kaz have been to Ferguson Prime, and the Empire is very likely currently preparing to invade and secure the IPC's best source of heliosite."

Now Ehreh had Nes Gow's full attention. "What makes you think so?"

"Howerath Mines has sensor records showing several Kaz exploring the mine shafts."

"Really? And they haven't done anything about it? Why wouldn't they have informed us of this?"

"I cannot say. Perhaps you could inquire of them?"

"Do you have these records? Can we see them?"

"They are not in my possession. I am sure Howerath Mines IP could supply copies. In any case, I suggest you prepare to defend Ferguson Prime to the best of the Fleet's ability."

"Yes, of course." The lieutenant pulled himself up and sniffed slightly. "Ehreh, I appreciate your concern, but I think you are unduly alarmed. That volume of space is very heavily patrolled. Sensors and drones are deployed throughout. I have a hard time believing that Kaz could have passed through there without our knowing."

"Yet, at least one Kazi was found to be right here on Midway, close to the very heart of Fleet operations. Regardless of how you feel about Howerath Mines' handling of security and information or how reliable you think this information might be, you must admit it is in our best, urgent interest to prevent the mine from falling into Kazi hands if possible. Err on the side of caution. I urge you to act quickly."

Nes Gow sighed quietly, but not quietly enough to escape Orian ears. "Wait here a moment," he said.

He went out, leaving the door open as if he wanted to keep an eye on his visitor. Ehreh could hear him talking to someone in the next room. ". . . I'm not sure. Maybe the base commander should hear this. Who's in charge of operations out in that sector? Get her in, too." After a pause, he continued, "Some crazy old geezer talking about an attack on Fergie Prime."

Ehreh pulled himself out of the chair, shook out his fur, stretched his aching back and straightened his tail. He could see these people intended to have discussions all the way up the hierarchy. The Fleet was unlikely to do anything on a time scale that would be useful. He went out through the door, passing silently behind Lieutenant Nes Gow and the person he was talking to, and was into the corridor and closing that door behind him before anyone thought to stop him.

THE BASE COMMANDER was on communications by then, hoping he would not have to go downstairs and listen to some old geezer's conspiracy theory. He had just said to Lieutenant Nes Gow, "Orian, you say. They're not usually given to flights of fancy. Get hold of the civilian authority, the liaison, what's her name, Nagy, Jamila Nagy, and ask if they have had any hint of Kaz on or around Fergie Prime. Also, ask if they have been in touch with Howerath Mines recently. I think the whole story's a load of natural fertilizer, but a little checking will keep our butts covered. No one should say we don't take concerned citizens seriously."

"Shit," Nes Gow said.

"I beg your pardon."

"Sorry, sir, but the old geezer just bugged out."

"Well, get him back."

Harassing civilians won't win us any medals, Nes Gow thought but got the office moving anyway. A certain amount of shouting ensued, and people charging around in all directions at once.

AS HE APPROACHED THE GATE, Ehreh saw the Higant who had brought him in.

The gate had been designed to keep intruders out, not to keep detainees in. Often, the builders of security systems neglected the fact that doors were typically functional in at least two directions. He nodded a greeting as he passed as if his exit were perfectly normal, and he crossed into the civilian part of Midway.

The Fleet would undoubtedly look for him once it got organized, but he did not believe they would put too much effort into finding some crazy old geezer, and even if they did catch up with him, they would not have much.

Back in the room he had just left, consternation ensued,

mitigated just a little when someone thought to check the sensors at the gate and noted that Ehreh had indeed left the facility. At least he wasn't wandering around in restricted areas getting into who knew what mischief. The downside was they had to call on the civilian police force to apprehend their man.

Often, that did not go well.

MIDWAY—RESIDENTIAL SECTION E

Michael slammed into his office, bypassing minions organic and mechanical, almost yelled at his virtual assistant to get his plant manager online, top-level encryption, you idiot, and told the plant manager to buy every scrap of heliosite she could lay her hands on before the price got to astronomical heights. Archie arrived in the midst of this, looking a little worn, with the news Michael already had.

"We've got to stop them," Michael said.

"Who, the Oriani or the Kaz?"

Michael spent a moment thinking about it, calming himself a little. "In the best of all possible worlds, both. In this world, Kaz first. Without heliosite, we're all screwed."

"Then we probably should think about giving the Oriani a hand."

"If they're successful, the Kazi threat ends, and we're screwed."

"There's a theme developing here."

Michael flopped down into his chair. Archie could hear the wood creak.

The IPCSPC meeting had dissolved into chaos after some local functionary got up and told the assembled delegates the rumour that the Fleet thought bad things were happening on Ferguson Prime, that Howerath Mines would be shutting down operations and evacuating. Michael had to query his implant to learn what was special about Ferguson Prime. The information didn't make him feel better, and he had joined the angry chorus demanding that the military protect their interests. But not for long. He was sure that a clamp on heliosite trading was coming as fast as the bureaucrats could get it together, whether the information was real or not. Securing a supply was far more important for the immediate future of Martin Enterprises IP than anything else at the moment.

"Why doesn't some smart chemist just make the stuff?" Archie asked.

"Don't think we haven't tried. Atom by atom, using nanomachines for the process, we've built a few small crystals. It takes forever, they don't work very well, and they're ten times the cost of the natural stuff. If you can explain the physics to me, please do."

"Not my area of expertise. Anyway, the Fleet will be mounting a serious assault on the Kaz at Fergie Prime, and the Kaz will fight back, so you've got that going for you. It should get you through the short term."

Archie hesitated then. He had debated with himself about telling Michael about Clough and decided that someone would do that in the next little while, and if he didn't get in there first, Michael would wonder why. "I hate to add to your trouble, but you probably should know that Clough is resigning from the IPCSPC."

"What? Why?" Michael asked. *Rats overboard*, he thought.

"All he said to me was that nothing he could do would help Whitby."

"What are his plans, then?"

"I don't know. It's all rather sudden, and he hasn't been forthcoming, which is not like him. He did say he can no longer support some of the policies the Council is determined to pursue. I didn't get a chance to discuss it with him. He just took off."

"Has he been talking to the Turgorn delegates?"

"I don't think so. Why?"

"Rhetorical question. Never mind."

In the morning, before all this other stuff had come down, Michael had spent an hour or more with the Turgorn, who were ostensibly asking his opinion on the wisdom of investing in several new start-up industries related to the war effort but were, in reality, trying to gauge his opinion about continuing the IPC's present course of action regarding the Kaz, considering that it was more than obvious the Kazi Empire was advancing, rapidly in some places. Was he open to a different approach? they wondered. Could manufacturing operations like his be reprogrammed to produce different weapons if the need arose? How much would it cost? How long would it take?

When Michael mentioned he could give them only limited information without non-disclosure agreements and lawyers, and even then, they would have to be more specific, they changed the subject. They had departed in apparently good humour, but Michael was not misled. They were feeling him out, trying to decide what he would do in case Turgorn changed course and backed Ehreh's plan.

"Clough has been meeting that bunch of Oriani who are talking about a new technique for fighting the Kaz with biologicals," Archie said. "I couldn't get close enough to hear what they had to say. Maybe you should give me that little bug back. I could probably plant it on him somewhere."

Michael hesitated. Archie was willing enough to sell out Clough. No doubt he would be equally willing to sell out Michael should a sufficiently affluent buyer come along. "Let me think about it for a while. Do you know where this little band of troublemakers is hanging out?"

"I know where they are right now. They move quite often."

"Present whereabouts will do for the moment. I'll get back to you in a bit. Don't hesitate to get in touch if there are developments."

"Sure." Archie let himself out. If nothing else, the kid knew when to leave.

Millions of credits, Michael had told the Turgorn. Months, if not years, depending. And he wasn't exaggerating. The difference between explosives and biologicals could hardly be greater. The Martin Industries' AIs had been labouring faithfully for decades, and therefore they were decades old. Hardly state of the art. Could they even understand such radically different programming?

And if he delayed, and the fight did take on this different character, maybe he wouldn't be able to change fast enough. Some minor brewer of probiotic yogourt could tool up faster, bump him out of the comfortable place in the world he now occupied and bounce him to the periphery, where he would end up building freighters for mineral haulers, doing not much more than making ends meet. Not a prospect that appealed.

He chewed it over for a time, looked for whatever data he could find about the Orian plan (next to nothing), and came to no satisfying conclusion.

Therefore, as much as it rubbed his ego the wrong way, he told the virtual assistant, "Please get my mother on an encrypted hyperspace link. Tell her I need her advice. Urgently."

She'll get a kick out of that, he thought. *But maybe not so much when she hears what the problem is.* Michael and his mother had what might be called an interesting relationship. Marietta was the avatar his virtual assistant adopted when it had a visual presence. Michael thought it helped to keep him motivated.

"Michael," Marietta said, responding almost immediately. "It's so nice to hear from you. You sound stressed. Are you taking your pills? How is the conference going?"

Michael hurried through the small talk and started in on the explanation of the problem. Though there wasn't much chance the communications system would cut *him* off, he was anxious to get past the embarrassing part of this call and hear what his mother might offer in the way of advice.

When he was done, the infinitely thin, imaginary connection between Midway and Earth hummed and spluttered in the void for a moment or two.

Then Marietta said, "So you need to know if the IPC and the Fleet will be able to protect Fergie Prime, and if they can, are they going to change direction in the war effort; if they are, then when; and how can Martin Industries be ready for any of these eventualities?"

"That's about it."

"If they do change direction, will they still need heliosite? Will Fergie Prime still be of strategic importance?"

"Pretty sure it will be. No matter what, the IPC will need to move around. And the military will be anxious to keep heliosite out of Kazi hands as well. If the Orian scheme works out as planned, they will still need warships, just not nearly so many."

"So, while that's not good for us, we're not going to go out of business right away. In the short term, you need time. You need to delay any decision until we can evaluate the probabilities. Given time, Martin Industries can stay on top of this for any possibility except perhaps a hundred-percent Orian success. That could be quite a setback. So, who is lobbying for this change? Can they be deflected? Bought?"

"Hard to do with Oriani."

"Yes." Another brief pause. "Is it the kind of problem that might be solved by cutting its head off? So to speak."

Martin wasn't that shocked. He had always known Marietta

was a savage; look at the business she went into. But she wasn't often quite so blunt. Did that mean she was as worried as he was?

She was tougher than her son, always had been, and she reminded him of this fact from time to time. He was a little bit afraid of her, too. Even though she couldn't see it, he put his finger on the jumpy little muscle above his eye to hold it still. "I'll give it some thought," he said.

"Do that. Call me back when you've decided," she said.

His first answer was no. Not ever. No way.

His second answer was that his mother was probably right. It was the only thing that was quick enough and decisive enough to give Martin Industries the time they needed.

Dread at the prospect welled up, clamped his stomach, iced his heart. While he was more than willing to play power games, wreck careers and reputations, absorb or destroy competitors in what was described as a cut-throat business, in truth, actual throats were rarely cut.

Michael Martin, the biggest, most prosperous constructor and purveyor of the engines of war, had understood what his mother was saying but was utterly repulsed by the image of getting his hands bloody. In his life, war had always been an abstraction. He was many layers of protocol and bureaucracy and hierarchical business levels separated from the act of killing anything. Weapons were lines on a balance sheet. He very much preferred it that way. It was like going to a restaurant and ordering a natural steak. One thought about the extravagance; one didn't think about the cow.

But then, he thought, *you don't actually go out there and kill a cow.* As Marietta had told him often enough, one of the best uses of money is to get other people to do the things you don't like doing yourself. It was what he did in a restaurant, leaving the butchery in the back room, in the hands of others; it was what he could do here.

Michael got onto the intranet, civilian Midway's local communications.

Ben Lawada also answered promptly.

"I have another job for you," Michael said.

"What?"

"Not on an open net."

"On my way," Lawada said.

MIDWAY—DOCKSIDE

Among the noisy crowds that frequented the myriad small shops, eateries, pubs, and whatnot that clustered around the docks, Ryet found the individual it was looking for amid a knot of humans at a sidewalk table. The human in question was still acting a bit surly, for all he appeared to have put away a fair portion of available intoxicants. As was usual for ships' crews, the crew of *Mercury's Daughter,* for the most part, clustered together; they commiserated with one another over their lost commission.

"Good evening," Ryet said, speaking to the shuttle pilot.

"You again. You know it took me more than an hour to find my way back here?"

"Oh, my," Ryet said with all the sincerity of a smiling crocodile. "And yet look at you, not in jail."

"What the f—" The pilot looked across the table at a stern-faced woman glaring at him. *Leader*, Ryet thought. "What the blazes do you want, then?" the pilot amended.

Ryet addressed the stern-faced woman. "I understand you have geared up for a trip to Ferguson Prime that was cancelled.

I know of others who need to go there. Are you still able to make the journey?"

"Yes," the captain said. "Kiri Narang. Captain of *Mercury's Daughter.*" She held out a hand. Ryet, somewhat puzzled by this, did not respond. The captain shrugged. "And you are?"

"Interested in getting a party to Ferguson Prime as soon as possible."

"If you have the money, we can go. It will take a day or two to deal with the Port Authority. And I'd be much obliged if perhaps you could tell me why everyone is so all fired up to get to Ferguson Prime suddenly. Not exactly a tourist spot."

"Money is available, though perhaps not as much as you were going to charge Stanton Clough." Not quite true, but Ryet could see no reason to spend more of Clough's money on transportation than necessary when there were other uses it could be put to. "But something is better than nothing, I believe the saying goes." He watched the captain's reactions carefully, trying to gauge how much he would need to concede.

"People who make up sayings don't have to pay my bills."

"True. I am sure we can come to an agreement. And, no, I am sorry, I cannot tell you about the renewed interest in a small, dry world."

"Because you choose not to or because you don't know?"

"One or the other, certainly. Do you wish to discuss terms here or perhaps somewhere more private?"

Captain Narang considered the creature across the table. Something vaguely sinister about it led her to say, "We can talk right here, right now." In public, she thought, surrounded by her people, who would stick up for her.

Maybe.

This was not Ryet's first choice. Alone, the captain might be more flexible. In front of her crew, she would have to look like a tough bargainer, working hard for their interests. Ryet thought the sooner into the bargaining process it could give her an opportunity to make her point, the better; that would be when it would cost him the least.

After a fair bit of back and forth, they did reach an agreement, due in part to the fact that Ryet, perhaps inadvertently, disclosed the information that the journey was in aid of an unofficial plot against the Kaz. The captain had had her own run-in with Kaz and was not averse to giving them grief whenever she could, even if it meant carrying a somewhat dicey-looking creature into deep space. She had no great love for officialdom, either.

When the negotiations were over, and some credits had changed hands under careful supervision by the crew, and Captain Kiri Narang had finished complaining that it wasn't the full agreed-upon amount, and Ryet Arkkad had explained that he wasn't about to pay all the money up front just to have his people abandoned in space somewhere and a modicum of trust was needed on both sides and that the captain could rest assured that when everyone arrived safely on Ferguson Prime, all accounts would be settled and, if all went well, perhaps a bonus was possible, Captain Narang briefly consulted her crew and then agreed, though still a little worried she had made a risky bargain. Something about the Nsfera suggested it was not quite what it appeared to be. Yet nothing it said or did gave cause for alarm. If she refused the hire, she would be hard-pressed to explain it to her people.

They each signed the agreement on the flimsy the Nsfera presented, and it transferred her one copy and transferred another to an escrow cloud. Then she looked up, and her brow furrowed. "What's this all about?" she asked and pointed to a group of Oriani making their way through the crowds, looking like they had serious business to discuss, though, with Oriani, it was hard to tell; they always looked like they had serious business. She tried to think of them having a party. It boggled the imagination.

When it became apparent that Ryet was the object of Oriani interest, the captain signalled the crew of *Mercury's Daughter,* and they withdrew into the crowd and left the Nsfera at the table to cope with the Oriani on its own.

Ryet didn't know any of those people or what they might want, but, being an optimist and curious, it waited for them.

The female in the lead said something, and the person beside her translated, "You are Ryet Arkkad?"

"I am."

"You know the Orian Ehreh?"

"Why do you ask?"

"I need to find him. It is most urgent."

"I do not know where he is." That was true. Ehreh had left earlier, on his own, without telling anyone where he was going. Ryet could guess where but could honestly say he didn't know.

"He lives somewhere? He has business here? There are people he meets?"

"Most probably all of those things are true."

"Your answer is not helpful." The female sounded a bit cross, unusual in an Orian. The translator's tone remained calm.

"How unfortunate. But I have no reason to be helpful. I do not know you. I do not know that you have this person's best interests centred. Why would you think I know any of these things? And why would you think I would tell you any of them if I did know? You assume a great deal for a reputedly logical creature."

The female's ears flicked, starting to flatten and then coming upright again.

One can provoke Oriani, Ryet thought. *Good to know.*

The crowd began to thicken, bored people stopping, drawn

by an argument, chittering among themselves, finding interest in anything even slightly out of the ordinary.

Ben Lawada arrived on the scene just in time to see the group of Oriani confront the Nsfera. He stayed a bit farther back, away from the crowd. The discussion was brief and not, as far as he could tell, particularly friendly, and ended when the Nsfera turned to leave, its attitude indicating annoyance, but Lawada, from his position on the other side of it, watching from a convenient doorway, thought he saw a smile on its face. Would he know a Nsfera's smile when he saw it?

He was about to step in front of it, hoping to have better luck than the Oriani, when two Turgorn Constabulary officers beat him to it, demanding to know where Ehreh had gone.

The Nsfera listened politely, declined to answer, and made to walk on by. One of the officers reached out to hold it. Ryet turned and hissed at him. Startled, the Turgorn leaned back. Everybody nearby was a bit startled.

All right, then, Lawada thought. *It sounds like an angry cobra the size of a horse. Maybe I won't step out in front of it. Maybe I'll just follow it and see if it will lead me to Ehreh.*

The police officers took a moment to collect themselves. Those in the crowd started to recover and resumed their chatter. The Oriani were muttering among themselves. The guards were phoning home for instructions, and Ryet was once more about to leave when the man of the hour appeared.

From somewhere out of a hallway, Ehreh slowly made his way through the crowd and hobbled up to the Oriani. "You are here for a reason?" he asked Murr.

By the time Lawada thought to look for it again, the Nsfera had left the scene. Once more, Lawada revised his plan of attack.

"Ehreh." Murr had regained her composure.

"Yes?"

"I have come here to stop you from taking an action that is irrevocable and wrong. I want you and Mawuli to return with me to Orion. I want the organism that you developed destroyed. You may need to face the governing council since you have defied their instructions."

"Yet I want none of those things. You intend to force them on me?"

Murr stopped for a moment, not sure how to proceed. She had prepared arguments but certainly had not considered force. "Surely civilized discussion is possible."

"Yes, of course, though we have had this discussion before. I do not expect to be swayed by old arguments. I do, however, suggest a venue less public."

"These ones have a space on the upper level. We can use that."

The ones referred to jostled a little and muttered among themselves, obviously not entirely in agreement with Murr's assumption of authority. *They are young*, Murr thought. *They need to learn to respect their elders.*

The Oriani left together, giving Lawada no opportunity. The crowd began to disperse. Lawada looked around for the Nsfera, but he couldn't see it anywhere. Well, he didn't really need it anymore. He knew where the Orian was. He phoned Michael Martin.

"Progress report," he said.

"You are on a public network," Martin said.

"Okay. I found our guy. I can't reach him right now, but it's just a matter of time."

"Cancel this connection," Martin said and hung up.

Not exactly the pat on the back Lawada had been hoping for.

It didn't get better. A few minutes later, a couple of official-looking individuals and a police officer made their way to the upper level and knocked on the Orianis' door.

When they came out again, they had Ehreh among them. They headed off across the wall and left Lawada fuming on the other side.

MIDWAY—MARTIN INDUSTRIES OFFICE

After thinking it over a bit, Ben Lawada went upstairs and knocked on the door where he had last seen his target. A young Orian answered. He asked for the old man. The youngster said he was not there.

"I know. I saw them taking him away."

"You seek one here whom you know is not here?"

"Do you know when he is coming back?"

"No."

"Can I come in and wait?"

"No."

"Not the friendliest people, are you?"

"I do not know how to answer that question." She shut the door and left Ben on the outside.

With nothing else to do, he sat down on the top step and tried to ignore the irritated looks he garnered from passersby. Much as he hated the thought, he was going to have to go to Michael and tell him. Michael was a bit short-tempered, and he hadn't had a lot of good news lately. Ben didn't know how that was going to work out. He was just about to get up and go to his doom when he saw Mawuli start up the stairs. He slipped on the persona of the friendly helper and stood up to meet the Orian.

"Ben Lawada, greetings. I did not expect to see you here."

"Hey, Mawuli. I didn't expect to see you either. What's going on?"

"I am to meet Ehreh here. You have seen him?"

"Well, actually, yeah, I did. Um, gee. . . ."

"There is a problem?"

"Yeah, I guess. The cops just came and picked him up. Took him over into the new part of the building, where average joes like you and me aren't allowed to go."

"Joes?"

"People. Regular people."

"Irregular people would be admitted?"

"Oh, look, never mind. Just say Ehreh's out of reach for the time being, okay?"

"No, Ben Lawada, that is not okay. I must get him from there. A mechanism is available by which he can be returned to this area? Or one exists by which one could gain access to the other, forbidden area? You know how that might be done?"

"I don't. You probably need a lawyer."

"You know how to access a lawyer?"

"Nope." A little brainstorm struck Lawada about then. "But I know somebody who knows lots of lawyers. Come with me."

Lawada started off, elbowing his way toward less crowded spaces, and Mawuli followed in his wake. *The guy's a grown-up, he's been around a bit, but he's trusting as a kid*, Lawada thought. On the other hand, Mawuli knew Ben as a person who had tried to help with Ehreh's transportation problem, a friend of the project. Ben thought he probably should feel bad about taking advantage, but it was hard to feel bad about saving his own life or at least his job.

"Why are you so anxious to find Ehreh? You know, they'll probably let him go eventually." Lawada led the way into the warrens of old Midway, following his well-worn route to Michael's place, keeping an eye on the sensors.

"He is very old and very ill," Mawuli said. "I do not believe 'eventually' is his best option."

"He's that bad off?"

"If I understand the question correctly, yes. He has little time left to him."

"No kidding? So what're you doing, fulfilling a last request or something?"

"I do not understand this. He asked for a quantity of the virus, and I am bringing it to him. Neither of us was comfortable about entrusting it to a commercial courier."

"Yeah, I guess you wouldn't be. Okay, here we are. Now, this guy's a bit touchy, so better you should let me talk. We may have to stretch the facts a little, and I'm better at that than you are, right."

"Stretched facts are lies, Ben Lawada."

"There, you see what I mean?"

Michael Martin opened the door himself with a less-than-welcoming look on his face. "Idiot. You're not supposed to be here."

"Michael, this is Mawuli. He is Ehreh's colleague, and he is looking for Ehreh, too. He has something Ehreh needs. If we were to let people know he was here, perhaps Ehreh would find us."

Michael stood squarely in the doorway.

"Let's get on inside," Ben Lawada insisted. "We don't want to be discussing this on the street." He meant that as much for Michael as for Mawuli. Michael stepped back and let them in.

"Cops came and took Ehreh across the wall. I haven't been able to find out what they want with him."

Michael was about to say something like, "So what?" but Lawada didn't give him a chance. "Why does Ehreh want the virus here?" he asked Mawuli. "It seems a long way from his usual stomping grounds. What's going on?"

"A ground for stomping seems an odd requirement."

"But you know what he plans. Is he still looking for a vehicle?"

"I have not spoken to him for some time."

"Mawuli, stop messing around with me. I'm pretty sure you know what Ehreh has in mind, so tell me."

"I would do that for what reason, Ben Lawada? If Ehreh wanted you to know, he would have told you himself."

"Hey," Michael said. "Somebody want to tell me what's going on here?"

"It seems the old guy is about to die on his own," Lawada said. "Mawuli here has the virus Ehreh was waiting for. That's what's supposed to kill off the Kaz. What are we going to do with it?"

Mawuli had been following the discourse, ears swivelling from one speaker to the next, but so far, had not given any indication of how he was going to respond to the situation. "Ben Lawada, you brought me here with the promise of help to retrieve Ehreh from 'across the wall.' If that is not what you intend to do now, I will go to seek other means." He stepped around Lawada toward the door.

"You need to stay here," Ben said.

"I do not," Mawuli answered. Lawada made to grab him, but Mawuli evaded him with a little twist. Lawada made another grab, and Mawuli gave him a push that sent him stumbling into the door frame. Lawada reached for his blaster, but then Mawuli had one ear in his teeth and both of Lawada's hands pinned to the small of his back.

There was a thump. Mawuli staggered, knocking Lawada down. His bite loosened, and he fell to the floor. Michael put the wine bottle back on the table.

"Jeez," Lawada said, getting to his feet. Blood was seeping out of his damaged ear.

"There better be a damned good reason why we're doing this," Michael said. He glared at the blaster laying on the floor. "What the hell did you think you were going to do with that?" The muscle above his eye jumped like a wild thing.

"Is he dead?"

"Let's hope not. The Oriani give us this picture of being strongly rational pacifists but irritate them enough, and the old tiger instincts surface. You don't want to be in the line of fire when that happens."

"Yeah, I kinda got that," Lawada said, looking for something with which to staunch the blood. "What're we going to do with him, then?"

Michael gave him a handful of tissue. "I don't know. Has he got the virus with him?"

"Not unless it's up his, uh, nose."

"What?"

"Dude, no pockets."

"He must have stashed it somewhere."

"I guess." Lawada thought about it. "He didn't have anything with him when I found him, so it must be in the port area somewhere. Where would he be able to leave it for safe-keeping?"

"What are we actually looking for; what does it look like?"

"Don't know."

"Is it bigger than a breadbox?"

"I don't know what that is, but I guess viruses are pretty small."

Michael studied the other man, suspecting sarcasm, but he seemed genuinely ignorant. "Let's secure this one, then we'll negotiate with the other Oriani. Somebody will know where it is."

"What'll we do with it when we have it?"

"Sit on it for as long as possible, then sell it to the highest bidder."

"The Oriani know how to make it. They'll just make some more."

"But the Kaz don't know what it is or how to make it or counteract it, and the IPC would give a lot to not to let them get a sample to work on, don't you think? The Kaz, on the other hand, would give a lot to get one."

"That's wicked, man."

"Good business."

Not that good, Lawada thought but kept it to himself. "What are we going to do with Mawuli?"

"Lock him in here. You backtrack him, find out where he might have left the stuff. I'll see if I can get him to tell me. Keep in touch."

After a quick, sharp knock at the door, Archie stuck his head in. "Michael, I—" Then he spotted Mawuli laid out on the floor. Then he looked at Lawada and his bloody ear. "Who're you? Jeez, Michael, what's going on here?"

"Damn," Michael said.

MIDWAY—RESIDENTIAL DIVISION D

Stanton Clough brooded alone in his miserable little room. He had never liked it, but lately, he had come to truly hate the place. He should be making arrangements to return to Earth after the funeral, where he had a proper apartment and a few luxuries. The sooner, the better. He took a deep breath. Later. *Tomorrow*, he decided.

He should get something to eat, but it took too much energy.

Archie had gone off somewhere, which was a good thing because Clough was tired of being nagged about how many people he needed to contact. In the morning, he would try to meet Bengit merondebar Bengit, the crabby Rosshay aristocrat appointed to the committee overseeing commercial port operations. When he first got to know Bengit, Clough wondered how Rosshay society survived if Bengit was typical. He opposed everything. But he was also the only person Clough knew who was currently on that committee. He wasn't optimistic about persuading Bengit to convince the committee to convince the Port Authority to ignore a small civilian craft heading off into deep space without a flight plan or clearance. But he felt he owed Lauren Fox a genuine attempt.

Archie had left more things for him on the flimsy. Beatrix was arriving in the morning. Archie had arranged accommodations, flowers, a light meal. Was there anything special he should add? Should he arrange somewhere for them to meet? Stanton shuddered.

The schedule of events for Whitby's funeral was waiting for his final approval. He should note any changes in a special file for Archie.

A long, angry voice-mail from Michael Martin came very close to threatening physical harm. Stanton had heard Michael could be vindictive, but he couldn't work up a lot of concern.

The rest of it, he just couldn't be bothered with. The deals and intrigue that had sucked up most of his life seemed so pointless now. He still believed attacking the nidus worlds was the most effective way to deal with the Kaz, but it didn't seem to matter much if he garnered political support because of that or if someone else did it better and a new faction developed in the government over which he would have no influence. He just didn't have the energy to care. The world seemed a dark and hopeless place.

He left a note for Archie: the funeral arrangements were fine; no, he did not want to meet Beatrix; tell Michael Martin to go fuck himself and tell everyone else he was in mourning.

Then he rummaged around until he found some sleeping pills, found a glass of water, and swallowed enough pills to make sure he was going to be dead to the world for a good long time, if not dead altogether. It wasn't all that important either way.

He woke up with Archie shaking his arm and looking more than a little alarmed.

"Christ," Archie said when Stanton's eyes opened. "I was

beginning to think you were gone. You need to be careful with those pills."

"What time is it?"

"Just after noon."

"Today?"

"Tomorrow. You slept about twenty-six hours. Beatrix is here."

"I told you—"

"Wasn't me."

"How did she find me?"

"I don't know. I guess if your name is Mrs. Stanton Clough, people tell you what you want to know."

Stanton levered himself to his feet and staggered forward.

"You might want to tidy up a little," Archie said. "Clean underwear and a clean shirt in the bathroom."

Half an hour later, he felt as ready as he could be to meet his ex-wife.

In the years since they had gone their separate ways, Stanton often thought the grey in his hair had spread too fast, his jowls had sagged too much, and his eyesight needed repair far too often for a man his age. Beatrix, on the other hand, looked exactly the same, exquisitely dressed, perfectly made up, poised and angry.

She sat gingerly on the edge of Stanton's chair, as out of place as a wax flower in a war museum. "I don't know what to say to you," she told Stanton.

"You'll think of something, I'm sure," Stanton said.

"Our child is dead, and all you can do is make a smart remark. Oh, that is so like you."

"Could we not fight, just this once? It won't help Whitby."

"Nothing can help Whitby. He's dead, and it's your fault. I never wanted him in that awful Fleet, with those awful, coarse people, but you couldn't let him alone to live his own life. He could have been so much more. I will never forgive you, Stanton. And I want you to know I don't approve of a military funeral, which is utterly wrong for him."

Some nasty things on the end of Stanton's tongue jostled for release, but he held them back. Nothing he could say would help Whitby or change one damned thing in his own life. Once upon a time, he had cared for this woman. It was hard to imagine now. "The funeral will be a formal affair. You should try to be decent to his colleagues for that. Afterward, I will be going home to Earth. You are welcome to go to hell."

Beatrix stood up and walked out without another word. *I could have been kinder*, Stanton thought, but couldn't work up much regret.

He shut the door behind her. Then he had nothing much to do.

He was alone with his ghosts.

So much of his life had been so busy, so involved with the intricacies of pushing agendas, fighting for policies that, when you came down to it, meant any number of young people had been sent to their deaths. In all the heated debates, the compromises, the anger both real and theatric, deals forged and broken, favours given and taken, this reality had never been on his mind until now. When some correspondent asked, he would say trite things about "our brave fighting forces and the debt we all owe them," but it was never real. He had rationalized his actions as the best way to protect the Interplanetary Community. He told himself it was how it had to be done. Was it true, or had he just been burying his conscience deep while cultivating his own influence? Had he never made the leap between a policy paper and its implementation before?

Often, the road before him had looked like a maze, so many needs of so many people, all clamouring for attention. Sometimes, the wrong path looked right until a drastic event made him look back, and then he saw where he had missed a turn. And now, it was too late. Now, it didn't matter anymore.

The road to hell was paved with good intentions. Or inattention.

Well, he'd washed his hands of it. And maybe he could go a little way toward making amends.

He poked around the room, looking for the flimsy. When he found it, he realized he didn't really know how to make it do anything. Where was Archie?

He got the display to start and found a big question mark, which, when he touched it, brought up a menu: "Help with" and a list, but nothing on the list said, "Finding Lauren Fox."

He gave up after a bit and thought he would go back to sleep instead. But he had slept himself out earlier, and so he lay on the bed and stared up at the grey ceiling owl-eyed.

Then he heard Archie's quick knock, and the young man came in.

"Archie, can you—" Stanton sat up, about to ask his aide how to work the flimsy when he realized the young man was in a state.

"What?" he asked.

Archie sat on the chair. He was pale. For once, he didn't have anything to say.

Stanton brought a glass of water and one of the tranquilizer pills. Archie took the water but declined the pill. After a moment, he said, "I think Michael Martin killed one of the Oriani." His voice was high-pitched and strained.

"That can't be true."

"I saw him lying on the floor of Michael's office."

"Who? The Orian?"

Archie nodded.

"What did Martin say about it?"

"I didn't ask. I just ran."

Stanton decided it was not a good time to ask what Archie had been doing in Michael's office.

"When?"

"A few minutes ago."

"Call the police?"

"No."

"You're a silly kid."

"I was scared." It was quite an admission from Archie and probably the first time in his young life that it was true. "Michael knows I saw. He's going to come after me next."

Stanton fetched the flimsy. "Show me how to work this thing." Archie didn't move. "If I have to go looking for a cop up and down the hallways, it's not going to do either of us any good."

Archie took the flimsy and spoke briefly to the Constabulary. "They want us to meet them there."

"Okay, then, that's what we're going to do. But first, get me Lauren Fox."

Archie did his thing and also pointed out a message from Bengit merondebar Bengit waiting for Stanton's attention. *People surprise you in many ways*, Stanton thought. He decided he should talk to Bengit before he talked to Lauren. First, they had to satisfy officialdom.

When they arrived at Michael Martin's office, a considerable crowd had gathered, and the police were trying to keep them away from the scene of the crime. It took Stanton trading on his status to even get anyone to listen, and at that point, one officer pointed out to Stanton that they remained unconvinced that a crime had occurred. "This young man was there," Stanton said. Then Archie told a solemn Turgorn, who identified himself as Kam Nok, what he had seen.

"Come in here," Kam Nok said, and he ushered Archie into the room. Stanton followed. "Show me where you saw a dead Orian."

The room was empty. The walls were bare. The furniture was gone. No one would guess it had been occupied in the last century. Archie pointed out as best he could without landmarks where he had seen the Orian laying. The Turgorn looked carefully at the spot on the floor indicated, applied several instruments to the spot and its surroundings, then shrugged and summoned a colleague with a crook of his finger.

"The human says here. The spectrophotometer is ambiguous. What do you think?"

The Tuer got down close to the floor and applied its long, rubbery proboscis here and there, then stopped. "This place," it said. "Here is blood of Orian. Also, blood of human."

Kam Nok asked, "This human?"

The Tuer sniffed toward Archie. "Do not think so."

"Okay," the Turgorn told Archie. "You'd better go with these people and make a formal statement."

Archie gave Stanton a panicked look. "Go with them," Stanton said. "Tell them what you know about what you saw here. Don't tell them anything else. Get my lawyer on the flimsy. I'll ask him to meet you there." Archie was about to object. Stanton took the flimsy from him and went on, "At least you'll be out of Martin's way for a while." *And then*, he thought, *I'm so going to fire your treacherous little ass when this is over.*

More police people arrived with instruments and recorders. They gathered data from the onsite devices, measured things, chipped bits from others.

Stanton was about to leave, but Kam Nok stopped him. "What's your relationship to Archie Bennet?"

"We don't have a relationship. I'm his employer. Soon to be ex-employer."

"Why is that?"

"That's between him and me. I have to go. I'm late for an appointment."

"Leave contact information with one of our people." To Stanton's questioning look, he said, "We might have further questions."

MIDWAY—ACROSS THE WALL

hreh, back in the same room he had left not so long ago, sitting on the edge of the same chair, waited. He tried to be patient, but he was weary and truly hoped this renewed interview would not go on for long. He had debated with himself about how much to tell the lieutenant and decided he could be forthcoming to a degree. By the time the Fleet moved on any information he offered, the virus would already be on its way, or the plan would be dead.

Nes Gow, not about to leave him alone again, had called in a Lleveci soldier to stand at the door. He had listened thoughtfully to Ehreh's explanation.

"You're telling me this hybrid organism you've built kills Kaz."

"Yes."

"All of them?"

"Testing has been limited." Ehreh hesitated a moment. One can be strictly factual and still not be entirely truthful, but at this point, some accommodation had to be made. "In vitro, all Kazi cells were infected, and all were destroyed. As far as I am aware, all of the live subjects tested have died."

"That's brutal. And nothing else dies?"

"We have not seen it infect any cells other than Kazi."

"Interesting. In that case, the obvious question has to be, why are there still Kaz? And why didn't you proceed through official channels, end this war once and for all, and let us all go home?"

"You have another career at home that you are anxious to pursue, Lieutenant Nes Gow?"

Nes Gow was a little surprised to realize he did not.

"Many do not," Ehreh went on. "Official channels are largely closed to us because our government disagrees with our approach; the destruction of an entire species is considered an extremely immoral act, even as acts of war are measured. Powerful vested interests oppose us, many of whom are highly placed within the IPC government. Efforts to involve existing structures have been met with opposition at the highest levels and with threats to careers and even to lives. I believed it prudent to try other approaches.

"We have only recently finished development. Dispersal is our problem at the moment. You could help us with that if you were so inclined."

"Ha. Not going to happen, my man. How long have you been working on this?"

Ehreh thought about it. "Perhaps most of a generation by Turgorn standards." He became very still.

"Are you unwell?" Nes Gow asked.

"I am." He swayed a little. "I have missed my scheduled medication. I must go."

"No, I don't think so. I'll get a physician in here. Just wait a minute." Nes Gow picked at the board in front of him and spoke briefly to the system, then said, "A physician is on the way. You keep yourself together, damn it. We have had too many deaths on this station lately."

Some spark of curiosity remained. "Persons are dead?" Ehreh asked.

"Since that Kazi that no one even knew about was found dead a few days ago, an Orian was reported killed." The information had arrived on Nes Gow's newsfeed just moments ago. "Somebody you know, maybe? The coincidences are beginning to add up."

"You are aware of the Orian's name?"

"No, sorry. We have not found a body—" Nes Gow's voice trailed off as Ehreh slid off the chair and onto the floor. As he hurried around the desk, he could see no sign of breathing. He growled a few choice Turgorn curses, which, fortunately, no one in the immediate vicinity understood, then rushed to the door to look for the physician and nearly ran into her at the threshold.

She spent some time over Ehreh, then called for care-bots and a gurney and various drug dispensers. "You may have waited too long."

"Don't lay this on me. He said nothing about being sick until he was ready to collapse."

"If he had said nothing at all, would you have let him die?"

Nes Gow wanted to protest his blamelessness in all this— he wasn't a medical practitioner, after all—but by then, all the medical paraphernalia that had suddenly filled up his office was on the move toward the hospital, and nobody was listening.

LAUREN HAD BEEN WAITING for Stanton Clough in the dockside cafeteria for a while. She had been surprised that he had asked to meet her, less surprised that he hadn't shown up. All the others on the project had described him as a vigorous opponent to changing the IPC's approach to holding off the Kaz and, if she was reading them right, the beneficiary of a great deal of support from various entrenched military provisioners. Push come to shove, he had no reason to help her.

She was about to give up on him when she saw him coming toward her from one of the residential areas. He was alone, which was unusual; he usually had the redhead somewhere nearby.

"I'm sorry. Something came up that couldn't wait."

"Okay."

"I have an idea that might help get you off Midway. It's not without considerable risk and will only work if we can keep it among ourselves in the strictest way. It will have to be timed precisely while at least part of officialdom is busy with Whitby's funeral."

Stanton stopped and took a deep breath. "It might not be much of an advantage, but maybe a little. I have the schedule here." He dug in his pocket and found an iPage.

"You shouldn't fold those things. They'll break eventually."

"Yes. Archie keeps telling me that."

Lauren transferred the file to an old, somewhat battered device she stuck with because it was tough, and low maintenance, and fit in her pocket. "Thanks," she said.

"I have spoken with a member of the committee that oversees the civilian activity at the port. He's going to try to have the Port Authority give a pass to a small packet leaving on a secret mission. That's mostly true. We don't have to mention what the mission is or that it is not officially sanctioned."

"Thanks, Stanton. All this is good stuff, but we are still stymied by one major issue. We don't have the virus. Ehreh's friend Mawuli was supposed to have delivered it a couple of days ago, but no one has been in touch with him, and I can't find Ehreh either. So, all the prep may be for nought."

"What does he look like, Ehreh's friend?"

"I've never seen him. Young. Male. Orian. That's all I know."

"Oh. Damn. I might have bad news for you." Stanton recounted Archie's story of earlier in the evening.

"So, do you think that might be Mawuli?" Lauren asked when he was done.

"I don't know. There were no—uh—remains at the scene, and it's not like a cop is going to tell you anything useful. Is any other Orian missing?"

"I need to find Ehreh. This schedule is tight. There's no room for delays unless you can move the funeral back a few hours." Lauren saw Stanton's expression break and said, "I'm sorry, I shouldn't even say a thing like that. I've never been given high marks for sensitivity."

Stanton shook his head. "Maybe you can find Ryet. It stands out in a crowd and always knows what's going on in the world. I'm sorry, I have some things I have to attend to."

"Do you know if Ryet has an implant?"

"I don't. There's a list someplace. I'll ask Archie when I see him. I have to go and rescue him from the justice system."

Lauren followed Stanton out of the cafeteria and set off for the docks. While she walked, she contacted the office (if you could call it that) of the Orian delegate and asked them if they knew where Ehreh was. The person who answered the call had a thick accent, but Lauren thought he said that Ehreh had been taken into custody by the Civil Constabulary.

"Why?"

"Unknown."

"Are you going to get him out?"

"You mean get Ehreh out of custody? I am not sure that the delegate's intervention in a local matter is warranted."

"And everybody told me Oriani look out for one another."

"You cannot believe everything you hear."

Especially, Lauren thought, *I can't believe Oriani making jokes.*

Now she had two reasons to find Ryet. She called Aroull.

"Do you know where Ryet is?"

"I do not. But you should know that Ehreh is here, in the hospital. He does not know Mawuli's whereabouts, nor does he know where the virus is. I believe our only hope is to find Mawuli."

"Why is he so hard to find? How many Oriani are on Midway?"

"Thirty-one," Aroull answered.

ADVANCE BASE 5023

I n a large, circular underground chamber bathed in the soft greenish light Kaz most favoured, on the lowest of the benches that ringed the walls and dominated the space, the Kazi broodmaster leaned back on its hindmost legs and prepared to enjoy a rest.

Fortunately, today its juvenile charges had been well-behaved and attentive. As a reward, it had dismissed the brood early while the light remained high. The brood was still very young, barely past the second moult, and would enjoy a period of unstructured time. As they grew older, it would seem less attractive to them, but for now, it was still a treat.

And, truth be told, the broodmaster itself, even though it was in middle life, enjoyed a little free time. It was rare enough. The Empire liked to keep its members productive.

But no sooner were the youngsters gone than the field group leader arrived unannounced, weary from its journey, offering the properly respectful gestures of lower rank to higher, but presenting a sense of urgency and dismay.

The broodmaster was able to give the group leader the careful and immediate consideration and attention it could not have done if the youngsters were still milling around, causing confusion and asking questions. But it did feel a bit of resentment for the loss of its moment of leisure.

The first thing that was obvious from the group leader's account was that it was the sole survivor of its group. That was alarming. The broodmaster agreed with its assessment that so many deaths among so small a number should be investigated. Its superiors, however, were disinclined to waste resources unless advantage could be shown, so it would have to make a good argument. Knowing why all these died seemed important, but its superiors had noted previously that the broodmaster tended to get too attached to broodmembers, something they thought it should be working to overcome.

The group leader was anxious to get to the meat of its report. The fact that heliosite was confirmed on Ferguson Prime it considered far and away the most important part of its information.

But all who went there died, the broodmaster noted.

Yes, but they returned much useful data before that happened, the group leader told him.

Can one safely assume the security countermeasures were effective, then?

The intelligence gatherer and its assistant were able to arrive on Midway without incident. The scouts were able to land on Ferguson Prime safely. But Ferguson Prime is a hostile world, ill-suited to survival. I believe the environment killed them, the group leader said. It staggered a little, and the broodmaster realized it was exhausted. It called an assistant, but before the other arrived, the group leader sank to the ground in front of it, breaking all protocol.

The doctors did what they could, but the group leader died within a few hours. They had no theory about the cause. The broodmaster mentioned that the group leader spoke of the intelligence gatherer's assistant dying in much the same manner. The doctors had no explanation to offer.

The broodmaster decided to transmit the information about the heliosite deposit directly to the core worlds, bypassing most of the hierarchy, as soon as it understood the need to avoid delay. The Ferguson system was not that far from Kazi-held territory. A quick and decisive strike was surely possible. A coup for the Empire.

It would also mention the number of deaths that had already occurred.

The broodmaster's superior, however, was less than pleased with this willingness to disregard the chain of command and questioned the need to investigate the deaths of various members of a field group, units normally considered expendable. A short time later, it summoned the broodmaster to its own, smaller, chamber, taking a posture of irritation and skepticism.

That nine died on a hot, dry world where they were working without support, it signed, *does not seem sufficiently unusual to warrant the cost of investigation. It was all but expected.*

Two of two who went to Midway also died, the broodmaster pointed out. *Official investigation by the Interplanetary Community of one death produced no obvious cause. The other individual died shortly after returning to the group leader on Beta Ellgarth. The possibility that something lethal resides on Midway must be considered.*

The superior's attitude and scent did not suggest it was being persuaded. *The group leader died here, among us, and we can assume nothing lethal is present here. Cause of a death on Midway is of no concern. We will not occupy Midway for quite some time, perhaps not ever. It is a useless place once its military base is destroyed. I do not see that we could learn anything of sufficient value to be worth the price. We must also consider the possibility the*

Interplanetary Community would present false information if they thought it would confuse us even in the slightest way.

I have a dead broodmember in my quarters, the broodmaster thought, not false information. But it had enough concern for its own welfare to avoid pointing that out.

However, I shall recommend that we occupy Ferguson Prime, the superior continued. *A colony there will supply a much-needed commodity to the Empire while denying it to the opposition and serve as an outpost inside enemy territory.*

Which the enemy will vigorously try to dislodge, the broodmaster pointed out.

A judicious distribution of forces could make the attempt very expensive for them.

And for us, the broodmaster thought, but again kept the thought to itself.

The superior preened itself a little as if it had thought of something extraordinary.

The broodmaster was preparing to return to its quarters when the superior's assistant arrived with an urgent hyperspace message from the core worlds. The chief military science adviser was asking for as many of the bodies of the deceased as could be retrieved as soon as they could be brought to the core. It included a long list of instructions about how to approach the bodies and how to isolate them from contamination.

The broodmaster's superior was not pleased, but it could not refuse the request. The broodmaster went to its evening meal with a sense of minor victory, only to discover it had not much appetite.

KING GEORGE XIII HOSPITAL

E hreh came back to the world in a white hospital room, attached by tubes and wires to many machines. The pain was extraordinary, as if his nervous system were trying to burn its way out of his body. Aroull was nearby, and some machine or another alerted him to Ehreh's return to consciousness. Aroull busied himself for a few moments checking things, then said to Ehreh, "You are trying to kill yourself? You have neglected your medications."

He pressed a hypo against Ehreh's neck, working it through the fur. The spray was sharp and cool all at once. Ehreh didn't answer Aroull's obviously rhetorical question, but he thought about it. Then he went to sleep.

He woke again, not knowing how much later. Aroull was not in the room. Ehreh began systemically detaching the machines. Immediately, Aroull was there.

"Stop," he said. "This is not to your benefit."

"It is time," Ehreh said. His voice was hoarse.

"No. It is not. Much remains to be done, and you are needed, old friend." Aroull began reattaching things.

"I have done what I can."

"No one can find Mawuli or the virus. All our work here depends on having the virus. Where could Mawuli be?"

"You have asked Murr? She was looking for him as well."

"Murr is here?"

"I met her in the delegate's office."

"I will try to get in touch at once. Harl has been trying to reach you."

"She was angry with me when we last saw one another."

"I shall arrange communication?"

"Perhaps later. She is an exhausting person."

"Tell me you will do nothing rash until I return."

"Do not be long.

AROULL'S WORKLOAD was not so demanding that he couldn't transfer most of his scheduled duties to a combination of other technicians and a pair of care-bots. There was some grumbling, not from the bots, but most of the technicians owed him a favour or two. He looked in on Ehreh one more time, then made his way into old Midway and the Orian delegate's office.

He found the office in something of a turmoil, by Orian standards. One person informed him that they had discovered Ehreh had been taken into custody, and Stanton Clough, a person they did not normally consider an ally, had asked the delegate to use his influence to get Ehreh released. They did, of course, wonder why.

The delegate was currently in discussion with Clough and the civil authority. They had found from the police that Ehreh had been given over to the military. The military had not been cooperative regarding inquiries about Ehreh's whereabouts.

"He is safe," Aroull said. "You may inform the delegate. He arrived at the hospital earlier today in the care of someone from the military liaison. He is resting."

A little of the tension bled out of the room. "He was damaged during his captivity?"

"I do not believe so. He has been ill for some years now. He has a malignancy growing near his spine. Treatment has slowed the progress, but now, nothing more can be done. I do not believe he will survive more than a few days.

"For Ehreh's sake, it is important that I find Mawuli. Ehreh said that Murr might have seen him here. That has happened?"

Murr shook her head. "He should have been here shortly before I arrived, but he was not."

"No one here has seen Mawuli?"

"Yes," one said. "He was here shortly before Murr arrived. He asked for Ehreh, but did not stay once he found Ehreh was not here. I do not believe anyone here has seen him since."

Murr said, "This one who has an illicit connection to the security system has found a record of him in the company of a human some hours ago. A search for him at a later time has been fruitless."

"This one has a name," the one said. "Ihosh, she is called."

Murr went on, "We are now searching for the human. Finding one human among the many is a daunting task."

Aroull looked over Ihosh's shoulder. "You do know that humans have developed software to allow an artificial intelligence to distinguish one of them from the others in records such as these?"

"I did not," the youngster said. "One could find a copy?"

"I would be surprised if the Civil Constabulary did not have at least some version of it, and since you are in their system already, acquisition should not be difficult."

The operator busied herself with the task.

"You are inciting this person to perform illegal acts," Murr complained.

"You seem willing enough to accept the benefits of those acts."

Murr's tail swished a bit, but she did not continue the argument.

"You have encountered images of a Nsfera?" Aroull asked the operator.

"This creature?" she asked, leaning over to activate another display.

"Yes." In a rapidly changing series of images, Ryet ambled along from the dock area toward a residential district, after which the system lost track of him.

"Who lives in that district?"

"Dockworkers, low-level civil servants, shop clerks."

"Ryet would go there for what reason? Rhetorical question," Aroull added when he saw the others were attempting to formulate an answer. "Keep me updated if you find newer sightings of the Nsfera." He left the crowded room and headed in the direction Ryet had taken.

MIDWAY—STORAGE AND MAINTENANCE

Mawuli came back to consciousness in the dark. Very dark. His eyes strained and could not capture a single photon.

He was lying on a bit of dusty, smelly carpet. He lay still because movement hurt. He listened but heard nothing. His whiskers detected not a hint of movement, as if the very air had died. It smelled of metal and mustiness. He catalogued his various pains, a great thudding anguish in the back of his head, the lesser hurts of bumps and bruises. He remembered Ben Lawada.

Moving slowly to minimize the discomfort, he began to explore his surroundings by feel. The walls were close by, so the space was small. The ceiling was above his reach. A large box that could be a cupboard and a door were the only features he could detect. The door seemed ordinary: a flat surface and a frame, a knob, and an electronic lock. The knob turned, but the lock held firm.

He felt his way back to the box. It had flaps that opened and shelves inside. The shelves held several items, some plastic bottles and small boxes, but most of the things he could not identify by touch. Something he brushed against gave him a small prickle of static. Nothing there was suitable for prying open a door.

He tried once more pulling on the knob with no success. He felt for hinges but found none. They must be on the other side or hidden. He tried to remember what he knew about electronic locks. Not much. He had never had a reason to study locks. Oriani rarely used them.

He sat quietly by the door. If people did put electronic locks on doors, would they connect them to the building's network? Security systems were often constructed ad hoc, so rules were not likely. What happened to electronic locks when they were damaged? Did they send out a distress call? Did they fall open so people were not locked into places, or did they fall closed so the places were kept secure?

He could try an experiment. He did not think he had a lot to lose however it worked out.

He felt his way back to the cupboard and felt around until he found the staticky object. It was rubbery to the touch, a flat, thickish sheet. He rubbed it vigorously against his arm and, in a moment, felt a tingle in his feet.

He pulled the bit of carpet over to the door, stood on it, rubbed the sheet against his body until every hair was standing on end, and then grabbed the metallic part of the lock. A spark crackled, and he got a painful jolt. The pounding in his head got worse.

He turned the doorknob and pulled. Nothing happened.

He repeated the experiment and got the same result. *Idiot,* he thought, *what did you expect?*

He considered it totally unreasonable that he should suffocate in some unknown place for an unknown reason. He sat down by the door to think what else he could try.

IN THE ROOM where she and an aged AI monitored a large part of Midway's infrastructure, Kiska Babina nodded at her station, jerking awake when her supervisor came in. On the panel in front of her, a number had come up, and the AI was generating a discrete ding, asking for her attention.

"What's that?" the supervisor asked. The supervisor was Higant, crabby, temperamental, and difficult, who constantly criticized Kiska and would like nothing better than to find an excuse to fire her. They did not like one another.

Kiska answered as quickly as she could get her wits about her. The numbers were coded by type. "Storage unit," she said.

"Whose?"

Kiska punched the number into her board. "Leased to Martin Industries IP." She turned the alarm off.

"Well?"

Kiska looked her question to the supervisor.

"Don't you think you should check it out?"

"Can't the AI—"

"I think Martin Industries deserves our personal attention."

Sighing, Kiska got to her feet and started down the corridor to the unit in question, grumbling quietly to herself all the way. It was a long walk, and Kiska was probably twenty kilos above her best weight. But she really needed her job.

When she arrived, the door stood blankly before her, the green indicator showing the lock undisturbed. Nothing she couldn't have learned from the office. She was about to turn back and report a false alarm when she heard a couple of loud thumps.

Querying her implant for the override code, Kiska opened the door and swung it wide. A bedraggled and bloody Orian holding a plastic bottle full of cleaning fluid fell out, almost into her arms.

"What're you doing in there?" Kiska asked.

"I do not know," the Orian said. He staggered a few steps, dropped the bottle, and collapsed.

For a moment, Kiska just stood there and looked at him. She had no idea how to check for a pulse with this kind of creature. She touched his neck where it wasn't bloody and felt only the thick warm fur. Finally, she struggled down to her knees, put her cheek close to his nose and felt his breath. Not dead, then.

She pushed herself to her feet again, closed the locker door, and tried to think what to do. If she called the medics, they would blame her. The supervisor would blame her. There would be a thousand questions about how this person got trapped in a locker, why he was there, how long he had been there, and what had happened to him, and she had no answers, and they wouldn't believe her, and she wouldn't get home for hours, if at all.

And the supervisor would finally have his excuse.

If the Orian would just return to consciousness, he could answer all those questions himself. He would know none of it was her fault. Maybe all he needed was a little time.

They couldn't wait in the corridor; it was monitored by cameras and patrolled by bots. She had to get him somewhere private until he regained his senses.

Here and there among the storage units, platform dollies were parked for the convenience of customers. She pushed one to where the Orian lay. It had a little crank in the front that retracted the wheels so it lay flat on the floor. With a great deal of shoving and grunting, trying all the while to keep from inflicting more damage, she rolled him onto the bed of the dolly, placed his tail over his legs, cranked the wheels out again, and trundled off down the corridor. A little farther along, she found a furniture blanket and threw it over the top.

She stopped at her workroom to let the AI know she would be away for a while and to pick up her lunch box and the reader she brought to while away the boring hours of her shift. She put those items on top of the laden dolly, put her ID code into the patrol-bot she met on the way, and headed home.

Home wasn't much, but it was hers, and it was private. Leo, an ex-boyfriend, had objected to the sensor and deactivated it. "Dose vatchers, dey vatch somebody elze, eh?" Leo didn't stay long, but Kiska never saw the point in reactivating the sensor.

Once the door closed behind her and her burden, she didn't know what to do next. She did have a flash of concern that what she was doing might not be her smartest move. She nudged the thought away. No one had ever accused her of being smart. And all she needed was for the Orian to wake up.

She decided she could get some food ready while she waited. She had no idea what Oriani ate. *Cat food, maybe*, she thought and giggled to herself. *And water.* Every living thing in the known worlds needed water.

Her implant dinged, and the supervisor's voice came on, spitting angry even in the abstract.

"Babina, Martin Industries are saying something is missing from their locker. I told them there was an alarm, but inspection showed nothing amiss. That's true, is it not?"

Kiska looked at the silent bundle on the dolly.

"Babina?"

"Yes. Yes," she said, too forcefully. "The door was locked when I got there. There was no sign of any trouble at all." Almost true.

"The log shows the door opened at that time."

"You told me to check. I checked. Nothing in it but cleaning supplies."

"Very well," the supervisor said and disconnected. *Very well for him*, Kiska thought, but now she was in an even deeper hole. The Orian had to wake up. There was no other hope for her.

But he hadn't moved a muscle. Kiska was getting seriously worried. What if he died there in her living room?

She polled her implant for a rarely used number and pinged Ryet.

"I will be there shortly," it said.

PACING IN A RENTED ROOM, Michael Martin was furious and more than a little alarmed. Only two people knew where the Orian had been stashed; he was one, and Lawada hadn't been out of his sight until he sent the man out this morning to inquire if anyone had seen a wounded Orian. So, how did the bugger get away, and where did he go?

Lawada had returned with no information.

Building management said they had no idea; there had been an alarm, they had checked it out and found nothing amiss. False alarms were not all that rare. The system was old.

Too much coincidence.

Michael annoyed people on communications until he could speak directly to the Building Maintenance head office. They assured him neither cameras nor patrols had reported anything out of the ordinary in the storage area.

"Nothing? Not the slightest thing?"

The supervisor said, "The only entry in the day's log for that area other than the false alarm was the encounter of a patrol-bot with a worker on her way home. This is a frequent happening. The worker entered the correct code."

"I need to talk to that worker. Who is it?"

"I'm not allowed to give out that information."

"Who is allowed?"

"No one."

"We'll see about that."

He called the Director of Midway Supply and Services but didn't get an answer. He called the constabulary. "Where is Archie Bennet?"

"No idea."

"He was in your custody. Don't tell me you lost him."

"He was released about three hours ago. We have no more interest."

He turned to Ben. "What did you find?"

"Nothing, boss. There's blood in the locker, but none any place else. No trail. The cleaners come by pretty often. No gossip around that I heard."

"I want to know who went to inspect the alarm, and I want to know who met the patrol. Somebody knows where that damned Orian is, and he better tell me."

Lawada touched the bandage on his ear. "Maybe he's dead," he said without any sign of regret.

"Then we need to find the body and dispose of it."

"How far do you want me to go with this?"

"As far as you need to, so long as it doesn't come back to me. Understand?"

"Yep."

Michael set himself the task of finding Archie. *Recruit him or shoot him*, he thought. Life was becoming fraught. The muscle above his eye jumped around and made concentration difficult.

LAWADA HAD no intention of dealing with the "usual channels." Martin would have done that long ago. The usual channels looked in the usual places, and obviously, Mawuli wasn't in one of them, or he'd be found by now.

He looked up Assiffah.

"If you want to get back at the guys who beat you up, this might be your chance. I need to find an Orian called Mawuli, and the sooner, the better. He seems to have disappeared. Anyone who can tell me where he is could earn a nice piece of change."

When Assiffah had scuttled away into the nooks and crannies where he was most effective, Lawada repeated the offer to the bartender he had spoken to earlier, then he went to the dock area and spoke to a couple of thugs he knew. He figured once enough eyes were on the job, Mawuli would turn up. But after several hours, he had nothing, so he decided to take action on his own. He went to the offices of Building Management, to the department from which he and Michael had previously rented a locker, rather in a hurry. The supervisor had accepted a consideration to bypass the usual vetting, which gave Lawada a lever. Not a big one, but he thought it would be adequate. The lower a person is on the totem pole, the more nervous he is about shit coming down.

The Higant was as hostile and cantankerous as he was before, but the threat of bringing to the attention of *his* boss the taking of bribes for favours settled him to the point that business could be done. The name and address of the unfortunate who had investigated the alarm at the locker were Lawada's in a relatively short time.

"But she assured me there was nothing in the locker."

"That's kind of the problem," Lawada said. "There should have been something in the locker, and I really want to know where it is."

"The other human who was with you has the key. You should ask him about anything that is missing."

"Yeah, I'll do that." It had occurred to Lawada earlier that Michael could be sending him on a wild goose chase, but he couldn't see how Michael would gain any advantage from that.

He was sufficiently familiar with Old Midway that once he knew what district, the search for the actual address was relatively short. He knocked politely at the door.

He got no answer.

INSIDE THE ROOM, Kiska Babina held her breath. Who would be knocking on her door? She had no friends here, or anywhere, for that matter. Would the supervisor actually come to her house? She didn't think so.

"Open up, sister," a rough voice shouted from the other side. A human. "I'm not playing around here. Open the door, or I'm going to break it to pieces."

Kiska bit her knuckles, trying to think what to do. She didn't need to be in trouble with the housing directorate over a broken door on top of her other troubles. But as soon as the door opened, the Orian on the dolly would become horribly obvious.

The knocking renewed, closer to pounding now. "Wait, wait," she shouted back. She threw the furniture blanket back over the still form and wheeled the whole thing into the bathroom, then pulled that door shut.

By the time she got back to the front door, the pounding had resumed. She opened it partway and stood in the opening.

"What do you want?"

"I want the Orian."

"I don't know any Orian."

"Yes, you do, and wherever he is, I want him."

"Please go away and leave me alone."

Lawada pushed on the door. Kiska had had the presence of mind to set the chain.

Lawada hit the door harder. He could hear splintering.

"Go away," Kiska said.

"That ain't going to happen."

"Oh, but it is."

Lawada whipped around to face the ivory grin of the Nsfera. It was leaning against the wall as if it had always been there. "I don't like people threatening my friends. You should leave now and never, ever come back."

Lawada bristled. If there was bullying to be done, he

expected to do it. The thing was tall but skinny. It made a lot of noise over by the dock but didn't actually hurt anything. Really, it didn't seem all that formidable when it came down to cases. And to be honest, he was much more afraid of Martin than of the Nsfera. "And if I don't?"

It didn't even shift its position on the wall. "I do not know. I should be able to devise a suitable retaliation." The Nsfera's dark tongue swept over its long teeth. "I haven't had lunch."

"Jesus," Lawada said. And it might have ended there, with Lawada searching out the better part of valour, except that Mawuli chose that moment to open the door wide and stagger out of the apartment and into the passage. He sat down hard on the doorstep.

Kiska immediately rushed in and came back with water. Mawuli sipped a bit.

"Ben Lawada, please explain this situation. How do I come to be here? This human and this other—person," he looked at Ryet, "they are?" Still believing Ben Lawada to be a friend of the project, he wasn't alarmed, though an itch in the back of his wounded brain insisted that Lawada was somehow at least partly responsible for his current condition. The ear. He thought he remembered doing that. He had a reason for that?

Lawada said to Kiska, "You're a lying little shit."

Ryet said to Kiska, "Call the medics."

"I'll lose my job," she said.

"No, you will not. Trust me." When she still seemed reluctant, it added, "Your situation will be worse if Mawuli dies here, don't you think?"

Her fear, lessened when Ryet first appeared, renewed itself. Jerkily, she nodded and activated her implant.

Mawuli began to slump as if he were about to pass out again.

Aroull came around a corner of the passage and called when he spotted Ryet.

"A faster-than-expected response," Ryet said.

Aroull was about to ask Ryet what it meant; then he saw Mawuli. Then he was all med tech for a while. The summoned medics arrived, and Mawuli was taken off to hospital. Aroull went with him.

Ryet still hadn't moved from its spot against the wall. It watched Lawada like a well-fed cat deciding if the mouse was worth the trouble.

Lawada swallowed hard and walked away, back down the passage. It wasn't a retreat, exactly. Mawuli had been the person he was after, anyway, and now he knew exactly where Mawuli was. He would deal with the Nsfera later when he could tip the odds a bit more in his favour.

Once Lawada was out of sight, Ryet turned to Kiska. "Now, we will get you a better door and a new lock."

KING GEORGE XIII HOSPITAL

n the hospital, Mawuli struggled to tell Kam Nok and other members of the Civil Constabulary what had happened to him. It became obvious he didn't remember the event very well. He had been with Ben Lawada, meeting a person Ben Lawada knew. He had been attacked. A blaster had been involved. He was hit on the head, and then he woke up in a box. He met a human who hauled him away on a wagon.

He could describe Ben Lawada—an average-sized human, dark, black hair, brown eyes—and his friend: also human, lighter-coloured, taller, hairless, but he couldn't remember the friend's name or where he lived. Eventually, Kam Nok gave up and went to pursue the investigation elsewhere.

"I find this quite strange," Mawuli said to Aroull. "My memory has holes in it."

"Loss of memory is not unusual after a concussion. It will probably improve with time."

Mawuli shook his head. He looked at Aroull with some alarm. "I cannot remember where I left the virus."

Stifling his own alarm, Aroull said, "Give yourself time." He had the sense of being less than totally honest. If Mawuli's memory loss extended that far back, it seemed indicative of deeper damage, more than might be quickly recovered. "You remember what the container looks like?"

"Two sealed glass vials inside a padded aluminum box, eleven by thirteen centimetres. Each vial contains about ten millilitres of black powder, the virus on an inert substrate."

"You obviously remember that quite well. Think about the box and where it might be, but don't push yourself. Let the memory come on its own."

This wasn't particularly sage advice, but for the moment, nothing else could be done except work to prevent further swelling in Mawuli's brain and wait.

Once he was sure the care-bots could take over monitoring Mawuli, he looked in on Ehreh. The bot that was minding him had increased the dose of sedative, and the old man was sleeping. *Probably for the best*, Aroull thought. He felt confident about leaving the hospital for a few hours.

He returned to the delegate's office and the person there who had worked her way into the Constabulary's surveillance web. He had a challenge for Ihosh.

"I found the software," Ihosh said when Aroull arrived. "The available AI is rather primitive, but it can do this. We can follow any human we need to."

"Can you follow an Orian?"

"I do not know. It has not been tried. Some modification might be necessary."

"I do not have much time. Let us try the program as it exists."

Ihosh shrugged. "Who shall we look for?"

"Mawuli. You found him leaving the dock area. I would like to know where he went from there."

Ihosh bent to the task, jollying the AI along as it searched a multitude of records, her whiskers bent forward as she followed events on the screen. At first, the task was simple. No great number of Oriani were on Midway. The AI thoughtfully drew a red ring around the appropriate image where it could find one. They watched Mawuli come to the delegate's office, pause at the door, then turn and leave. He was not carrying anything.

"He asked for Ehreh," one of the others said.

"Can you find that first image again? He had something with him?"

But at that time, he was in a crowd. It was impossible to tell.

They saw him meet Ben Lawada on the steps for a brief conversation, then go with him, proceeding across the concourse into an upscale residential district. In that area, he was harder to follow, sensors being less prevalent. They found him one final time at an intersection, still following Ben Lawada, and then they could not find him again.

"You know where this place is?"

Ihosh showed him the map on the next screen, where the spot was marked at a crossroads. It was no great distance from Kiska Babina's apartment, even as things were measured on Midway, and likely not beyond the ability of a damaged young Orian who was otherwise fit to travel. The question had to be, why?

"Keep searching for further sightings."

"And keep you apprised. I am learning the procedure. It may happen that the delegate will want his assistants to return to their prescribed chores."

Aroull nodded his appreciation and left.

When he arrived at the marked intersection, he could see down one of the roads a collection of police people and equipment gathered at one of the residences. Curious, he went in that direction. It was as likely as any other.

A bot stopped him at the periphery of the police presence. *Who are you?* its screen displayed.

Aroull told it.

The bot fetched one of the investigators. "We are investigating the murder of one of your kinsman. Perhaps you know him? His name was Mawuli."

"I know him. He is not dead. He is in the hospital. I left him a short time ago, talking to Kam Nok. You thought he was killed?"

"We have an eyewitness report."

"Your witness is mistaken. Mawuli is damaged but not at all dead."

"I guess I better go talk to him."

"Kam Nok is there. Communicate with him. Mawuli's memory has been affected, so he may not be able to tell you much."

"And why are you here?"

"Mawuli lost something of great value. I have been following his movements to see if I could find it."

"Describe it to one of the bots. They'll keep an eye out." The investigator's tone suggested he had very little expectation of its recovery.

"I will do that," Aroull said but had equally little expectation it would produce useful information. A problem with bots was that although their factory-fresh programming made them scrupulously honest, many had been altered to favour their handlers with information about any valuable objects found at crime scenes. Given the usual mob of inquisitive onlookers where they worked, who often enough stooped to picking up souvenirs, the change could go unnoticed if the handler was the least bit judicious about what went missing from a site.

On the other hand, following Mawuli's journey through Midway increasingly appeared to be futile, producing more questions than answers. The more he thought about the images he'd seen on the security records, the more certain he became that Mawuli did not have the virus with him.

For all that his encounter with the Nsfera had put Ben Lawada into a deeply foul mood, it didn't mean he couldn't follow up on his task. And fortunately, the civilian wing of the hospital had a pretty lax sense of security. It was there to heal the sick and repair the wounded. It did not expect to be attacked. Finding Mawuli was the work of a few minutes.

Getting to him, on the other hand, was a bit more complicated.

He seemed to be worse off than Lawada had imagined, given that the last time he saw him, Mawuli was walking and could talk, even though he seemed a bit confused. Lawada thought he'd be more or less okay by now.

An unmoving bundle on a hospital bed, he was surrounded by care-bots and technicians and police people, and an actual physician looked in while Lawada watched, trying to work out a way to bypass all that.

A care-bot rolled up to him. *Can I help you?* flashed on its screen.

What the hell, Lawada thought. "That's my friend," he said. "Is he going to be all right? Can I get in to see him?"

The bot consulted its data for that patient. *Your friend is suffering the aftereffects of a concussion. Security restrictions are in place. What is your name, please?*

"Bill Smith," Lawada said.

I am sorry, Bill Smith is not on the cleared list. You will need to apply at Administration for clearance.

"Right, I'll do that then."

To your left, fourth door on the left.

"Okay, thanks." Why did he thank a machine, he wondered. *The stupid thing is going to watch me and make sure I go to the right place.*

He started off down the indicated hallway. About halfway,

he looked back. The machine had gone on about its business. *Good.*

But it didn't help him with his problem.

He could barge in, but that would likely get him nothing but arrested.

He could wait until local night when the people went off shift, but the bots never did, so that wouldn't work.

He meandered over to a visitors' lounge and called Assiffah.

When Assiffah had heard his idea, he said Lawada's plan would cost a great deal since it seemed that he, Assiffah, would end up damaged or in jail, and possibly both.

Lawada contacted Michael and told his boss he had found Mawuli but that the Orian was inaccessible at the moment in the hospital. "'Security restrictions are in place,' according to the bot. What do you want me to do?"

"How much has he told the police?"

"Don't know. He's either sleeping or unconscious. I can't get close enough to be sure."

"Don't tell me you are baffled by a medical robot." Michael was feeling particularly cranky.

"Damned right. They're built tough, they can get as much help as they need at a moment's notice, and they're armed with needles and sprays and who knows what drugs. And there's more than one. But I do have an idea. It's going to take a bit of money."

"Every time I want you to do something, you want money."

"Yeah, that's kinda how it goes."

———

LATER, at night, Assiffah brought a friend, a Sgat he said was knowledgeable about hospital circuitry and electronics. The first thing the Sgat did was deploy a gadget it said would neutralize the sensors. It bought the machine from a Rigan, it said, who stole it from a Kazi, who had no more use for it on account of being dead. It was an odd-looking thing, and Lawada had his doubts.

Then the Sgat considered the care-bots. "About this kind bots, programmed for pay attention to certain things, which are many. For miscellaneous, like what's on floor, no cycles left over. That's for cleaner bots, right."

"Okay. So?"

"So, for doing job of you, first to know is how long for help to arrive if one distressed."

"And then?"

"Then make brain freeze, yes? CO_2 cartridge we drop underneath and freeze small electronic brain. Now is known you how long for work."

Lawada frowned.

"Down near wheels is processor, right. Gears and mechanical and instruments and supplies in top of housing. First task you and Assiffah to make bot stop in right place. 'Kay?"

"You think this'll work?"

"Not first time doing so, I. Rogue bots not so rare. Take this you."

It looked like one end of an electrical cable.

"Across hall is making test run. Clock you have?"

Assiffah ducked into a bedroom, came back, and threw a sheet over Lawada and one over himself. "Ffor the ssenssorss." The Sgat looked a little annoyed. "Can not hurt to be ssaffe, yess?"

Lawada pulled part of the sheet over his head like a hood, but he didn't feel adequately disguised. Across the hall, Assiffah and Lawada each took an end of the cable, laid it on the floor, yanked it up to tip over the first bot that came by, then scrambled down the hall to see how long help took to arrive.

It took a discouragingly short time.

"Damn," Lawada said. "Looks like all we'll have time to do is snatch the guy and work out what to do with him later. No time for questions, for sure."

"All ready?" asked the Sgat.

The unlikely-sounding procedure went surprisingly well. Lawada walked up to the bot in question, and as before. it stopped him. *Nothing has changed* came up on the screen. Meanwhile, Assiffah knocked on its other side like an impatient visitor, and the Sgat rolled the CO_2 cartridge between the bot's wheels. A sudden white cloud and an aborted beep, and Lawada walked past the bot to where Mawuli lay.

Now what? Lawada wondered. *Boy, sometimes you ought to think these things all the way through to the end.*

He threw a sheet over Mawuli and tried to pick him up. Mawuli roused a little and peered out from under the sheet as Lawada worked to get him over his shoulder.

"Ben Lawada. You are doing?"

"It's okay, just relax."

Surprisingly, Mawuli did to some degree.

Assiffah came, urging speed. "Bugger's heavy," Lawada complained. "Something with wheels would be good."

"Hass no time."

Sure enough, buzzing and clicking were emanating from the bot. Lawada staggered past it with his burden and on into the hall.

"Hhere," Assiffah said and guided him toward another room.

But before Lawada could get there, there was Ehreh, right in their path. Ratty-looking and bent, he barely seemed to be holding himself together, swaying just to stand.

"Ben Lawada, you are here for what reason?" His voice rasped. "Hanging head downward is not good for Mawuli. He is suffering from a concussion."

"Get out of the way," Lawada said.

"No."

Assiffah came hurrying up. He gave Ehreh a shove, and the old man collapsed as if his bones had turned to dust. "Now go, now," the Roothian insisted.

But it was too late. Rescuers were arriving from every quarter, and they were soon surrounded by people and bots.

Ehreh, carried a few doors down the hall as if he were made of soap bubbles, and Mawuli, gently returned to his room, were the rescuers' priority, but Lawada and Assiffah were not neglected by any means. By the time anyone thought to look for the Sgat, it was gone, taking its gadgets with it.

The Constabulary arrived and took Assiffah and Lawada into custody. Lawada demanded to speak to Michael Martin. The police officer told him if he could provide information about Martin's whereabouts, they would be happy to put him in contact.

Aroull arrived back at the hospital just in time for all the excitement. He looked in on his two charges. Ehreh had been sedated. Mawuli was awake and trying to explain something to the care-bot in attendance, which had a hypo poised, about to administer some medication.

Aroull told it to wait. "Mawuli, you are further injured?" Aroull asked.

"No. No. I remember. Aroull, I need to tell you, Harl has the virus."

"Harl? That is odd."

"I think she was going to bring it here. She has come?" Still struggling with his memory, Mawuli looked distressed.

"I will inquire."

Standing at the bedside, Aroull got in touch with the delegate's office and let Mawuli listen in on the conversation. After some discussion, he could talk to Murr, and he asked her if Harl had come with her.

"No. She said she would go home to her family. They are near Owr-Lakh, I believe."

"Aroull, something is not right here," Mawuli said. "Something else happened at the Academy."

"You had no companion with you?" Aroull asked Murr.

"Raish. What are you seeking, Aroull?"

"A small aluminum box," Aroull said, thinking he was becoming quite adept at being truthful without being honest. "Mawuli thought Harl would bring it here."

"I have seen no such thing. I will ask Raish. I do not understand why Mawuli would think Harl would come here, she who never wants to leave home, an attitude I am appreciating more and more as time goes on. I came here at considerable inconvenience to bring Ehreh back to Orion and find Mawuli and recover the virus, and so far, all I have been able to do is answer unreasonable questions."

"Events do not always proceed the way we would prefer."

Murr sniffed.

"Ehreh is here in the hospital. He is in no condition to travel."

"You might have said so earlier." Murr broke the connection.

Well, Aroull thought, *Harl had tried to contact Ehreh. An inquiry might be worthwhile.*

MIDWAY—DOCKSIDE

Mercury's Daughter turned out to be a trim little vessel, but "little" was the operative word. Lauren was willing to use Stanton Clough's name with a right good will to get her outfitted. Almost everyone on Midway knew him, and many owed him something, so items in short supply, like extra-bright battery-powered hand-held lights, became suddenly available. Not cheap, however.

Captain Kiri Narang had been more helpful than Lauren had reason to expect. The captain held business meetings in the Dockside Bar in the mornings when the place was empty of everything except cleaner-bots washing away the smell of old beer, erasing the stains of the previous night's fun, gathering together forlorn chairs and tables, tidying as best they could before evening came and messed it up again. Efficient through long experience, over the noise of the bots, she made suggestions, helped Laura find things, cautioned her about what to avoid, and calmed her down when the task seemed overwhelming. Members of the crew came and went.

But today, she had a more serious point to discuss.

"Sit down for a moment. We have some issues with the Port

Authority. They are routing all traffic away from the Ferguson system."

Lauren stared at the captain. "Did they say why?"

Narang shook her head. "There's some non-zero chance they'll shoot us down if we try to take off without clearance."

"So, how do we get clearance?"

Narang straightened her back and stretched. She could see this job slipping away from her. "To a place where the Fleet is about to set up a no-go zone? I'm thinking we plain and simply don't."

"Jeez, really? Kaz come and go, and nobody does anything. Here we are out to save the day for God, motherhood, and apple pie, and they'll shoot us down?"

"Don't take it personally. It's the military, and they don't play nice with people who don't do what they say. No matter what our reason, we're not going to get approval for a flight plan to Ferguson Prime without divine intervention. And yeah, I'd really like to know how the Kaz have been sneaking under the radar, so to speak." She smiled a little. "Could be useful now and then. I'm sorry. I really should have thought of this sooner. Usually, it's just routine."

Lauren was quiet for a long time. She tried to think of a way around this new, enormous obstacle. "I wonder if Stanton Clough has any friends with the Port Authority."

"Now would be a good time to find out."

"Yeah."

The captain raked her fingers through her short grey hair and came to a risky decision. "We could file a flight plan to the Eta Circini system instead and hope the big boys don't track us. Same initial trajectory into hyperspace, just twenty or so light years short on a wider arc."

"It's not legal."

"No."

"Well, how much more trouble can we be in?" Lauren said.

"Me? A lot. But my guys have to eat, and *Mercury's Daughter* is too expensive to keep as a hobby, and I don't like Kaz."

"Okay, if you're willing, let's do that. Eta Circini, here we come. I'll see if I can find Clough and get us some official sanction."

She stood up, intending to go look for Clough, but she got distracted. John Kim was approaching. Lauren was actually glad to see him. She thought she might like to hug him just for the comfort of it, but she restrained herself. She left the bar and met him at the entrance.

"Bit early in the day?" he asked.

"It's where our captain does business." They walked across the dock area toward the shuttle bay.

"Are we making progress?" he asked.

"I don't know," Lauren said. "Nobody seems to know where Ehreh is, and we still don't have the virus. Getting us off Midway without a flight plan apparently invites the Fleet to shoot us down, but filing for one is a problem. So, I'm thinking not so much. We could be working our butts off for nothing."

"Can I help?"

"Jeez, I hope so. I need help. I don't know what I'm doing here."

John walked around the pile waiting for the shuttle to carry it up to *Mercury's Daughter*. "Whoa. How long are you planning to be on Fergie Prime?" he asked, eyeing a big barrel of water.

"If we don't encounter complications, probably a day or two. Depending on how thorough Nathan has been getting the settlement packed up and away, I think we should take everything with us we need to survive. Life-support facilities will likely be shut down. And I'm thinking it won't hurt to maintain a margin of error. Sunscreen, damn, don't forget a bucketful of class-A sunscreen," Lauren said. "And Nathan. I need to talk to Nathan. He needs to hold up the fireworks until we get there. I wonder if he or Marc can pick up my belongings?"

"Hold on. Take a deep breath."

"Don't you get patronizing with me, John Kim."

"Don't you be so touchy. Take this as you will from someone who knows a little about spacecraft, okay?"

Lauren did take a deep breath. "Yeah, okay, sorry. I'm as tense as a Caparan on tax day."

"Okay. So, you do realize this little ship won't lift a lot of mass, don't you? I think you're going to have to scale your plans back quite a bit, limit the number of people, and cut your margin for error razor-thin. You don't need the whole gang for this. Two or three people, quick in, quick out. No hanging around, no camping out, no picking up souvenirs."

"Oh." Lauren looked blank for a few moments while her vision of a dozen or more of Ehreh's group spreading out like Vandals over the mine site, wreaking as much havoc as possible, was pared away to a couple of ninjas setting their trap and fleeing the scene. "Damn."

But that approach would immediately solve a number of supply and space problems . . .

"I guess you're right," she admitted. And, a cooling thought, if worse came to worst, and they got stranded on Fergie Prime, it would also limit the loss. "Don't look so smug," she said to John. "Anybody can be right once. Okay, then, Plan B. Three or four people. How do we decide who should go?"

"I have some suggestions. Just don't jump all over me, okay?"

"Mm."

"You have to go; you know your way around Fergie Prime. I'm going. I think we should take Ryet."

"Ryet?"

"It will be valuable as a scout. No Oriani. They would have to discuss every step along the way, and it would take much too long."

"I'm not so sure about Ryet. It's kind of crazy. We could discuss the plan with the Oriani before we left."

"You know that's not how they work."

"I wish we had more time. Planning on the fly is not what I do well. And I have this other thing that's bothering me. I need to talk. I really need to talk to somebody, preferably human, so I don't have to tiptoe around alien sensibilities."

"Well, don't knock yourself out with all that flattery."

"Oh. John, no, I didn't mean it like that. Anyway, can you discuss the change of plans with Captain Narang? You two can work out what all we need with us. I need to get everybody not busy with something else to look for Ehreh and Mawuli. Unless we find them, none of this matters. I should find someone who has connections on Orion to try to find out if Mawuli actually left to come here. Let's not be chasing ghosts."

"We have a few Oriani on Midway to choose from. You need to settle down and think a little. Flying off in all directions at once won't get anything done; you're going to end up with some kind of anxiety disorder or something."

"You're a psychologist on your days off, Carl Sigmund Kim?"

Kim shook his head. "Come down to the cafeteria. I'll buy you a coffee, and you can talk to me. If that'll help."

"It would," she said. "It really would."

HE BROUGHT HIS THERMOS AGAIN. They sat in the same corner of the cafeteria they had used last time. Lauren remembered to avoid the wonky chair. She started out with a jittery feeling about how she was spending the time but settled after a bit.

"What did you want to talk about, then? Or are you just here for the coffee? I'm not the guy who can tell the Fleet to stand down if that's what you're thinking. They refuse to listen to me." He regarded her sober face and added, "That's a joke, you see."

"Yeah." Lauren was quiet for a moment. "Could we talk about something else?"

"Sure."

"Here's a question: if you knew someone had done something utterly illegal but had maybe done everyone a favour in the process, would you feel obliged to tell the authorities about it?"

"Wow, talk about a change of subject. And a really vague question. Depends, I guess."

"On what?"

"Well, to start with," John scratched his chin, "did anyone get hurt?"

"Yeah, someone died."

There hadn't been many deaths on Midway lately. "Are you telling me you know that someone killed the Kazi? Do you know who?"

"Yeah, I do. But I don't know what to do about it."

John studied her. There was more to the story, he was sure. No one would normally be that upset about a dead Kazi, not even other Kaz.

"I know who killed the Kazi, John. I don't know how or why yet, but I know who."

"Have you told the police?"

"No."

"You probably should, so they don't go on wasting time and resources trying to find an answer you already know."

"It doesn't feel right."

"Because?"

"I can't prove it."

"That's their job, isn't it?"

"I guess." Lauren inhaled the fragrance from her cup.

Coffee at its best was a wonderful thing. No wonder humans planted it wherever they went.

"So?"

"Will they prosecute the killer, do you think? I mean, who really cares about a dead Kazi? Shouldn't we be cheering?"

"If that's what you think, why did you take the job?"

"I was bored. And they offered money. That sounds bad, but I'm hard up against it, John. Home and family seem farther and farther away all the time." She kept her eyes on the coffee cup, thinking she was saying more than she wanted to. "They should give it a medal," she muttered mostly to herself. "I don't want to sic the whole local law enforcement apparatus on the guy if I'm not a hundred percent sure."

"You're never going to be that sure."

"True."

"If you tell the perpetrator you know, maybe he would turn himself in."

"Maybe. Or maybe it would eat me. We'd lose a member of our team."

"Ryet Arkkad."

"I didn't say that. I probably shouldn't even be talking to you about this. You are the authorities."

"No, just a warrior in the field, lady. And I'm on the shit list anyway, given I've been working with the Oriani, contrary to established policy. Is this why you don't want it to go to Fergie Prime?"

"No." Lauren reconsidered. "Yeah, maybe. I don't know. Too much has happened, John. I don't know what I think."

"Let's talk to Ryet. Get this done. Get a load off your mind."

"If we use the communications system, everyone will hear about it."

"I think you're making excuses, but okay, let's go find it for a face-to-face. If it tries to take a bite, I'll shoot it."

She looked at him in alarm.

"Joking. Just joking."

RYET WAS HANGING around the docks, as it often was. As far as it was concerned, most of the interesting life on Midway occurred there, where the collisions of dissimilar objects produced unpredictable results. This was, however, a quiet afternoon, relatively speaking. Leaning against a wall near the Dockside Bar, it had found nothing to catch its attention until it realized it had been watching a human who appeared to be utterly lost and uncertain as she went from place to place, trying to talk to people but having no success.

It watched her suffer for a few minutes longer, then ambled over to offer its services.

"You seem to be having some difficulty. Can I help?"

The human turned to look at him, and her face became a mask of alarm. She backed away and stumbled into a Turgorn, who grunted at her and moved on. She squeaked something that Ryet didn't understand.

Ryet spotted *Mercury's Daughter*'s co-pilot and beckoned him over. "This person seems to be in trouble. I think she doesn't know Sindharr. Translate for us." The co-pilot started to bristle, but Ryet remembered the magic word. "Please."

"Right now, she's jabbering about a demon from hell."

Flattering in its own way, I suppose, Ryet thought. "Ask her if there is something she needs. Try to look friendly."

"I'm going to friendly you a pop on the nose."

"That would not alleviate her consternation."

"Make me feel better, though." But he turned to the woman, and they spoke back and forth for a while.

"Her ex-husband threw her out of his house, she had already given up her hotel room, and she has to attend a funeral tomorrow. She needs a place to stay."

"Beatrix Clough."

The woman recognized her name in Ryet's hiss, but whether that made her more or less alarmed was hard to say.

"Find her something to eat and a drink of whatever intoxicants are favoured by your species. I will look into accommodations."

"You paying?"

"Yes."

"Why?"

"One can never tell what will come in useful."

"You're weird, Ryet Arkkad."

"I know. Isn't it wonderful? Celebrate diversity."

Shaking his head, the co-pilot led Beatrix to a nearby eatery. Ryet understood the man knew nothing of irony.

It talked to the person who ran a general store nearby and had an extra space he let out now and then. That settled, it returned to tell Beatrix. The co-pilot said to it, "She doesn't drink. Lucky you. I do, however, so not so lucky."

"You worry about the wrong things." Once it was confident Beatrix knew she had a place to stay and knew how to get there, it started away.

The co-pilot said, "She says to tell you you are kind."

"Okay."

Then it heard its own name and turned to see Lauren Fox and John Kim. They were often with one another these days. That was interesting. Something was brewing there.

"I need to talk to you," Lauren said.

"Please satisfy your need in any way you see fit."

"You're a nasty creature, Ryet Arkkad." The woman had changed colour slightly around the cheekbones.

"With a variety of personalities, it seems."

"You want to do this out in the open, or would you prefer some privacy?"

"Since I do not know the subject, a decision is difficult."

"A dead Kazi."

"A delicate topic, perhaps best kept among us. Come with me." Ryet led them a short way down a lane and into a tiny shop whose walls to the rafters were hidden by shelves filled with boxes and bottles and cans and canisters of condiments and spices from many worlds. The colours and smells were amazing. "This is one of my favourite places," Ryet said. It spoke to the person doing accounts behind a tiny counter, and the person closed up his machine and disappeared through a rear door barely visible among the shelves.

Lauren took a box down from a stack of them and tested it gingerly as a place to sit. John leaned against the stack. Ryet squatted on its heels. Its folded wings stuck up behind its head, giving it the look of a medieval gargoyle. "What do you have to say to me about a dead Kazi?"

"You killed it."

Ryet said nothing.

"The Constabulary has a record of you coming and going from the place the dead Kazi was found; they just don't know it's you. Yet. You need to tell them," Lauren said. "You need to tell the police you killed it."

"I do not. I did not." Ryet displayed its toothy grin. "Not directly. The argument might be made that I provided the means for the person who did kill it. I did not urge that individual to apply the means, however."

"Who is this person?"

"I do believe that that person was not aware of what he had done."

"How could he be that dumb?"

"Ignorance is rife in these worlds. Everyone should support a better system of education."

"Not funny, Ryet. Either you tell the police what you know, or I will tell them what I know."

"Threats and bargains? Considering the enterprise you are

embarked upon, flirting with the Constabulary is ill-advised. Considering your intention to destroy Kaz by the countless billions, harassing me over the demise of one strikes me as picayune."

"It's not the same thing," John said.

"Because war is different?"

"Well, yeah."

"Well, no. You think that government-sanctioned mass killing is morally good, but the unsanctioned death of one is evil? Between dead and dead is a subtle distinction I do not believe I understand. Bear in mind your project is not sanctioned by most governments, and, as it happens, the weapon you are about to deploy on Ferguson Prime is the weapon used to kill the individual here. Ehreh's virus is the cause of death of the Kazi in question."

"You're saying an Orian killed the Kazi?"

"No, John, I am not." Ryet stood up and stretched but made no effort to spread its wings in the confined space.

"But you know where the virus is."

"I know where a small sample of it used to be." It said to Lauren, "Mention the virus to your Turgorn friend, and he will think you are a genius. However, I suggest you do it from deep space because officialdom is currently pretending it knows nothing about the Orian plan, so it will have its wings in a twist if it is forced to admit knowledge, and all sorts of people will be caught in the outfall while it tries to divest itself of responsibility." Ryet turned and walked out of the shop.

"It didn't agree to anything," John said when it was out of sight.

"I think we hurt its feelings," Lauren said.

"I'm not sure it has feelings, but I am sure it is willing enough to manipulate the feelings of those that do," John said.

"Well, you talked me into this little encounter. Where do we go from here?"

"I don't know. Let me think about it awhile."

The proprietor returned from where ever he had been. "How do you know Ryet?" Lauren asked him, thinking to make polite small talk. She stood up and replaced the box on the stack.

"We have done each other favours now and then," the proprietor said and turned back to his accounting.

John and Lauren left the shop and headed back toward the dock. "Let's stop somewhere for food. I can't remember when I ate last."

CAPTAIN NARANG CAME to meet them when they arrived at the dock quite a bit later. She consulted the device in her hand. "Lauren, you are a popular person. Nathan wants you to call. Stanton Clough says he needs a word. Aroull has information for you. A police officer needs to get in touch, and you, madam, need either an implant or a secretary 'cause this here ain't in my job description."

"But you don't have an implant." John nodded toward the device in her hand.

Kiri Narang flipped her hair away from the socket behind her ear. She said to John, "One hole in my head is about all I want to cope with. I'm sure you understand."

"I guess I do."

"All righty, then," Lauren said, "seeing as I'm the only one here without a hole in her head, I vote we start with Aroull. Let's hope he has the information we need."

Aroull, answering his implant with typically Orian direct-ness, said, "I know the location of the missing item. Recovering it will be challenging."

"Where?"

"Open network," Aroull said.

"Yeah, okay. I'll get there as soon as I can."

Stanton Clough asked about her health and discussed the prognosis before saying he had been able to get a minor concession from the Port Authority. It was Lauren's turn to stop him and remind him that Midway's communication system was far from private.

"Damn. I'm beginning to believe ancient wired telephones had something to recommend them."

"Not going to help us much right now. Are you at home?"

"Yes, that's what they call this place."

"Mm. Can you stay there? I'll be around in a little while."

She thought that the talk with Kam Nok would be the most fraught, but he sounded happy to hear from her.

"I have had an interesting conversation with one Ryet Arkkad, who said it was your recommendation that sent it to talk to me. It gave me an odd story about how the Kazi died."

"Do you believe it?"

"Should I not? As much factual data as we have is not inconsistent."

"Are you satisfied the case is solved?"

"Yes. We can put it to bed. Thank you for your assistance."

Lauren told John what Kam Nok had said. "He's happy to be shut of it. I wonder what Ryet told them."

"Probably better not to know."

"Yeah. Come with me to talk to Clough, please. He's going to tell me something about how we're going to get off Midway, and I think you will understand that better than I will."

"Okay."

"Then we'll go on to see Aroull. He says he has discovered where the virus is but that it is going to be difficult to get our hands on it."

CLOUGH SEEMED disoriented when they got there and a bit dishevelled. "I miss Archie," he said. "I've become very reliant on the kid."

"Where is he?"

"In the clutches of the Civil Constabulary. He was a witness to the aftermath of a crime—they say an Orian was killed—and they've been questioning him ever since."

"Well, the good news is, the Orian isn't dead, he's recovering in hospital, and with luck, he will be able to tell his own story soon enough. That should let Archie off the hook."

"Good," Clough said, but without the enthusiasm Lauren expected. "Now, I have been speaking to a member of the committee overseeing port operations. If you can leave at exactly 12:55 after noon local time, when the Fleet will be busy doing its salute to Whitby," Clough paused, then carried on, "this person will attempt a temporary blur of focus over there, a small diversion, and you will have your best chance to slip away unchallenged while they are distracted. It's not much, but it might help a little."

"Not what I was hoping for," Lauren said when they left Clough, "but better than a kick in the head."

"Maybe Aroull will have better news. Why don't you go talk to him? I have some things I need to do."

"Yeah, okay." Lauren found herself feeling disappointed.

AROULL WAS TENDING Ehreh when she arrived at the hospital. To Lauren's unspoken question, he said, "He is near death. I will take him home soon."

"I'm sorry," Lauren said.

"You should not be. He has lived a long and fruitful life, and he is ready." Aroull spent a few moments instructing the care-bot and putting things away, then led them out of the room into the hallway.

Lauren leaned against the wall and closed her eyes briefly, feeling tired. Aroull whipped out an instrument to measure her respiration and temperature and peered into her eyes. "Come." He led her back to the room she had been occupying.

"What?"

"I want to be sure all the nanites in your system are idle."

"Is it likely some are not?"

"You are a unique case. I do not know the risk."

While he worked, Aroull said, "Mawuli is recovering bits of his memory, and one of the things he has remembered is that he was attacked at home, on Orion, near the Academy. This unheard-of occurrence stands out in his mind. Oriani simply do not attack one another."

"But it was an Orian who attacked him, not some other species."

"Mawuli is not certain. In some ways, an outsider would make more sense. In any case, because of this attack, which gave Mawuli to understand that he had become a target of those trying to prevent Ehreh from reaching his goal, he thought it wise to find another person to deliver the virus to Ehreh whom no one would suspect."

Aroull put his things away. "All is in order."

Lauren got off the bed and arranged herself, thinking she really needed to find some better clothes.

Aroull continued, "Mawuli and Harl concocted a rather baroque scheme in which Harl would plant the container on Murr after she had induced Murr to travel to Midway to confront Ehreh. Harl led Murr to believe Ehreh had the virus."

"It sounds like a freaking soap opera."

Aroull paused to parse that sentence. "I do not know what 'soap opera' is, but I have spoken to Harl. She said she put the virus in its container into the carryall Murr takes everywhere she goes."

"Wouldn't Murr have found it by now? What else is in the carryall that she wouldn't notice?"

"Harl believes some computational devices—Murr is a mathematician and fills idle time with work when she can— and some items of food since she did not know if suitable foods could be found on Midway. I understand she is quite selective about what she eats."

"And they actually expected this to work?"

"Harl and Mawuli are both young and not yet convinced that chance owes them no favours. If Murr has found the container, then we have lost. If she has not, we need to recover it."

"Will she give it to us?"

"I doubt she will. Her aim from the beginning has been to destroy it. We may have to apply some schemes of our own. You know where Ryet Arkkad is?"

"I don't think it's talking to me right now. We've had a bit of a disagreement."

"It will talk to me."

"It probably won't be hard to find. I have a question: Ryet claims that Ehreh's virus killed the Kazi that was found dead. If that's the case, don't we have a Kazi full of virus? Could we recover some from it if needs must?"

"If Ryet Arkkad is correct, the dead Kazi could be a source of the virus, though not in a readily dispersible form. Recovery and preparation would take some considerable time, with no guarantee of success, nor do we have access to the body."

"Yeah. Just thought I'd ask. Time is what I am rapidly running out of. We're supposed to take off after noon tomorrow. And I don't even know who Murr is or what she looks like. "

"I do. Let us find the Nsfera at once and see what can be done."

"Okay. Give me a few minutes. I need to call Ferguson Prime and see how they're getting on."

Nathan was slow to answer the phone. Lauren was afraid for a moment that he had already left, in which case she didn't know how she would accomplish the task. But he did come on, sounding breathless. He was nervous. Having made the commitment, he was anxious to be gone.

"Leave the demolition set up and tell me what button to push. I need the shaft open," Lauren said. Nathan dithered. "Listen, I know you don't think I'm the brightest light on the string, but I can push a button, okay?"

"Okay."

"Is Marc still there?"

"Yes."

"Ask him to pick up my stuff, okay?"

She looked over her shoulder to make sure Aroull wasn't watching over her shoulder, then prepared the message for Marc—encrypted: *see what you can dig out of your databases about Fleet Lieutenant John Kim, currently stationed on Midway, please and thank you.* She was not unaware of the irony.

Then, just as she was about to send it, she changed her mind. She had been outraged when he did this to her. How could she justify committing the same offence?

In the Orian delegate's office, Ihosh said Murr and Raish were out arranging Murr's passage back to Orion, and Murr was not pleased with the way things had turned out.

"Do you know if she has her carryall with her?" Lauren asked.

"I would think so. I have not seen her go anywhere without it."

"Does either of them have an implant?"

"No. Raish carries an external communications device. Your interest in these things is puzzling."

"Can you ask them to meet us somewhere?"

They met at the security gate as Murr and Raish were about to leave. Murr had her carryall with the strap over her shoulder and the bag tucked securely under her elbow.

She listened to Raish translate Lauren's request, and Lauren watched Murr draw herself up as if offended. "You want to go through my possessions?"

"All I want is for you to look and see if there is anything there you don't recognize. We are looking for a small metal box."

"For what reason?"

"It would satisfy you to know that it is important to a project we are working on?" Aroull asked.

"It would not."

Go for broke, Lauren told herself. "The box contains a quantity of Ehreh's virus. We need it."

Murr reacted with a little shudder of revulsion the way Lauren might if she had found a slug in her salad. She slipped the bag off her shoulder and began gingerly to look through it. Out of the corner of her eye, Lauren saw Ryet coming toward them, walking rather fast and studying the device in its hand. It bumped into Murr, apologized profusely, and helped her pick up some of the things that had jounced out of her hands. Then it went on its way.

Digging further into the bag's contents, Murr did not find a little metal box.

"It is not with me." She started putting things back in the bag.

"Okay, sorry to have bothered you. But there is one other thing."

"I do not believe I want to hear anything further from you. I do not wish to lose my place on this vessel."

"Just listen a minute. Aroull says you are a mathematician."

"Aroull is correct in this one instance."

Ryet was back, trying to interrupt. Raish asked it to wait. Ryet being the creature that it was, did not. "I wish to speak to this female," Raish translated, only because Murr asked. "Does this belong to you?" It held up a metal box. "It was on the floor near the wall there." One could imagine the box dropping from Murr's bag, sliding across the floor, and arriving at that spot.

"Give it to me," Lauren said.

"Do not. It belongs to me," Murr said. Ryet looked from one to the other as if trying to decide, then handed it to Murr.

"Again, my apologies."

Murr took it and tucked it into the bag.

"You're welcome," Ryet said. He wandered off toward the Dockside Bar.

Lauren closed her open mouth. There was nothing she could do short of wrestling Murr, a contest she was sure to lose.

"You had a question for me?"

But half-certain Ryet had given the box to Murr because it was annoyed with Lauren, she felt utterly defeated. She couldn't see the point of going on.

After a moment, Aroull said, "Solving this could save many lives, even if we are not able to defeat the Kaz."

"I guess. Okay. Yes, I have a mathematical problem. At least, I think it is. Would you look at it?"

Murr's own huffiness subsided a little as curiosity took over. She inclined her head. Lauren took that as being not outright rejection. She gave Murr the flimsy with the DoubleChek technicians' calculations. "We have discovered the Kaz are finding ways around our sensors. This has been offered as an explanation of how they are doing it. Does it make sense to you?"

Murr looked over the file for a minute or two. "Superficially, yes. I would need to study it more thoroughly to give a definitive answer."

"If it is what the Kaz are doing, can you devise a way to undo it, so to speak?"

Murr was still studying the file. It obviously interested her. "I might be able to suggest a theoretical approach. Transistors and wires are someone else's domain."

"That's great. If you could treat this as an industrial secret, my company, DoubleChek, will be very happy to pay for your time. I'll ask them to get in touch."

"Payment is not required."

"Donate the money to your Academy, then. Humans tend to value what they have to pay for."

Oriani can't smile. They don't have the facial muscles for it. But whatever Murr was doing, Lauren felt sure she was amused by the concept.

"Come," Aroull said. "We have places we need to be."

In the Dockside Bar, Ryet put two glass vials into Lauren's hand.

"I thought you were angry with me."

"I am not, however, suicidal."

YALLAH RULLENAHE INTERPLANETARY SECURITY SERVICE MILITARY GARRISON

Across the wall, in the commander's tidy office without Nes Gow listening in, the commander said, "I understand our little scheme is about to bear fruit."

"That's still uncertain, sir," Kim replied. "The Oriani seem to have mislaid their supply of the virus, and without it, nothing much can happen. If we stop them at this point, we don't have much to hold them on."

"I've always thought of the Oriani as a very well put together people. Not like them to lose something."

"I need to know something. What side of this are we on?"

The commander leaned back in the chair and brought a fist to his chin. "Good question. Our political masters are saying two contradictory things: one, that they know nothing about the Orian scheme; and two, that it is ill-thought-out, dangerous, unproven, ineffective, expensive and slow, and, of importance to politicians, contrary to the Community charter."

"That's a lot of contradictions," Kim said.

"Yeah. Personally, I think that if it has a chance to prevent a few casualties on our side of this business, even if it just distracts the Kaz for a while, it's worth pursuing. I don't see where there's much to lose if it fails. On the other hand, those with stock in the armaments trade have plenty to lose if it succeeds.

"I have kids in service. I'd say give the Oriani their chance."

"In that case," John said, "if the Oriani manage to find their virus, we need to give a pass to a vessel called *Mercury's Daughter*. And I want to go with it, so I'll need a reason to not be at the funeral tomorrow."

"We should be able to work something out. But if this goes sideways, I don't know you from a hole in the ground."

———————

THE NEXT DAY, people gathered, by invitation only, across the wall in for the funeral service being held in a small observation room. The attendees faced a floor to ceiling window that looked out over the launch site where the Fleet's 5th Battle Group was preparing the missing man formation.

The flimsy, folded into his pocket in spite of Archie's warning, dinged for Stanton Clough's attention. He stepped outside, against the flow of traffic, to answer. Bengit merondebar Bengit said, "I'm not going to ask for any kind of pass for that vessel, *Mercury's Daughter*."

Of course, you're not, Stanton thought. *I suspected as much.*

"It's been flagged three times already," Bengit went on. "There's something odd going on there, Clough. Should the committee be taking an interest?"

"Oh. Well, no, don't bother then. I guess it's being taken care of. Thanks."

"Sorry to hear about your boy, Stanton. That's a hard thing."

"Thank you. I appreciate you looking into this. I have to go now."

A bot came to the doorway to summon Clough inside. Stanton called Ryet and told it what he had just learned.

"How strange. I did not expect we would be afflicted by too many friends. "

"I have to go," Clough said.

"Of course. I will take care of this over-abundance of solicitude."

Inside the room, a preacher of unknown denomination droned on, obviously having never met any of the dead. But he did manage to remind Stanton Clough that two others had perished with his son, and that Walter and Amelia Brown, who sat next to him, were mourning their daughter Amy every bit as much as Stanton missed Whitby. Further along, four stiff-backed Lleveci were there for Tafillah Rullenahe. On his other side, Beatrix was holding together better than he expected she would. He had anticipated hysterics.

During a lull in the proceedings, Beatrix leaned toward Stanton and said, "Thank you for sending that strange person to rescue me yesterday. I don't know how I would have managed without it."

Stanton had no idea what she meant, but had the good sense to pretend he did. "You're welcome," he said. A minuscule chip broke off the iceberg between them, which would never thaw completely, but might become smaller and less debilitating. Then, beyond the observation window, the starships lifted with the obvious gap in the pattern and everyone got emotional.

⸻

ELSEWHERE, Midway Port Traffic Control was suffering a little anxiety because an official from the Port Authority had been hanging around, getting in the way, and questioning decisions.

When the call came, "*Mercury's Daughter*, preparing to lift off," the official said, "Tell them to wait."

"*Mercury's Daughter*, stand by." The icon for that vessel changed colour and a soft beeping commenced, reminding everyone that it was there and waiting. The AI on the job asked for instruction.

"*Mercury's Daughter*, standing by," the ship's captain repeated.

The chief controller came across the floor. "What?" she demanded. They had very little traffic this morning. The AI indicated it had deferred to the official. The chief glared at him.

"There has been so much chatter about that ship--that Rosshay on the oversight committee, the Terran delegate, the base commander, all kinds of people have suggested *Mercury's Daughter* is special and shouldn't be interfered with. I want to know what the shit is going on here."

"With that much brass behind her, we should probably let her go. She has an approved flight plan for Eta Circini."

"Why would it want to go there?"

"None of my business, nor yours either. Unless you can give me a good reason not to, I'm going to let them go."

To the pilot, who was serving as second for this journey, Kiri Narang said, "What's that all about?" Behind them, the passengers muttered among themselves. Everybody on the little ship was holding his breath, metaphorically speaking, half-expecting the Port Authority to refuse to let them leave.

The pilot shrugged. "They'll tell us soon enough."

"*Mercury's Daughter*, please say who is aboard."

"*Mercury's Daughter*, who is aboard. Kiri Anna Narang, captain, Jagadish Chandra Bose, second, Lauren Fox, John Kim, Ryet Arkkad, passengers."

There was a hissy little silence for a moment, then Traffic Control said, "*Mercury's Daughter*, you are cleared for Eta Circini. Have a good trip."

"*Mercury's Daughter*, cleared for Eta Circini. Thank you, Control."

The little bump as the engine came on was a relief for everyone.

FERGUSON PRIME

They came out of hyperspace with the twin stars blindingly bright, one on either side, and a little residual speed in roughly the right direction. The pilot was about to ask about the early exit, since they would have a bit of a haul to reach Fergie Prime, but he didn't get the chance.

"Shit," the captain said, and everyone was sure bad things were happening, because Kiri Narang just did not use that kind of language.

"'Sup?" the pilot asked.

"AI dumped us into space normal. We've got no sensors."

"Nothing?"

She showed him a screen with two bright spots representing the stars and a scattering of lesser stuff. "IR," she said. "That's all."

"Space is mostly empty. With a little luck..."

"In the region of a double star system where two big boys have been spitting at each other for a billion years, not so much. And as your average Orian would say, luck's a poor thing to depend on."

"What's the plan, then?"

"Good question. Running an obstacle course blind isn't a fun game. Sitting here isn't going to save us either. If we don't run into something, something is liable to run into us."

"I have a suggestion," Kim said.

"Give it up, man."

"If you mask the stars, you could increase gain until you can see the IR emission from the larger, warmer bodies. We can at least avoid the big stuff. Get in behind something big and follow in its wake until we figure out a strategy," Kim said."

The captain instructed the AI and gradually, with a little experimentation, the stars were reduced to dull spots and a host of lesser IR sources appeared on the screen. She and the pilot tried to map them to the chart of the system in the navigation display tank.

"It's not all trash they teach you guys in the Fleet. Okay, cowboy, any other ideas? Are we just going to cross our fingers and wing it?" Narang asked. "We're about a light year out. Short hyperspace jump. Long, long way in normal space."

"Any way I can think of to get from here to there is risky."

"Can you communicate with Fergie Prime? If they've been evacuating, they must have a usable route," Lauren said.

"Or there are a lot of dead ones. Jag, see if you can raise them. Tell them what our situation is, ask about a safe course, nav markers, ephemera."

"We got a f--, a blasted auto-responder. Some data, orbital parameters. All we're going to get, I think." The pilot entered the new data into the nav tank. "Overriding the AI," Narang said. Following in the wake of some chunk of rock, they built up speed.

"Okay, everybody hold your breath."

"You think that will help?" Lauren asked.

"Nope. But if you die, you'll think you suffocated and your ghost won't blame me."

Two of those disorienting little twists in space-time in and out of hyperspace came almost on top of one another, and then Fergie Prime was there, covering most of the visual field.

"That's just too close," Kiri Narang muttered to herself. "Nothing from the ground. Guess nobody's home. We'll have to land our baby all by ourselves"

The pilot tapped an indicator on the board in front of him. "We got fuel on the surface?"

"Better hope so."

"Any Kaz down there?"

"Better hope not."

⸻

LAUREN DIDN'T THINK she had forgotten how hot it could be on Fergie Prime, but even in the ship's shadow the heat, reflected from the landing pad and supplemented by the heat of the ship's engine, hit her like a wall when she stepped out onto the surface. Her eyes watered in the blaring sunlight. The wind made the heat seem hotter, and past the landing pad, dust devils whipped the dirt around. Ferguson B was setting. Ferguson A was still an hour or more above the horizon.

A hundred or so metres away, the buildings that served the port looked shuttered. Declan's van was parked there.

"Is that-- ?" John asked, pointing to the dark stain and a pile of debris a kilometre or so along, the scar that the *Senator Alice Hester* had made as she fell out of the sky. The wind had begun to scour it away. No effort had been made to recover the dead. The dune building up over the wreckage would become their memorial. John stood quietly for a moment, biting his lip.

For once having nothing much to say, Ryet had come out to stand on the pad, turning this way and that, moving away from the others and finally extending its wings to test the air, then just lifting off the ground like a big black kite, finding the air currents it wanted with a few heavy flaps and sailing away.

"Wow," Narang said. "I never thought I'd actually see that. Where's it going?"

"Don't know," Lauren said.

"Oh." Narang obviously considered this a failure of leadership. "Well, you guys better get going, do what you have to do," she said. "I'm going to look for fuel and a bit more in the way of navigational aids so we can actually get out of here when the time comes."

Lauren said, with much more confidence than she felt, "We shouldn't take more than three or four hours, if everything goes according to schedule."

"Yeah, nothing ever does," Narang said. "We'll be here for as long as it takes, unless, and I'm going to say it right up front, if it even looks like any Kaz are about to show up, we're gone, and you're on your own."

"Are you sure you want to hang around? Did Ryet--"

"Never mind Ryet. I know guys like that. I'll get my due out of it, one way or another. You're trying out a way to beat the Empire. I'm willing to do my bit to help."

"Isn't staying on the ground dangerous for you?"

"Yeah, but what the shriek isn't these days."

Lauren thought she should offer some expression of appreciation, but didn't know what to say so instead she climbed back into the ship and picked up her backpack then said to John, "Let's go see if Declan's crappy vehicle will go."

"Don't we need a code or something to get in?" John asked as they came up to it. Lauren waved her arm in the empty window space. "Probably not. Getting the engine to start is another matter. The system won't recognise us as legitimate drivers." Dust was everywhere. A miniature sand dune had built up on the back seat.

"My Dad had a machine something like this. Allow me to offer the fruits of a misspent youth." John found his way into the engine compartment, fiddled around for a while, and got it going. "You drive," he said.

They sped down the road between the port and the mining town, disrupting the fingers of dirt sneaking out onto the tarmac as Fergie began to reclaim its territory.

The town was deadly quiet and exhaled an abandoned air. But by the time they had reached the office, some snarly little drones had lifted off from the roof of the building and were buzzing around overhead.

"Tell me those things aren't armed," John said.

"Don't know. They're new to me. But we can hope they recognise Declan's van, unless Howerath was out to get every-body." They waited, baking inside the vehicle.

In a few minutes the drones buzzed off and Lauren and John felt a little safer about getting out.

The office door was locked, the window boarded up.

"I hope Nathan didn't think door locks were going to keep the Kaz out." Lauren picked up her backpack and looked around inside the vehicle. "Do we have burglary tools at hand?"

"Got a blaster on my belt."

"Seems like overkill."

"Yeah?"

"Like getting a backhoe to dig the flower bed, but, hey, this no time to be refined and delicate."

The door didn't stand much of a chance.

The room was dark with the window covered over, the only light coming in through the doorway. It was much emptier than when she last saw it. Most of the equipment she had comman-deered to study the sensor records back then was gone. The big screen had gone back to the process monitor. All the displays were dark, indicator lights out. The AI was still there, encased in a protective box now, with a smiley face drawn on it, displaying Marc's sense of humour.

It was so quiet. Creepy quiet. No movement, no fans, no motors, no beep and bop of gadgets trying to get attention.

"What are we looking for?" John asked.

"Mine access control override. And the detonator for the explosives in the shafts."

"No power in here, you've noticed."

"Some essential units have a back-up power supply of their own." Lauren poked a button, hoping Nathan hadn't prudently pulled the power packs out of everything. A display came up with a rough map of the mine and a limited number of options for action on backup power. It showed both the access points sealed. "I'm thinking we should work in the number two and three shafts, which was where we found the Kaz before."

"Okay."

She swiped the icon of the man-sized door in the entrance building and got a green light.

Noise, sudden, a lot of it, on the roof. Startled, she ducked like a scared rabbit.

John was at the door, weapon in hand, looking up.

Ryet dropped down in front of him. It had one of the drones, a little worse for the encounter, in its hand. "These things have no sense of self-preservation."

"It's a machine, Ryet. And you need to look after your own self-preservation. You almost got shot."

Ryet tilted its head at John like a bird eyeing a snack. "Really."

"Yeah, really."

Ryet shook the dust out of its wings and folded them away, and by then its annoyance had dissipated. John put his gun away. "Kaz have been to the mine site, and recently. A small group, I think. An advance party? Their tracks have not blown away yet. I don't know if they have been into the mine itself. I did not see any open doors and I did not see any Kaz on the ground."

"Well, I just opened a door for them," Lauren said.

"Why?"

"We need to get in there. I didn't think the Kaz would be here yet. I really thought they'd wait for winter."

"And you didn't think to wait for your scout's report?"

Caught off guard, Lauren sputtered.

"Who knew, Ryet?" John said. "You just took off."

Ryet eyed John again, but then continued, "I saw signs of preparations to begin excavation, possibly habitat. I admit I was unwilling to get too close."

"You think they have weapons with them?"

"They are well inside IPC space. They will be prepared to defend themselves." Ryet said.

"So what do we do? We can wait for dark. I think we will only need a few minutes once we're in." Lauren found her backpack and passed bags of water around. "But we are close to the pole. The night is short at this time of year."

"How long until dark?" John asked.

"Less than an hour until Ferguson A sets. Full dark will be awhile after that." Stepping into the inner office, she found what she needed, sitting in the middle of Nathan's desk with her name on it. "Meanwhile, we could go see if Declan left anything for us in the bar."

"Do you think that's a good idea?"

"John, my friend, not one damned thing about this enterprise is a good idea. I'm still not fully my old self; I need a rest and it's not so hot in there."

Ryet declined their invitation. It took to the sky.

———

Breaking into Declan's bar was no harder than breaking into Howerath's office. The silence of it was equally disconcerting. Lauren found a bottle of red wine in the back room that was closer to blood heat than a wine should be, but, she thought, burglars can't be choosers.

John brought glasses from behind the bar that was already beginning to show signs of neglect. The brass that wasn't brass was looking a lot like plastic. Modern illusions erode fast, Lauren thought. They need constant attention.

They dusted off a table near the back of the room and sat quietly with the wine for a time. Then John said, "Since you don't have any excuse to run away for the next few minutes, tell me about the homicide charge on your record."

"What? Why do you want to know? I don't want to talk about it."

"Who died?"

"Beau Merriweather."

"Hanna's father?"

Lauren nodded.

John waited patiently. After a long moment, Lauren said, "I shot him. I guess you already know I was exonerated. Justifiable, they said. Public freaking service, I'd say. I was charged, went through the process, and came out of it free and stony broke. That's the wonderful thing about the Terran justice system. Even if you're innocent as a lamb--I wasn't--you're screwed."

"What did Merriweather do to you?"

"Plenty. But it was what he did to Hanna that was the straw. I really don't want to talk about it. You were right; wine wasn't a good idea. It's probably time for us to get moving."

THEY STARTED off for the mountains after sunset. Declan's van didn't have good headlights; they were yellow and dim and one was directed toward the wheels and the other out toward the horizon. As twilight faded, the track went from sandy to rocky, and progress was slow as they bounced over stones. Squatting in the back to accommodate its wings, Ryet suffering the most, its wing joints banging against the roof every now and then. It complained, but suggestions that it fly or walk were met with flinty silence.

They stopped the car between hills a kilometre or so away from their destination and scrabbled overland from there, trying not to raise too much dust and hoping to not attract Kazi attention. Again, Ryet had the worst of it, stumbling along from stubbed toe to banged ankle. It occurred to Lauren that it couldn't see as much as humans could by starlight.

The structure at the entrance to the mine was a bulky darker shadow against the shadow of the hill it was built into. Designed for security rather than beauty, without windows and with only one big overhead door for machinery, and a smaller person-sized door along side, it looked much like a prison. The lights that would normally flood the area were dark. That was good. It meant that the Kaz wouldn't be active around the outside of the building and also that they hadn't become well enough organised yet to put up their own lights. Other big shadows in the night were likely the Kazi machinery Ryet mentioned, being made ready as the Kaz prepared to dig in.

They squatted down behind a line of boulders, some of the first stone taken from the mine when it was being built. The fifty metres between this rock wall and the entrance had been kept flat and clear.

"Are they inside?" John asked.

"The small door should be open. I don't see any light from there."

"Alarms and so forth?"

"The sensors are out of commission. That's why I was here in the first place."

"We going in?"

"Let's wait a minute. The mine is full of bots, some AIs, that the Kaz could reprogram as guards."

"You said we didn't have much time." John picked up a handy-sized stone and threw it in the direction of the entrance. It flew and bounced about half way across the flat area. Nothing happened.

"Okay, let's get this done." Lauren tried to sound more confident than she felt. All the hairs on her neck prickled as they crossed the flat ground. She half expected a Kazi to jump up and say "boo".

Closer to the structure, it was darker, and Lauren was relieved when they passed through the door and she could fish around in her backpack for her light and switch it on. She turned it up to max and swung it around, examining the space. It was a higher, broader construction than one might have expected to be carved out of the rock, and better finished, with several interior doors, and several arched passages leading off under the mountain.

"Close the door," John said.

"I'm trying to figure out how to do that."

"I thought you knew your way around here."

"I've never been in the mine before. I worked in the office."

"Great."

She found a panel covered in icons of one kind and another, and two of them had appropriate looking arrows printed beside them, so she punched one and the door slid shut. Near the panel, a map of the facility was on a display set into the wall, and around them the walls were well supplied with direction signs.

Lights came on, a dim, dotted line down the tunnels. Backup lighting. Near another wall panel, Ryet smiled.

"We good?" John asked.

"Ventilation fans?"

"Would they be set up at each dig as it's worked?"

"Maybe. Let's look."

The tunnel slanted gently downhill. The floor changed from dressed stone to packed dirt. In a hundred metres or so, it bifurcated, one branch labeled #1 and the other #2. They followed the #2 tunnel. A little way in a bay had been dug into the wall and a tractor and a pair of general purpose bots were parked there. The control panel this time was just screwed onto a support and the conduits attached to the ceiling alongside thick bundles of pipes. The display wasn't lit. Lauren poked the icon with two blades beside a group of short lines anyway.

Gradually a tangible flow of air built up.

"Where do you want to put the stuff?"

"Where they're working, I guess."

"That could be many kilometres away."

"It didn't look that far on the diagram in the front."

"Okay, let's get going. Time's awasting."

They trotted along the tunnel which now showed ruts on the floor and grooves on the walls made by the mining machines. It wasn't long before Lauren couldn't trot any more, so then they walked. They passed the place where #3 branched off, after which the slope was steeper, and Lauren thought it was much longer than it should have been from the map. They came to little piles of rubble, then chunks of rock and then finally to the end wall. A digger had stopped there, left to fend for itself when the miners evacuated.

"How are we going to do this so the virus doesn't just blow back out with the exhaust?" Lauren wondered aloud as she dug one of the glass vials out of her backpack.

Ryet paced around a bit, up to the end wall and back around the rubble and forward again. "Air flows from here downward," it pointed at a vent near the roof, "along the floor turbulently, and up at that grate. Spread your powder near the top of the end wall for maximum distribution. We should turn the fans off when we leave."

Lauren thought about how to get up there. "You do not need to be neat," Ryet said. "Just throw it."

She did, hard because the glass felt thick. It shattered nicely about two thirds of the way up."

"On to the next," John said. He was getting nervous. The idea of a short night, a long tunnel, and Kaz wasn't sitting easily.

"Give me a minute to catch my breath," Lauren said.

"One minute."

The #3 shaft was mercifully shorter, but unfortunately steeper, than #2, but the process was the same. Climbing back up left Lauren breathless. "Wait." She panted while the cramp in her diaphragm eased.

Back at the beginning of #2, she remembered to turn the ventilation off, stopped to rest, then continued along #1 and was about to go into the entry room when Ryet stopped her.

"What?"

"Kaz. Do you smell them?"

"No. My nose isn't that good. A lot?"

"More than one. Not a great many."

"Can we get by them?"

"I believe they are in one of the other main passages. But as I mentioned, the air flow is turbulent," Ryet said.

"We turned the fans off."

"It takes a few minutes to settle."

"Since they went down the wrong tunnel, I'm guessing their sensors don't work any better in here than ours do," Lauren said.

"Rejoice. We have a precious few minutes to gloat. We need to turn the lights out," Ryet said.

"Unfortunately, the control is in the wrong place"

"Can we cut the wiring?" John asked Lauren.

"I don't know, John. I don't know a lot more about this place than you do, really." She was scared herself now, and still panting too much to be answering a lot of questions.

"Come on," John said. They went back to the alcove. "Give me your light." He shone it onto the roof, following the conduits around the control box. "This one seems to be going to the entry."

"But the power supply could be on either side of it."

"Let's find out."

He climbed up on the tractor, balanced on the superstructure, grabbed hold of the conduit and pulled on it, but it was armoured in anticipation of rock falls. Even when he swung on it with his whole weight, it didn't move.

"You have a blaster," Ryet said.

"The noise will bring the Kaz running," Lauren said.

"Not if the lights go out."

"We need to do something. We can't stay here." John got back on the floor, aimed the weapon at the conduit and fired. After a lot of noise, smoke and sparks, lights on both sides of the break went out.

Then beyond the reach of the hand light it was very dark.

Lauren took the light back, dialed it down to its minimum, slightly brighter than a candle, and aimed it at the floor. "Can you see?" she asked Ryet.

"Not well."

She directed the light just in front of it.

They shuffled along half blind, hands to the walls, across the entry until Lauren could reach the controls for the door.

The door slid open and daylight poured in.

"Oh, shit," Lauren said. She shut the door.

"Well, what do we do now?" she said into the blackness.

"Do we have Kaz out there?" John asked.

"Don't know. At the moment, I don't know how to find out. We could wait for night," Lauren suggested.

"How long will that be?" John asked.

"About thirty hours if I remember correctly."

"Waiting would be ill-advised," Ryet said. Near the mouth of one of the arched tunnels small sparks were coalescing into a larger light, and beginning to illuminate the walls. "They have found a power supply and are assembling display lights from the machinery."

"So," John said, "Kaz for sure inside or Kaz maybe outside?"

Lauren didn't answer. Her head hurt and she felt less well than she had. She her pack down on the floor, leaned her back against the wall and slid down until she was sitting beside it.

John squatted on his heels facing her. "Hey, don't flake out on us now."

"I need a few minutes to think."

"Do you know how to work the bots? Maybe we can use the bots. They have cameras. Send one out and have it look around, see if there are any Kaz outside."

"And if there are some outside, what do we do? And since sensors haven't been working around here, I'm not confident we'll get any information back."

"Regardless," Ryet said, "if Kaz must shoot something, let them shoot robots."

"That's not a bad idea." Lauren stood up and shouldered her bag. "Get a few together to run interference."

"I do not understand the expression but if it means we have an opportunity to leave here safely, I am in favour."

"Okay, let's round up some bots."

They managed to find six of various kinds without getting too close to where the Kaz were building up their light. It was quite bright in the darkness by then; at any moment, the bad guys would be ready to go.

The simplest bot controls were intuitive and could be linked, so they opened the door and walked out behind a robot defense.

"Can we close the door?"

"No controls on the outside."

Ryet went back in, pushed the control and slipped out again, beating the closing door with a millimetre to spare.

They followed the robots toward the stone wall. Ferguson B, split by the horizon, glared between the bots and glinted off their metal frames, making it hard to see past them. John had the blaster ready in his hand.

Lauren thought she saw movement out of the corner of her eye.

It might have been a swirl of dirt. It might have been imaginary, created out of fear and tension. They reached the wall, where the machines, having no climbing ability, stalled. Lauren turned them around and sent them back toward the mine entrance, maybe a distraction, maybe no use at all, but surely no harm. The people hopped over the wall and turned back to look, expecting to see a mob of Kaz coming across the flat ground, but there were none, just a little dust in the sunlight raised by the bots.

Ryet could make better time in daylight. They reached the van much more quickly than they had gone the other way. Poised on the height of land before the small valley where the van was parked, Lauren pulled Nathan's detonator out of her bag, armed it, and fired.

A mighty thump hit her feet from below. A plume of dust rose over the mountain and bent in the wind. "Let's go."

They just got started in the van when they heard aircraft overhead, circling the mine site. Lauren pushed the van as fast as she dared in spite of Ryet's complaints. Finally, as they topped another small hill, it got out of the vehicle and took to the air.

The buildings of New Towne were a welcome sight, but Lauren didn't stop to appreciate it. She drove on to the port and parked the van next to the landing pad.

As soon as she and John left the vehicle, she spotted Ryet, a dark spot in the shadow of *Mercury's Daughter*, working at something. Ferguson A had risen; the air was getting hot. Lauren was thankful she wasn't soot black and absorbing heat the way Ryet must be.

She took a moment to register that several dead Kaz dotted the tarmac and what Ryet was working at was first aid for Kiri Narang. The pilot was nearby, bleeding. He appeared to be unconscious. An exhausted blaster lay beside him. A long black streak marred the ship's side.

"We need to get everyone aboard and get going. The Kaz have aircraft. They'll be here any minute."

"Unfortunately, our captain here is incapacitated," Ryet pointed out. It had sprayed antibiotics and then slathered artificial skin copiously over her wounds. It had her feet propped up on the first aid kit. "She is going into shock. Who will drive?"

"I guess that will have to be me," John answered.

Narang roused a little, and said, "Nobody gets my ship. Especially not Kaz."

"I need to borrow it for a while, to get us home, okay."

"Can you actually fly this thing?" Lauren asked.

"Never know 'til I try."

"That's not the answer I wanted to hear." By that time, Lauren was sure she could hear aircraft in the distance.

THEY GOT EVERYONE ABOARD, taking care with the wounded. John took the pilot's seat and studied the instrument panel for a few moments. Lauren took the seat beside him, though she knew she would be not much use as co-pilot.

John found the com link that would connect him to the AI and plugged it into the socket in his head. Then he yelled and jumped and yanked it out again.

"Jesus."

In a barely audible whisper, Narang said from behind the pilot's seat, "I told you nobody gets my ship. Give me that."

"Um," Lauren started to protest, but John handed the com link over. The captain plugged into her own socket. A few seconds later, she handed it back. "Okay," she croaked. "You're good now."

John plugged in again, a bit gingerly.

"Do we have a way to avoid rocks this time?"

"Rocks or Kaz, take your choice."

"Rocks."

"That's what I thought."

"Our choices have been erased." Ryet pointed to the view forward.

"Okay, not good. Really not good," John said.

The aircraft looked like the sort one would ship in pieces and bolt together on site, a minimalist machine, and it was headed straight for them. At the last possible second it pulled up.

"What would be the outcome of a collision?" Ryet asked.

"Not good for either of us. We're not armoured and that thing looks like it's made of spit and string."

"Let me out of here."

"No way, Ryet. No martyrs, okay."

"The alternative is to wait until we are shot to pieces, which would be a martyrdom in its own right, just a pointless one. Be ready to leave. Reinforcements will not be far behind."

John hesitated. "I don't want to fight you," Ryet said.

John wondered how such a contest would turn out, but he opened the hatch.

Ryet stood poised in the open hatchway, facing out. "John," Lauren said, "You can't let it do this." But before John or Lauren or anyone else could stop it, Ryet threw itself into the air.

Its wings spread with a pop as it headed straight for the aircraft which had come around for another scare-you run.

Ryet landed with a hard thump, covering most of the front, and dug its claws in. Lauren got an awful feeling in the pit of her stomach, thinking that the impact must have shattered most of Ryet's slender bones. A volley of energy charges fizzed away from the craft, but they were aimed by guess and only charred a few rocks. Ryet started tearing pieces off, anything tooth or claw could pull away. The Kazi pilot tried to shake it off, but Ryet was picking away at the control surfaces, and the pilot had all it could do to keep its craft in the air until then it could not and aircraft and Kazi and Nsfera went ass over teakettle into the port buildings.

John fired up *Mercury's Daughter* and headed out.

It wasn't the hyperspace transition that left Lauren feeling sick to her stomach.

KING GEORGE XIII HOSPITAL

Lauren Fox was sharing her hospital room with Kiri Narang now, and it was all sealed up in an imperme- able membrane just in case the Oriani virus was dangerous to other life. The hospital would take no chances despite Orian reassurances and even though the virus had been in Midway once before, and no one but a Kazi was affected. Aroull was all got up in biohazard gear, like some bizarre Halloween figure, with his tail tucked down beside his leg.

"You know that gear is pointless, don't you," Lauren asked.

"Yes. None the less, I am expected to abide by even foolish rules."

"Is the captain going to be okay?" she asked.

"Yes." Then Aroull realised something else was expected. "She lost much blood, but no irreparable damage has been done."

"John?"

"John Kim is in good health. He will be discharged as soon as the quarantine is over."

"Can I talk to him?"

"Yes."

While Aroull worked on the nanites, Lauren admitted her feelings of guilt about leaving Ryet behind. The Orian had become her confessor in a way. It was good to talk to someone who wasn't a part of the station gossip cloud.

"We should have been able to do something. We just left it there. That's so wrong."

"It was certainly dead." Aroull's voice through the speaker in his gear had a tinny sound. "To risk lives to recover a body would negate its sacrifice. It obviously though its act was worthwhile."

"It was an act of desperation."

"So many things are. You are feeling well?"

"Better. Less exhausted. How long are we going to be in quarantine? Can I communicate with the outside world? Can I talk to Ehreh? I want to tell him what happened."

"Of course. He is sleeping now, but he should rouse soon. I will let him know you want to speak to him." He left a communications device beside the bed. "At some time, you might consider joining the modern world and get an implant."

Lauren had considered it, but the thought of a piece of machinery in touch with her actual brain made her shudder.

She slept then, and when she woke up, Ehreh's bed was wheeled down the hall. All the machines that had been attached to him were disconnected but a care-bot hovered near by. The bump on the bed looked too small to be the old man, but she could see the white-tipped ears on the pillow. He had to stay on the other side of the plastic barrier, so Lauren found a chair and sat as near to him as was allowed. The head of his bed was raised, so they could see one another.

"I thought you might like to hear what happened on Ferguson Prime."

"Yes." His voice was a hoarse whisper.

Lauren told him, about the mine and how they spread his virus there, that Kaz were already there, and they would be carrying it back into Kazi territory right away. She told him how they nearly got caught and about Ryet Arkkad's sacrifice. At times he may have drifted off for a few minutes, but it didn't really matter. At the end of the story, he said, "We all owe Ryet Arkkad a great debt," so Lauren understood he had been paying more attention than she thought.

"Yeah, we do. Some of us more than others."

"Thank you," the old man said.

"It's going to work, Ehreh."

Divested of the gear, Aroull came to Ehreh's side of the barrier. "Are you ready, old friend," he asked. He said to Lauren, "We are going home. I have observed no problems with the reactivation of your nanites. My colleague will look after their removal in a few days. Your passage to Centauri is booked for thirteen days from now, at the end of this arbitrary quarantine. Your daughter is expecting you to call soon."

"I didn't think you really meant it, that you would get me home," she said.

Aroull gave her that golden stare that said he couldn't be held responsible for what she thought.

"You have visitors."

Aroull and Ehreh left. Shortly thereafter, Stanton Clough appeared on that side of the barrier. He looked less tense than Lauren had ever known him, as if he had found some peace.

"I'm on my way home, to Earth," he said. "I thought I'd stop in and say good-bye. I understand you were successful,"

"I think so. Time will tell."

"I'll leave contact data. I have a project or two you might be interested in."

"Honestly, Stanton, I don't see myself going to Earth anytime soon. I need to spend time with my kid, and deal with some problems at home, and that's the extent of my ambition right now."

Time passed. She was more relaxed than she had been in a

while herself, in spite of the spectre of the Merriweathers hovering in the background. She slept a lot, and chatted with Kiri Narang as the captain regained her strength, and she talked to John. It was hard at first, getting past the awkwardness caused by her impromptu confession in Declan's that seemed like years ago, but was in reality, only a few days. "Don't stress," John said. "It's what people do in bars. It's a tradition."

"Maybe you're better at the espionage business than I originally thought. I do tend to tell you stuff."

"Joke, right?"

"Yeah."

After eleven days, Aroull's colleague came, introducing herself as Eva Flynn, and began the process of removing the nanites.

Getting them out was more difficult than getting them in; they had to be herded to an accessible vein, deactivated and then sucked out with what seemed like way too much of her blood. Lauren imagined she could detect them protesting their eviction.

By the third iteration, she wondered if she had would enough blood left to sustain life. Eva gave her some odd tasting smoothie-like thing to drink and told her, "Plenty of fluids. Stop worrying. You'll be fine."

And she was. Just a few hours later, she felt stronger.

Lauren obtained access to a hyperspace link and started calling people. She told Nathan an abbreviated version of the story she told Ehreh. He was only interested in when the mine could reopen. It wasn't up to her, she told him.

She told DoubleChek she was taking a leave of absence, and that it looked like the Kazi threat had been pushed back, at least for now. She talked to Sillah to start with, but then the boss came on, grumping about time off and wanting to know when she thought she might be able to come back to work, hers not being a part time job.

"I don't know," she said, "but listen, get in touch with a mathematician called Murr at the Academy in Owr-Marl on Orion. She could have some interesting information for you regarding the sensor malfunctions."

"I'm going home," she told John.

"I know," he said. He didn't sound happy about it.

Then she phoned home.

"Mom, mom, mom."

CORE WORLD 97

The senior biologist stood inside the 3D display, beside the AI that generated it. Around it a forest of coloured lines of light represented a million deaths, tracing connections, branch upon branch, and the biologist studied them, trying to find the meaningful thread. Often a trace simply began somewhere and ended somewhere else, disconnected from the rest. The biologist recognised the possible, or perhaps inevitable, fact that natural forces accounted for some of the data, and were unrelated to the enormous die-off that was killing Kazi at a great and accelerating rate. If one died while travelling, the death might as likely be attributed to a traffic accident as to the disease even though it was sick. Or vice versa, if it was not sick. The biologist asked the AI to sift through the data and remove any connection that also could be related to accidents, crime, age-related disease or suicide.

One by one, a few of the disconnected branches disappeared. Crime and suicide were rare in Kazi communities. Other branches, previously connected, became disconnected.

That this was a contagion was established early on. It followed a well-established pattern. Comparing autopsies of the dead, medical people found the same inflamed guts, damaged organs, fluid-filled cavities over and over again. Tissue cultures often showed evidence of a common respiratory disease organism, to which most Kaz had been exposed at one time or another in their lives, and which caused mild discomfort and was usually overcome in a few days. The medics thought it was possible that individuals who were infected were more likely to succumb to this new thing.

Could it be that the respiratory disease left a residue which became active later in life? Why would that suddenly show up now, so widespread and so virulent? Many young had died. It seemed unlikely.

The biologist turned in its cage of light. There were anomalies. One isolated case had occurred on Beta Ellgarth. Nothing preceded it. But it started a branching chain that reached into the core worlds. An individual had died on Midway, but since the Empire had received neither the body nor a report, it was hard to say if that death was also due to the disease.

Most of the earliest known cases clustered in space and time. As much as it could follow by eye, these seemed to connect to almost everyone else. The biologist told the AI to remove all cases that did not ultimately connect to that cluster. The disconnected branches all disappeared, as did the Beta Ellgarth string. Hardly anything else did.

A messenger arrived, and paused outside of the display. Its gestures were barely visible through the lines of light. *The Emperor's chief science advisor requires your presence.*

The biologist, sensing it was on the verge of an insight, regretted the need to leave its deliberations, but it could not deny the command. It stepped out of the display and followed the messenger through the tunnels to a larger chamber with built-in benches where a number of the Empires best scientists and medical people had assembled.

What have you discovered? the advisor asked.

The biologist realised it had grasped the inference it had been searching for in that moment. *I believe the contagion began on Ferguson Prime. Many died there early on.*

A battle is being pursued for control of Ferguson Prime and the heliosite mines. Many deaths would be expected. The oldest member of the group was a medical practitioner, and did not have the high status that would give its opinion weight. Medicine was a minor science among the Kaz, who tended neglect the individual in favour of the group. It was speaking outside of its field, and its pheromones were weak.

I suggest we urge the Emperor to move our people away from the region of Ferguson Prime and quarantine any person who has been there, the biologist said.

The advisor said, *The Emperor is determined to take Ferguson Prime. A proven source of heliosite is extremely valuable, and denying it to the enemy even more so.*

The Emperor should be made aware of the connection between Ferguson Prime and the disease.

Is this connection more than a hypothesis on your part? What evidence can you present? The old one was leaning back on its legs. It looked about to fall asleep.

If I can bring in my equipment, I can demonstrate my reasoning.

The messenger was sent to fetch the AI and the 3D projector. Once set up, the biologist retraced the steps it followed to its conclusion. The advisor was unconvinced. *Go one step back.* The AI did so. The advisor pointed out the branch that began on Beta Ellgarth. *This is in a different place and earlier in time. It appears to have no connection to Ferguson Prime. Do you neglect it because it does not fit the supposition?*

The biologist admitted it had no explanation for that anomaly.

The advisor said, *We will not disturb the Emperor until we are certain we understand what has happened, which explanation must include this anomaly.*

I believe this to be unwise, the biologist said.

Less unwise than disturbing the Emperor for no reason.

We must quarantine Ferguson Prime.

Find the reason.

With that, the meeting ended and everyone prepared to go back to what it had been doing, except the old medical practitioner, who did not move at all. All of them stopped and turned toward the room as they felt the cold rush that marked the end of life.

ACKNOWLEDGMENTS

The author would like to acknowledge the assistance of Dr. Fawziah Gadallah, who steered her away from the more egregious misrepresentations of biological science. She is a good guide and an excellent daughter. The errors and omissions that remain are all my own.

I would also like to thank Lawrence Gadallah, technical advisor of skill and patience and excellent son.

Thanks also to Five Rivers Publishing, original publisher of *Cat's Game* in 2018, and editor Robert Runte. Without their encouragement, this book would not exist.

ABOUT THE AUTHOR

Leslie Gadallah grew up in Alberta and is currently living in Lethbridge with her geriatric black cat, Spook. Educated as a chemist, she has worked in analytical, agricultural, biological, and clinical chemistry. She has written popular science for newspapers and radio, has served as a technical editor, and is the author of four SF novels and a number of short stories.

ABOUT SHADOWPAW PRESS

Shadowpaw Press is a small traditional, royalty-paying publishing company located in Regina, Saskatchewan, Canada, founded in 2018 by Edward Willett, an award-winning author of science fiction, fantasy, and non-fiction for readers of all ages. It is a member of Literary Press Group (Canada) and the Association of Canadian Publishers. It publishes an eclectic selection of books by both new and established authors, including adult fiction, young adult fiction, children's books, non-fiction, and anthologies.

In addition, Shadowpaw Press publishes new editions of notable, previously published books in any genre under the Shadowpaw Press Reprise imprint.

Email publisher@shadowpawpress.com for more info.

AVAILABLE OR COMING SOON

SHADOWPAW
PRESS

The Good Soldier by Nir Yaniv

The Headmasters by Mark Morton

Shapers of Worlds Volumes I-IV

The Downloaded by Robert J. Sawyer

The Traitor's Son by Dave Duncan

Corridor to Nightmare by Dave Duncan

The Door at the End of Everything by Lynda Monahan

The Sun Runners by James Bow

Ashme's Song by Brad C. Anderson

The Wind and Amanda's Cello by Alison Lohans

Thickwood by Gayle M. Smith

The Emir's Falcon by Matt Hughes

One Lucky Devil by Sampson J. Goodfellow

Paths to the Stars by Edward Willett

Star Song by Edward Willett

NEW EDITIONS OF NOTABLE, PREVIOUSLY PUBLISHED WORK

SHADOWPAW
PRESS *Reprise*

The Canadian Chills Series by Arthur Slade

Let Us Be True by Erna Buffie

The Glass Lodge by John Brady McDonald

Cupboard Love: A Dictionary of Culinary Curiosities by Mark Morton

Duatero by Brad C. Anderson

Phases by Belinda Betker

Blue Fire by E. C. Blake

The Legend of Sarah by Leslie Gadallah

Stay by Katherine Lawrence

Dollybird by Anne Lazurko

The Ghosts of Spiritwood by Martine Noël-Maw

The Crow Who Tampered With Time by Lloyd Ratzlaff

Backwater Mystic Blues by Lloyd Ratzlaff

Small Reckonings by Karin Melberg Schwier

The Shards of Excalibur Series, The Peregrine Rising Duology, *Spirit Singer, From the Street to the Stars* and *Soulworm* by Edward Willett